THE CINE STAR SALON

LEAH RANADA

THE CINE STAR SALON

A NOVEL

NEWEST PRESS
EDMONTON, AB

Library and Archives Canada Cataloguing in Publication

Title: The Cine Star Salon / Leah Ranada.
Names: Ranada, Leah, author.
Series: Nunatak first fiction series ; no. 55.
Description: Series statement: Nunatak first fiction series; 55
Identifiers: Canadiana (print) 2020040556X | Canadiana (ebook) 20200405594 | ISBN 9781774390320 (softcover) | ISBN 9781774390337 (EPUB)
Classification: LCC PS8635.A475 C56 2021 | DDC C813/.6—dc23
Classification: LCC PS8609.G36 T46 2021 | DDC C813/.6—dc23

NeWest Press wishes to acknowledge that the land on which we operate is Treaty 6 territory and a traditional meeting ground and home for many Indigenous Peoples, including Cree, Saulteaux, Niitsitapi (Blackfoot), Métis, and Nakota Sioux.

Board Editor: Anne Nothof
Cover design & typesetting: Kate Hargreaves
(photo creative commons by guogete via Unsplash)
Author photograph: Betsy Morales Photo
All Rights Reserved

NeWest Press acknowledges the Canada Council for the Arts, the Alberta Foundation for the Arts, and the Edmonton Arts Council for support of our publishing program. This project is funded in part by the Government of Canada.

201, 8540 – 109 Street
Edmonton, AB T6G 1E6
780.432.9427
www.newestpress.com

NeWest Press

No bison were harmed in the making of this book.
PRINTED AND BOUND IN CANADA

1 2 3 4 5 23 22 21

In memory of Lola Leonora "Luring" Pangan

I
SHARP
INSTRUMENTS

I

THE CLANGING OF WOKS AND HARRIED CALLS FROM the cooks seemed louder that Sunday, the bustle carrying a more frenzied air. Sophia felt like a caged animal. She looked up at the ceiling, wishing to float above the flood of noise. Across the table, her parents sat straight-backed and elegant—they dressed up on Sundays for mass. At this dim sum place along Fraser Street, they were familiar faces to servers who were used to serving them efficiently. Her father always brought them to the same place after the service; he enjoyed the anxious, deferential treatment. Sophia wished everybody would just slow down, that the plates of deep-fried rolls would land on the table without that haphazard clink, the tiny steaming bowls set down with some care. The world lacked in grace. There was no need for all this hurry.

There was also no need to talk so loudly. Sophia marvelled at how her mother's excited voice surfed above the noise level in the restaurant, while Samuel and their father hungrily served themselves with the newly arrived delicacies. What was it with men that could make them so indifferent when everything around them was chaos?

"There might have been a fight, some confrontation." Her mother looked to Sophia for confirmation. During last night's Skype call to Manila, every single detail had been dissected, with Sophia's mother embellishing with things remembered from the past, and Auntie Mila correcting her faulty memory, happy to fan the same topic as it kept at bay the other usual subject, which was her perpetual singlehood. They had harmoniously called it an *accident*. Sophia, who had been eavesdropping, missed the kindness of the word, its blamelessness, now that her mother was adding fresh angles to her younger sister's juicy gossip. "Maybe it wasn't an accident. Who knows?"

The feast on the Lazy Susan gave off the aroma of sesame and pork fat, all of which ordinarily made her day. Sophia had a voracious appetite. Adrian had once said that she wasn't like other beautiful women who ate like birds.

That morning she didn't feel like a single bite.

"Your Auntie Rosy," her mother waved her chopsticks at Sophia on *your*, stressing that the woman was just someone Sophia called Auntie, not a family relation, "has not seen a customer since the *accident*. The ale left with an unfinished haircut and a bleeding cut on her cheek. Fight or no fight, Rosy must have been drunk!"

Her father shrugged. "What's going to happen now?"

"For sure, she's going to lose the business. It's so sad."

But her mother didn't sound sad. She sounded cold, satisfied even.

"Where did Auntie Mila hear this?" Sophia made her
voice sound skeptical, poised to dismiss the story.

"Everyone in the neighbourhood is talking about it.
I'm surprised you haven't heard."

"I haven't been in touch with them." She avoided her
mother's gaze by looking up at the server who put down
a fresh teapot on their table before hurrying off with the
empty one. He brushed against another server pushing
a cart that carried towering piles of bamboo steamers.
Sophia herself felt like a tottering container in danger of
falling to the floor, her secrets tumbling out like meat filling from a breached dumpling.

How generous she had been back then, sending money and packages filled with salon supplies and
gifts to Manila. It had been three years, but Sophia was
remembering all of it too clearly. How, at the beginning,
it hadn't felt like a burden. Every amount she signed off,
every package she sealed and shipped, left her with a nos-
talgic glow from paying homage. It hadn't been hard to
keep these charitable efforts from her stingy parents—as
a child, Sophia had harboured bigger secrets. That Auntie
Rosy was grateful to the point of tears every single time
only spurred her generosity. Being left to run Cine Star
after Aling Helen's death had made her fragile and resil-
ient at the same time. Such contradictions were the stuff
Auntie Rosy was made of. Perhaps the end had been in-
evitable. Their friendship couldn't have emerged from their
dreadful misunderstanding unscathed. When everything

finally blew up, Auntie Rosy no longer wanted to speak to Sophia, who had been irked but ultimately relieved by this outcome. Through all of it, her family had been unaware and uninvolved. As always.

Outside the skies were bright, the leaves vibrant in the late-September showdown between summer and fall, but all Sophia could see were the smudges on the glass window, swirling traces of mist where the cleaning cloth had been. A cut on the cheek. Auntie Rosy had been a stylist for decades. What had taken so long, Sophia thought, for something like this to happen?

The scene played out in her head: the woman storming out of Cine Star, hand cradling one side of her face. Murmurs rising among onlookers lined up at the next-door pawnshop and the bakery at the other side. Auntie Mila would have pieced the story together from plenty of sources. Her account was so detailed that her mother, who knew nothing about the people living next door to their Collingwood area townhouse, would talk about it for a long time.

But it was Erwin's version that Sophia wanted to hear. It had been months since they had last spoken, but from what she could tell from his Facebook and Instagram posts, her childhood friend still lived in the same neighbourhood, worked at the same call centre outfit. Heard the same rumours. Erwin was Sophia's remaining link to Auntie Rosy.

By the time they left the Chinese restaurant, the morning's sunny skies had turned into a defeated shade. "It might rain," Sophia remarked, looking through the window of her father's Honda. Next to her, Samuel had earphones plugged in his ears, his slouch disguising his springing height. He looked thirteen instead of nineteen. As her mother went on questioning Auntie Rosy's life choices, Sophia found herself agreeing with the prevailing belief within the family that her brother was the clever one.

"Mila says Rosy and Soledad are still tight. They are still seen together at nights."

Aling Soledad! Sophia had not thought of her for years. When she was growing up, the rumours about the woman swirled around their neighbourhood like a swarm of bees. Back when she believed that being beautiful brought a woman a lot of trouble. The string of boyfriends. Affairs ending stormily. The next man a step down from the last. Sometimes a baby in their wake. Sophia wondered if Auntie Rosy still styled Aling Soledad at Cine Star like the old days. For free.

"She should be locked up," her father huffed. They were stopped at a red light. An old lady with a walker ambled across the pedestrian line. "Both of them."

"Vincent, naman. That's too harsh." Sophia's mother rubbed his shoulder. For the first time that morning she had reverted to her mellow and tremulous voice, which Sophia guessed was used at her job as a receptionist at the community centre. It sounded like she was shivering and was concealing it by being friendly. Polite. Auntie Rosy's accident had resurrected the loud, commanding voice she had once wielded against noisemakers as a college librarian.

The light turned green and the car eased forward, leaving the topic of Auntie Rosy's accident at the intersection.

Sophia waited for something within her to settle, her heartbeat or the food in her stomach, but her pulse had been fine and she had eaten very little at the restaurant. Her sigh created a cloudy patch on the car window, which looked out to hardware stores, parking lots, obscure office buildings rushing past. It was all familiar landscape, but what went on behind those vandalized stucco walls, those glass doors advertising hours of operation? Something always lurked behind the surface, every wall knew of some drama. Her father drove faster and the shops flew past with their untold stories, leaving Sophia with her faint reflection floating along the pavement. A lady's face with shapely eyebrows and lips, not belonging to the little girl she had felt like a few blocks ago.

BEAUTY SALONS WERE FOR WOMEN, NOT LITTLE GIRLS. Sophia had believed this until she was brought to Cine Star when she was nine years old. She would realize later that her mother had simply devised a lie so she could go to the hair salon without a child in tow. But Sophia would never see herself as a little girl again.

They had been visiting Auntie Mila, who had told them about the newest beautician in her neighbourhood. "The old woman, she's very skilful. It's time for your daughter to get a real haircut, 'no? You can't keep cutting her hair yourself."

Plastered on Cine Star's window were pictures of women sporting lush, wild-looking hairstyles that reminded Sophia of poodles. When they stepped inside, a harsh odour stung her nostrils, making her think of a witch's potion. She counted three mirrors, framing the reflections of three ladies wearing dark capes, sitting on cushioned chairs. More women were seated against the back wall.

The frail yet regal old woman fussing over the ladies on the chairs turned out to be the owner. Aling Helen wore a dark green blouse with puffy sleeves and a knee-length, pleated black skirt. A strand of white pearls peered from her collar. Sophia thought then that if dolls grew old they would look like Aling Helen. The title, Aling, seemed wrong for her; it was the same one her mother used for women in the market, whose hands were stinky from handling raw meat and fish, fruits and vegetables that still smelled of earth. Aling Helen was more like a *Madam*.

"Do we need an appointment?" her mother asked, observing the women sitting in the salon. "There's two of us."

"I recommend that but I work quick so I usually have time for walk-ins." Aling Helen's throaty voice was somehow audible over the whirring of the hair dryer. "My assistant just stepped out but she should be back soon."

Sophia and her mother leafed through magazines while they waited for their turns. The models on the glossy pages had eyelids like rainbow rays. They stared at Sophia with dramatic gazes. Some women had their hair piled up like a queen's or swept airily across their foreheads. Others had wavy tresses cascading like water past their shoulders. She swung her legs, impatient for her turn to be pretty.

More women arrived, whom Aling Helen invited to sit down as she glanced worriedly at the window.

When her mother's turn came, she said to Aling Helen, "My hair is limp and dry. I don't have much time to style it in the morning. Only for putting on rollers."

"Big ones?" Aling Helen put a cape on her mother.

"They take the least time."

When Aling Helen finished, her mother stood up with her hair in short, billowy waves that made her look like a TV reporter. Sophia felt like she was getting a better mom.

It was finally her turn. The chair was too high. One of her slippers fell to the floor, but she was too scared to ask Aling Helen to pick it up and slip it onto her dangling foot. Maybe her mother had been right about beauty salons not being for girls. "I'm thinking of the apple cut for her," she heard her mother say, and Sophia wondered what kind of transformation she was about to go through. She looked up at the mirror and arranged her face into a strong grown-up expression she had seen in the magazines: hard gaze and small lips.

Chimes jingled and a woman several years younger than Aling Helen appeared at the door. She winked at Sophia in the mirror. She was short and plump, and her dark skin glowed in the afternoon sun along with the ringlets that framed her smile. The housedress she wore was so sheer that sunlight streamed through, showing the outline of a slip around her thighs.

"Rosy, finally! Where have you been?" Aling Helen was suddenly stern.

"Just around," the younger woman chirped and turned to the waiting clients. "Okay, who's next?"

Aling Helen shook her head. "You can't keep leaving the salon during business hours!"

Sophia stared at her lone slipper on the floor. She felt bad for this friendly woman being scolded in front of everyone.

The neighbourhood felt different when they stepped out, as if it had transformed into a lesser place while they had been at Cine Star. Shirtless men and noisy women milling outside the stores and plywood-patched dwellings eyed Sophia and her mother as they waited for a tricycle that would take them home. Her time on Aling Helen's chair had seemed too quick. Sophia kept replaying the experience in her mind: sprayed water that tickled her nape, the pleasant tugging at her scalp as Aling Helen lifted sections of her hair, the steamy breeze from the hair dryer. When her cape came off, Sophia's eyes looked rounder and her cheeks popped out. The bangs on her forehead provided a shield for her secrets. Her mother clapped her hands at this new look as Sophia turned her head, searching for all other grown-up parts of herself that had finally come to light.

"Madam's haircut is so pretty!" someone called out. Her mother beamed, tightening her hold on Sophia's hand. A group of children nearby looked at them, their faces smeared with dirt and sweat. From the window of a sari-sari store, Aling Soledad peered out curiously between the hanging bags of prawn crackers and chocolate cookies. "She's a call girl after store hours," her Auntie Mila had said of Aling Soledad. Sophia imagined Aling Soledad calling out to people in the streets—she didn't understand what her mother and Auntie Mila found so interesting about that. She had always liked her bright doll-like face and her wavy hair that flowed to her waist. But now, Aling Soledad was following her mother with admiring eyes.

"I think we found our favourite stylist." Her mother had patted her waves to show off to her father that evening. She winked at Sophia. "Sofi and I will be going back there."

THAT HAIRSTYLE DEFINED HER MOTHER'S LOOK FOR SEVERAL years before she had her hair rebonded along with everyone else when straight and silky hair became the craze in Manila. Her mother had cared about her looks back then, but now Sophia wasn't even sure where she went for her haircuts, which only happened two or three times in a year. She had never set foot in Sophia's hair salon. "It's kind of far," she had told her once. Later on, "I don't want to take away time from your paying clients."

The rear-view mirror offered slices of her parents' reflections, the glances, the frowns. There were bigger mirrors in her hair salon, and Sophia was used to relying on those vast, clear pools to know her clients well enough to elevate their attributes. But she didn't need mirrors to see how much her parents had aged since arriving in Canada eight years ago. Gone were the smooth foreheads and the delicate cheeks and chins; the markers of symmetry had become faint. Lines at the corners of their eyes and lips had deepened. Sophia had always wished she looked more like Samuel, who had gotten the angular face of their father. Instead, she had inherited their mother's wide jawline.

Focused on driving, her father furrowed his brows, eyes steely, like those times he would peruse the column of marks on the report card Sophia brought home from school. She no longer feared that look; the bald patch had made it less severe. Years ago, Sophia had chuckled to herself when her father started combing over a thinning spot on his crown. Now he was past any kind of cover-up.

Things would be so different if she lived with Adrian. Her days, Sophia imagined, would be peaceful, uncomplicated. They had been dating for more than two years and had discussed living together. Sophia had turned down the idea. Her salon had just started breaking even; it felt unfair to move in when she had barely made a dent on her business loan. He didn't mind, but she was proud. And there were also her parents, of course, who would frown upon living together before marriage. "The surest way for him to take you for granted," as her mother put it. Staying with them until she wed was Sophia's last-ditch attempt for a grain of their approval.

She felt for the phone in her pocket, sent her fiancé a brief message: *You up*? She touched the ring on her left hand, felt the delicate tip of the princess-cut diamond. He had proposed last spring, tax season, and she had not quite decided whether the timing and manner he had chosen were cute or cheesy. They had been going out for two years. Discussions around marriage had been casual and speculative: a faint vision remote from the immediate realities of their hectic work hours and reliably frequent date nights.

Then on a crisp April evening, while waiting for their dinner on the patio of a Thai restaurant, Adrian handed her an envelope. "Done with your taxes. I added some deductibles we missed from last year. You might want to review."

Sophia had just gulped down her lychee cocktail and was growing impatient for the food. "I've looked at those receipts a hundred times."

"You need to sign a page."

"Can I do that later?"

"If you do it now, I can pop it in the mailbox tomorrow." Adrian sounded a bit too eager.

Pink rose petals fell out of the envelope when Sophia pulled out the papers. She looked up. Everybody on the patio was looking at her. Adrian knelt on the floor, holding up her ring in a small velvet box.

Women who came to her salon had told her that proposals never happen like in the movies. In real life, either an emotionally wearying discussion or a straight-out ultimatum would push the man to a state of clarity that he was ready for the next step. But here was Sophia's ring. No discussion needed. It was as if the universe had granted what she rightly deserved, sparing her the stressful confrontation. That was how things between her and Adrian worked. They sailed through the two years with a quiet understanding of each other's needs. Sophia was in love with his tenderness, his calming presence. He could only muster a low earnest tone during the handful of times they had argued. Even his smell was mild; Sophia would press her nose against his neck and catch a faint whiff of aftershave. Or the aroma of the food they had just shared. Sometimes her own perfume. He didn't have one hovering scent. She loved that Adrian's body didn't carry a history, as if each time they got together was a new, clear day, void of any past drama.

They were getting close to home. Outside, produce markets rumbled past, the colours of the vegetables and fruits leaping out of their skins, bright as her future. Same sights from the same drive from the same restaurant every Sunday. Her parents would wither without any rigid routine. When she and Samuel were growing up, even their weeknights had a specific schedule, as if the strict private school they attended wasn't punishment enough. After supper, the dirty dishes and the supper's bits and drips made way for textbooks, their plastic covers sticking to the moisture on the table. Their parents supervised as Sophia and her brother solved math problems and read passages from their lessons. They were not trusted to study alone in their bedrooms. These sessions had bored Sophia. She entertained herself by imagining the people mentioned in her textbooks: "How much of the pie would Alyssa have left if she gave a quarter slice to her mother and another to her uncle?" Alyssa, in Sophia's mind, was a thin girl with sharp eyes and long wavy hair. And wasn't a quarter slice of a pie too small for an uncle? Where was Alyssa's father?

Early in their relationship Sophia had instructed Adrian that if her parents were to ask him to join any of their family activities, he would politely decline and explain that he was busy with work. She cherished him for being a perfectly willing accomplice in creating the best impression for her parents while establishing boundaries, getting them accustomed to distance. They rarely need to lie. Adrian was always busy assisting senior accountants handling tax work and field audits for small-to-medium businesses while pursuing his CGA. On top of his job, he had courses to attend, examinations to write. His limited vacation days were reserved for studies and visits to his parents.

Sophia's parents could only approve of Adrian's dedication to his profession. Simply put, they approved of Adrian. Her mother liked his kind face. Her father, thrifty with compliments, had remarked that at least he had a serious job. Once they were married, it would be easy for Sophia to skip her parents' Sunday brunches. They would create their own routines as a married couple. She made a mental note to visit her parents every other week. Or every month.

Erwin had been one of the first people to know about the engagement. "That's great." He had flashed a knowing grin. "A white guy. You're going to have good-looking children!"

Annoyed, Sophia had retorted, "My kids will be beautiful no matter who I marry!"

"Ah, yes, my gorgeous friend. We know that already. It's just that your kids with Adrian will be tisoys. Half-bred. Like movie stars."

They reached another red light. "Did Rosy ever go to school?" her father asked.

Sophia's mother shook her head. "I think Aling Helen could have sent her to school, but Rosy wasn't keen on it. Right, Sofi?"

Sophia's father cut in before she could respond. "Probably a waste of money. She doesn't sound like a bright girl. Not even for cutting hair."

His last remark hung in silence. Her mother, Sophia saw in the side mirror, bit her lower lip.

When the light turned green, her mother turned to Sophia. "Oh, we probably should have dropped you off at work."

Sophia couldn't figure out which irritated her more: her father being eternally convinced that hairstyling did not require brains, or her mother always forgetting her salon's Sunday hours. She disguised her annoyed huff with a stretch of arms; she really was feeling tired anyway. "I'll drive out there myself. I don't open till one."

Within seconds of arriving home, Sophia logged onto her email. On her screen, "Inbox (1)" gleamed ominously. From Erwin, no subject. Sophia took a deep breath, clicked on the small envelope.

> Sofi,
>
> Kailan ka online? Auntie Rosy's in deep
>
> trouble. Chat tayo, pls. She's thinking of
>
> asking for your help.
>
> Erwin

2

BWISET! NOW SHE NEEDS HELP.

Sophia sighed, long and ragged. Her irritation was suffused with pity and guilt. Whenever Auntie Rosy was in the picture, a host of thorny recollections would crop up, which Sophia would weed out, only to discover more difficult sentiments clinging to the roots, squirming in her hands.

Years ago, Sophia had been the one who needed saving.

THE DAY AFTER HER FIRST HAIRCUT AT CINE STAR, ERWIN Perez had sat beside her on the school bus. "Aling Helen cut your hair."

Sophia whirled toward him. They had never talked before. Erwin was two grades older. "How did you know?"

He shrugged. "Basta, I just know. You look pretty."

Sophia wished everybody could see the frown she gave Erwin before inching away from him. She wanted him to leave her alone. Everyone made fun of him for being bakla. The meanest boys on the campus called him names and strutted with swinging hips whenever he was around. The same boys were rounded up at the principal's office weeks ago after Erwin was seen in the corridors with his white uniform stained with mud, hurrying toward the lavatories. If it became known around the school that he and Sophia were friends, maybe some kids would throw dirt at her too. She could imagine her father barging into the principal's office, demanding to know what had happened. If he found out who Erwin was, would he squint and shake his head the way he did whenever he saw gay people on TV?

But Erwin was still sitting beside her. Was that a smile she could see from the corner of her eye?

"They say you're gay." It came out hesitant. Sophia didn't want to accuse him outright. But Erwin stood up and planted his hands near the belt of his navy blue pants and declared, "And so what?" He regarded her with a raised eyebrow. "I hang out at Cine Star after school. Want to come with me?"

A spot in a game of hopscotch, a whispered secret about another girl. Those were the things Sophia had earned from her friendships with other girls at school. If she kept her foot off the chalk-drawn boundaries during her turn and sealed her lips about whose older sister just got pregnant in high school, she could sit with her usual group during recess, never having to be alone with her sandwich and juice box while wondering who whispered behind her back. Erwin, who barely knew her, was inviting her to a grown-up place where they were unlikely to be seen by other kids from school. When her friends would be home watching anime or opening their Hello Kitty notebooks, she would be surrounded by mirrors and ladies making themselves look beautiful. Besides, it was a safe place—her mother had just taken her there the day before. She just had to make sure to be home before dark so her yaya wouldn't worry.

But when Sophia and Erwin arrived at Cine Star that afternoon, Aling Helen glowered at them. "What are you doing here?" Sophia wanted to turn around and go home.

"Sophia's my new friend. We just got back from school," Erwin explained. "We want to watch you work."

"Susmaryosep! What if her parents look for her?"

"I will take her home," a voice behind them said.

"Auntie Rosy!" Erwin called out.

Sophia turned and recognized the lady with a big smile from the day before. She was cradling a litre bottle of Coke with one arm and holding a paper bag leaking grease with the other. The smell of fried bananas made Sophia's stomach grumble.

Auntie Rosy's kind eyes met Sophia's. "Of course, you can stay for a bit and have a snack first."

There were only three skewers of banana-cue. But Auntie Rosy offered Sophia her share and poured her Coke in a plastic tumbler. She drank slowly at first. Her father had said sugary drinks would make her teeth rot and fall out. But she was thirsty, and the taste went well with the sweet bananas. "Thank you, po," she told Auntie Rosy. Her mother was strict about manners.

But Auntie Rosy smirked as if Sophia had said something stupid. "Sus, it's nothing."

Aling Helen was too busy for a snack. On her chair sat a tired-looking woman with her hair gathered in a towel. Aling Helen took off the towel, revealing tidy rows of pink perm rods on the woman's head. Sophia watched closely as Aling Helen carefully unwound the rods. A shiny curl tumbled down from each one. Sophia was transfixed. In the mirror, the client was starting to look like a fairy-tale princess. By the time the last curl was released, the beautiful woman was smiling.

As she had promised, Auntie Rosy took Sophia home. She had ended up staying longer than planned and had phoned home to tell her yaya, Ate Liza, where she had been.

"Since when did you learn to hang out at places after school? Wait till your parents find out about this," Ate Liza had said tartly. "Come home! Now!"

Sophia's heart was beating hard as she walked with Auntie Rosy. It was getting dark; the street lamps flickered, their beams dotted by the frantic dancing of mosquitoes. The smell of roasting meat and beer fused with the loud babble from every storefront they passed. Sophia had never been out on the streets at dusk with an adult she barely knew.

"Rosy!" a booming male voice called out. "Have some beer with us."

Even in darkness, Sophia could see Auntie Rosy's smile. "Later," she said.

Aling Soledad was standing in front of her store. "Mare!" Auntie Rosy called out, spreading her arms as she approached. Sophia nervously followed, hoping no one nearby would tell her mother she was out late with a friend of the call girl. The two women kissed each other's cheeks like actresses did on TV. Aling Soledad's blouse and shorts were so tight they looked as if they would pull apart at her chest and hips. Quick whispers were exchanged, while Sophia stood aside, trying to decipher the secrets told by their bright lips.

When her house came to view, Sophia wished she could run away and never return. Her parents wouldn't be home until dinner time, but she could almost hear Ate Liza telling them about the missed curfew. Then the furious weight of her father's palm on the table and her mother's sermon that would last the whole night.

The gate to the house swung open and a broad-shouldered man stepped out wearing a shirt torn at the sleeves, exposing colourful tattoos on his big arms. Ate Liza followed holding his hand. Sophia had seen the man before. Ate Liza had sneaked him into their kitchen through the back door a few times. Sophia's mother had told Ate Liza that she would be replaced if she entertained her male friends at the house. The man turned around, held Ate Liza with his dagger-in-heart arm, and drove his lips against hers, before heading off in the opposite direction.

When Ate Liza spotted Sophia, her eyes blazed. "There you are! What took you so long?"

"She already told you she was at Cine Star," Auntie Rosy cut in.

Ate Liza yanked Sophia's arm. "Don't you ever do that again!"

"Does Madam know that Badong visits you at the house?" Auntie Rosy was looking at the street corner where the tattooed man had turned. Ate Liza's eyes widened and her grip on Sophia's arm relaxed.

Auntie Rosy's eyes glittered. "She's really well behaved. Can't think of *anything* else to tell her parents."

"It doesn't happen a lot." Ate Liza's small voice reminded Sophia of the time she had burned their supper.

"I don't mind looking after her." Auntie Rosy winked at Sophia. "I also think Badong's really gwapo. Can't blame you for looking after him more."

At school the following day, Sophia was sketching at the back of her notebook. A woman's face with long, curly hair. Her pencil turned dull after many thick spirals. She drew another face, this time with a wispy, shoulder-length hairstyle. But the drawing more resembled a melon covered with feathers. Sophia crossed it out.

During the bus ride home, Erwin sat beside her. "Joining me at Cine Star?"

Sophia shook her head.

"No? Why not?"

"My yaya's waiting for me." She felt ashamed as she recalled Auntie Rosy and Ate Liza's encounter the night before. While they were having supper, Ate Liza's eyes had darted nervously. Sophia's parents hadn't noticed the glances they exchanged, thick with knowledge of broken rules.

"Auntie Rosy can phone your yaya from the salon," Erwin said. "It'll be okay."

"She'll do that for me?"

"Of course," Erwin said. "You know, one time, Papa hit me for trying on my mother's dresses. When Auntie Rosy found out, she walked over to our house with her scissors. She threatened to cut off his dick."

"Really?" Sophia stared at Erwin. "What did your father do?"

"At first he just yelled at her to go away," Erwin said simply, as if talking about a storm that had long passed. "We knew she couldn't really do it. But the neighbours, along with her friends drinking on the street, heard her yelling, so they came to our house to cheer her on: 'Putol! Putol! Putol!' Auntie Rosy thrust her scissors toward my father's pants. No way Pa was going to beat her up with all those people watching through the windows, so he went to the bathroom and locked the door. Ma even said she'd call the pulis, but he said, 'wag, 'wag, there's no need!' Auntie Rosy left only when Pa promised through the bathroom door that he'd never hurt me again."

"Is this really true?"

"He doesn't hit me anymore."

The bus turned onto Cine Star's street. Sophia pondered the situation. Ate Liza would pick up Auntie Rosy's call. At least she would know where Sophia was. That was already a better scenario than yesterday's. She would probably phone Badong next.

And Sophia would be at Cine Star, eating sweet snacks while listening to Erwin's stories, watching women turn pretty instead of cartoon reruns that never failed to make her baby brother Samuel laugh just like the first time.

PIXIE. PAGEBOY. SHAGGY. SOPHIA LEARNED THE NAMES OF hairstyles from Auntie Rosy, who made a grand sweeping gesture with her arm every time she finished with a client, proud of her handiwork. Older women wanted their curls shiny and tight. Young ladies asked for stylish cuts that would slim down their faces. A girl requested a haircut à la Demi Moore. "Who's that?" Sophia whispered to Erwin.

"Don't you have a TV at home?" he asked.

She learned what a call girl was by listening to Auntie Rosy defend Aling Soledad against Aling Helen's accusation that she was throwing her life away. "The woman just wants to be able to support herself the best way she knows how. Besides, she has stopped now that she's with the congressman."

Sophia was relieved that Aling Soledad was no longer sleeping with different men. She hoped people, including her parents and Auntie Mila, would start seeing Aling Soledad as an ordinary woman, so she wouldn't feel so nervous when they stopped by her store during the evenings. Her mother seemed uncomfortable and gave Sophia wrong answers whenever she asked what a call girl was.

Besides, the other women who came to Cine Star were not that proper either. Sophia and Erwin listened to married women swear at their husbands' mistresses or talk dreamily of a male colleague they had lunches with, or whom they kissed before saying goodbye at the jeepney terminal after office hours. They had mean names for that flirty neighbour, their rageful bosses, a scheming colleague, everybody else they hated—the menopausal bruha, the smelly puta, the lecherous pig. Some mothers shook their heads angrily about their troublesome children who had learned vices from their friends at school. Sophia found herself nodding only when they lamented the horrendous traffic along EDSA, being the only grown-up topic her parents openly spoke about in front of her and Samuel. A fat lady with heavy makeup always came in with her equally dolled-up teenaged daughter whenever they had an audition for some film studio or TV advertisement. She bragged about her daughter's sweet singing voice that could hit the highest notes, and her growing bust that would eventually catch the eye of movie directors. A tall, quiet saleswoman who always asked for a short haircut— Sophia and Erwin agreed she could be a model if her skin was fairer and she wasn't so shy—was in love with another woman who worked with her in the shoe department. Sometimes, a teacher from their school showed up, and Sophia and Erwin would hide in the salon's backroom, where they would giggle about how close they were to being seen by someone who could tell her parents.

When she and her mother went back to Cine Star for their haircuts weeks later, Aling Helen and Auntie Rosy acted like they didn't know who she was, treating her like just another client. Sophia tried to suppress the smile that formed on her lips whenever her look met Auntie Rosy's in the mirror.

Aling Helen mostly ignored Sophia and Erwin, talking only to her clients. Whenever they explained the style they wanted, she would listen and nod her head before making her suggestions. It always amazed Sophia how gentle her voice could sound. "Are you sure, iha? You have a nice round face. What if I cut your hair just a little short but leave you with layers?" There was no force in her tone, but the client would turn to Aling Helen. "Would that look better?"

On a scorching afternoon, a woman with long, thick hair walked into Cine Star. Her housedress had mismatched patches for pockets and her rubber slippers left wet footprints on the floor. Sophia smelled laundry detergent.

Aling Helen was styling a woman who wanted to look like Princess Di. ("Who's Princess Di?" Erwin had asked Sophia, who replied, "You don't know Diana of Wales?") "*Psst!*" she called to Auntie Rosy who was engrossed in a romance paperback.

"Gupit-lalaki!" the woman said curtly as she sat down on the chair. Sophia and Erwin looked at each other with raised eyebrows, wondering why this woman with glorious hair was so angry and wanted to look like a boy.

"Okay!" Auntie Rosy's cheerful voice surprised even her client. She hummed as she fastened the cape behind her neck, sprayed her hair with water, and ran a paddle brush through the woman's tresses. "Tired of long hair?" she asked.

"Yes, with this heat, I just want to feel cooler." Thick black strands fell to the floor. After the woman left with very short hair, Aling Helen shook her head. "Tsk, tsk."

"What's the matter?" Auntie Rosy asked.

"Next time," Aling Helen said, "take a moment to study her and ask what she really wants."

"She asked for a boy cut."

Aling Helen started sweeping the floor, gathering clumps of hair onto a dustpan. "But she was also upset. Mainit ang ulo. I doubt she had thought her decision through. Can't you see she didn't even change to come here?" She dumped the hair into a trash can hidden under her station. "I just didn't want to interfere. Don't worry though, she'll blame herself."

On slower afternoons, they watched telenovelas. Stories of babies switched at birth, their paths meeting years later. Lovers separated by social standing and scheming rivals. A woman from an impoverished village trying her luck in the big brutal city. Convoluted fates, polarized characters, gratifying destinies. Sophia was convinced that adults had such complicated lives.

Auntie Rosy's face would be red with fury by the time the credits rolled. "That evil woman! She always makes her stepdaughter's life miserable. I hope she gets run over by a ten-wheeler."

To which Aling Helen would reply, "She will be when she gets tired of the script. Or gets a movie offer."

Sophia secretly devoured Aling Helen's remarks, trying them on her lips before falling asleep at night. Aling Helen needed to take only one glance at the woman on her chair to know what hairstyle suited her. Sophia marvelled at her skilful fingers, the way they fluffed graceful layers, tightened curls, sprayed chignons into place. It was like watching a machine at work, her quick and exact movements putting together a vision from a brilliant blueprint. She liked those brief moments when Aling Helen paused, betraying a studious expression, her tools suspended mid-air. Or when she adjusted ornaments, brushed off tendrils, her hands suddenly human and cautious again. Once, when Aling Helen caught her watching, she narrowed her small eyes, willing away Sophia's stare.

"She used to work in movies," Erwin told her during one of the bus rides from school.

"Don't make up nonsense." Sophia rolled her eyes, using a phrase she had learned from Aling Helen.

"Seryoso. Aling Helen worked with actresses like Charito Solis and Nida Blanca. She even styled candidates for beauty pageants."

More names she didn't know. Sophia was sure she could learn the world in Cine Star.

"Why did she quit showbiz?"

"How would I know?"

When they left the salon in the evenings, finally free from Aling Helen's inhibiting presence, they pressed Auntie Rosy about her mentor's mysterious past. They learned that the two women hailed from the same province. "What could I do? Aling Helen was so impressed with my skills she had to bring me to Manila with her." Auntie Rosy threw up her hands, as if helpless against her good fortune. "I heard she worked with the biggest stars, even went out with some hunks in her day."

"Who?" Erwin asked.

"Different guys, nothing serious. She worked with Gloria Diaz during her Miss Universe reign. Or with starlets starting out. The schedule was always super hectic with all that filming, TV interviews." Auntie Rosy shook her head. "She got so burned out she went back to our barrio for a break. At first, she was grateful for the fresh breeze and the quiet nights. Everything was slow and placid. But she grew bored like most city folks. What can you expect from someone who drank with PA's and managers, eavesdropped on stars and directors at the Aristocrat?"

In Auntie Rosy's hands, Aling Helen's fragmented glamorous past blended with her own humble origins. Days of being barefoot in the paddies weaving in with late-night soirees after the FAMAS awards. The ordeal of lugging hair products and styling tools along the halls of the Manila Hotel, ending with the discovery of Auntie Rosy's styling prowess in their barrio's only beauty parlour. The result was an ever-changing history of shaky memories, melding the lives of two different women, that left Sophia and Erwin wanting more.

They stayed at Cine Star until six, when Aling Helen and Auntie Rosy closed the salon. Before walking Sophia home, Auntie Rosy always fixed her own hair and put on heavy makeup. Glittery eyeshadow and dark brown eyeliner. Bright red lipstick.

"You look like a clown, Auntie," Sophia remarked once.

"She's right," Aling Helen said. "Are you and Soledad going out again?"

Auntie Rosy smacked her lips and smiled. "When will you join us?"

Aling Helen sighed and didn't say anything else.

When they were out in the streets, Sophia questioned

Auntie Rosy. "Are you and Aling Soledad looking for a boyfriend?"

Auntie Rosy laughed so loudly that people they passed on the street gawked at her. "Soledad has the congressman. They're in love with one another." She gave Sophia a pretend-angry look. "Are you giving me a hard time as well?"

"No." Sophia was looking at the sunset, its orange glow billowing from behind the jagged silhouette of rooftops and electricity poles. The thought of homework waiting for her slowed her steps. She had learned that Erwin would not be sympathetic with her complaints about her parents being so involved with her studies. "My father hates me and my mom works hard to send me to a private school," he always said. "They are too tired and just not as smart as yours. You should be thankful." He could be so preachy sometimes.

"Come on, it's getting late." Auntie Rosy tugged at her arm.

"I don't want to go home."

"Your Mama and Papa will be sad if you don't." Auntie Rosy was speaking to her like she was a little girl. "And you have your baby brother." When Sophia didn't answer, she continued, "You're lucky to be with your family. I miss mine a lot. I have small brothers and sisters. Sometimes, I cry at nights."

"Really?" Sophia hadn't imagined Auntie Rosy as somebody's child, let alone crying for her parents. She had always envied that she could stay at Cine Star the whole day and meet friends at nights without worrying about staying out late. "Don't they send you letters?"

"Sometimes. But they mostly ask me to send them money, gifts."

"How about Aling Helen? She is there for you."

Auntie Rosy sighed. For a moment, it seemed as if she was going to smile, but she straightened her lips as if suppressing something painful. Sophia wished she could make her feel better, but Auntie Rosy's sadness seemed vast and deep like the night, too heavy for a child like her to understand.

3

S HE'S THINKING OF ASKING FOR YOUR HELP.
Erwin's email was sent mere hours ago. This was the
kind of news he would send without delay. When
did the accident happen, exactly? How long did Auntie
Rosy wait before deciding to ask for help? Sophia's gut
clenched, sensing desperation flaring from thousands of
miles away. Her fingers itched to fill the space provided
for her response so she could push the correspondence
back to its source, unload herself of the burden. But any
word from her would mean that she was now involved and
could no longer turn a blind eye.

The computer clock blinked: 12:23. Time to go to work.

Downstairs, her mother told her that Samuel needed
a ride to the park where he played soccer with his friends.
He usually used their father's car, but he had driven to see
friends for the afternoon. Sophia decided she could be
a few minutes late, but it puzzled and annoyed her that

Samuel had not asked her directly.

She got her car second-hand with the loan she had taken out for the salon. It had given her parents the false impression that she was making decent income during the salon's first year, and Sophia never bothered to correct them. Her father had seemed wounded when she chose to take driving lessons from a company instead of practising with him in his car. Getting a licence had been a triumph in itself, silencing him about the issue of her owning a vehicle.

Sophia didn't know this person sitting in the passenger seat. Once a chubby toddler being chased by Ate Liza around their living room. Then the sharp-witted boy who recited the multiplication table without pausing or making a mistake. Now a sullen teenager in a sweatshirt and jersey shorts from which sprouted short muscular legs. With his head turned to the window, Sophia could see only half of Samuel's thin, pimply face.

Andy Livingstone Park was out of the way. She wanted to tell Samuel she would open late because of him, but her day had already begun on a testy note. No sense in carrying the same mood into the afternoon.

When did he learn to play soccer? Sophia couldn't remember her brother being into any sport when they were living in Manila. She could barely resist the snarky questions, *"Isn't soccer bad for your grades? Does Dad approve this?"*

Sophia wished Adrian was in the car. On one of the first few times he had visited their home, her usually quiet boyfriend went past brief hellos, directly addressing

Samuel, who was attempting a hasty retreat to his bedroom. "Sophia told me you're into video games."

A tight nod from her brother. "Yeah."

"What are you playing these days?"

"*WarZone II.*"

"Did you find the secret levels in the garrisons?"

Adrian would later tell Sophia that he had only been trying to be friendly. Samuel had nodded and after a few more words exchanged, coolly asked, "Wanna check out where I'm at?" Adrian was almost thirty. Samuel had just turned sixteen. They spent close to an hour completing virtual sieges. Sophia had acted annoyed, but she secretly relished that her boyfriend and brother were forming some sort of bond. A good sign.

Rain started to fall. "Still want to play soccer?" Sophia turned the wiper dial on.

"We always play in the rain," Samuel muttered.

By the time they reached the park, the droplets were drumming loudly on the windshield. Samuel hesitated before pushing the passenger door open.

"Thanks, Ate," he mumbled.

"Any time." Sophia looked straight ahead, only turning after Samuel had hauled his sports bag onto his thin shoulders and shut the door. He ran across the field toward a group of boys huddled beneath the sheltered portion of the bleachers.

She needed the traffic to be super light so she could open her salon on time. Fortunately, she was careful not to schedule appointments right at opening time. Sophia hated hurrying, the pounding in her chest as she push her way into the slow, oblivious pace of the world. To be a voice out of tune, an object out of place.

Eight years ago, she had been the messy, frazzled girl stinking up the SkyTrain with her hastily bought takeout, using her commute as a break between the full-day hairstyling program and her late-night fast-food shift. She barely made it on time, changing into her uniform in the rancid staff washroom, plumping up her tired face with layers of cheap foundation. When Sophia thought back to those hard, early years, she barely recognized herself. People changed to get by, or make do with a new life. What had helped her get by was the knowledge that it was all temporary. She could be herself again once she was a stylist.

"Do you really have to study *that* again?" her father had asked, eyeing her student styling kit. He and his mother couldn't believe she needed certification to work in a hair salon.

By that time, Sophia had stopped explaining herself. It helped that they had ceased being the family in Manila who sat together for supper. Samuel had begun the habit of using school work as an excuse to hide in his bedroom. Because what was there to share at the dinner table? Her parents, surely, were not in the mood to discuss the number of resumés they had sent out to jobs with the colleges and the school boards, for which they had deemed themselves qualified. Their eloquent applications were met with silence, their courteous phone calls answered with equally courteous rejections. They eventually had to lower their sights, aim for minor clerical positions. Weeks went by, funds dwindled, and optimism frayed. Sophia came home from her closing shift one night just in time to catch her father leaving for work, wearing a neon-coloured vest for a security shift at a construction site. Not long after, her mother joined an after-hours cleaning crew. They trudged in and out of their basement suite like tired, shivering machines. During those first years of being away from their friends and their hard-earned careers, Sophia never saw her parents shed tears, but noted their faces eroding into humbled expressions, their voices becoming softer, cautious, and subdued.

She's not too bright. Not even for cutting hair. Sophia gripped the wheel tightly. Her father had meant those words for Auntie Rosy, but that morning she had the urge to pull the thinning patch on his shiny head. Hair represented a person's youth, vitality, and glory. Living in Canada had made her father old, tired, and powerless. No wonder he had become so bitter.

It was only when she had turned into the street where her hair salon was located that Sophia got a sense that she had been driving angry. Not fast, thankfully, but her jaw was set and her joints felt taut. Now that she was in that tree-lined street, driving by walk-up apartments with large murky windows, she loosened her hold on the wheel.

When she had been hired by Olivia, the salon's former owner, Sophia was struck by the silence of the neighbour-hood and the salon itself. Clients who chatted during their appointments were rare; the exchanges never swelled in the same way she remembered happening in Cine Star, where one woman's story was feasted upon by every ear in the salon and rewarded with a biting commentary. In

Vancouver, people rarely invited themselves into a conversation. It seemed to Sophia that many clients came and went, treating the city like a launch pad for other places better suited for permanence. While those who stayed kept to themselves.

True, she had her regulars, even Olivia's once-regulars. But many of them had moved to other places. Then there had been several women who sat in her chair, giving off a foreigner's air. International students from Japan. Australian tourists with seasonal jobs. She spoke Tagalog to old women from back home who complained about their English-speaking grandchildren. Meanwhile, new hair salons were opening up along Broadway and Main, their large windows featuring the sight of hip, shiny interiors. Erica had been convincing her to create a Facebook account for the salon, and Sophia knew she needed to look into this option soon, on top of many things she had to think about.

Erica was already waiting at the locked back door by the time she drove onto the parking lot.

Sophia had been running the salon for half a year when she put up an ad for a chair rental. After showing the salon to students wearing exotic bleached cuts and to stay-at-home mothers wanting a little extra money but not too many hours, she was relieved when Erica Sloane coolly walked in. Erica was friendly, minus the put-on sisterly voice and crinkling smile. She inspected the station, peeked in drawers and the closet, and then asked to see the washroom. A gig for an independent movie had brought her to Vancouver, and she had been a mobile stylist since then. She wanted to have a space for a change. Sophia couldn't detect need in Erica's voice. There was a hint of pickiness, even. "Looks nice," she said as her fingers lightly touched the station she would be working in. "Four hundred a month, right?"

Sophia wanted to share the salon with someone composed, not given to volatile emotions. Businesslike but easygoing. Like Erica with her brunette elfin crop.

"I'm sorry. My brother needed a ride," Sophia called out in the rain.

"Guess who was here," Erica said.

"Who?"

"Adrian. You just missed him. He thought you'd be here before me."

"Oh. What did he want?"

"I dunno." Erica grinned. "A quickie, I guess."

"Did he say anything?"

"Nope. But he looked a bit heavy. Like he wanted something off his chest."

"Really?" Was something troubling Adrian? The past weeks they had spent time together, he had seemed drained; date nights were spent on his couch. Sophia checked her cell phone. There was no new message. Strange. Sophia swallowed the apprehension balling up in her throat. She often dropped by at Adrian's place after work so there was no reason for him to come to her salon before she opened unless he wanted to say something important. "You should have asked him to stay."

"I don't work here as a fiancé sitter," Erica teased, unaware of Sophia's unease.

"Some friend you are."

"Poor guy. Why are you still living with your parents, again?"

Sophia threw Erica a pretend-annoyed look, masking her actual displeasure at this usual jab. Erica had moved out of her parents' home at eighteen and lived in four cities since then. Gone out with boys since she was twelve, and for as long as Sophia had known her, was taking a break from men. Her face seemed always cynical, like she had known too many disappointments. She wondered what Erica would make of her curfewed past, the scant under-whelming men she had dated.

She was grateful for the friendly dynamic they had reached now. During their first weeks of working together, they had been cool and impersonal, often just talking about the weather and things that needed to be done around the salon.

A row of tiny potted succulents on the glass counter greeted her as she opened the door. The scent of citrus-infused cleaner hovered in the air. In this space, many women had confessed to Sophia that their jobs were the easiest part of their day, that work was their break from their families and the endless list of tasks that waited at home. Sophia nodded truthfully at such assertions. Now that she had arrived at her salon, she was feeling lighter. Capable and in charge.

The first thing she had done after taking over was to get rid of anything that looked heavy and oppressive. The fabric sofa with chunky armrests and chaotic whorl-like prints made way for a plain black vinyl replacement with thin chrome legs. She discarded the fake plants she had dusted leaf by leaf, the jars of scentless potpourri. Wide and square-backed moss-green stylist chairs were replaced by hydraulic seats with chrome-plated legs and gleaming black cushions with rounded backs and armrests. The tall glass shelf housing the hair products for sale took a lot of floor space because Olivia had used it as a divider between the work area and the back of the salon where she kept their cleaning supplies and the boxes products were delivered in. Sophia removed its contents and pushed the shelf against the wall, opening up space for two shampoo stations, which she planned on using more often. She hated that Olivia never offered a wash for a basic haircut and used a spray bottle of water instead. The unsightly heap of odds and ends at the back was sorted—mostly useless junk; boxes were flattened; the mop and broom hidden in a closet. When she returned the hair products to the glass case, Sophia didn't cram them side by side the way Olivia used to do. The bottles were arranged with even spaces between them, which looked neater, more presentable.

She peeled off the posters of heavily made up models with stylish cuts and tall dramatic updos, leaving the two newest-looking ones: the tousled copper pixie, and the jet-black, silky mid-length bob highlighted with a sliver of navy blue. The front window was also stripped of posters, brightening the space inside. For the longest time, Sophia had held her tongue from pointing out to Olivia that the place had way too many posters. After scrubbing off the adhesive stains left behind on the wall, Sophia installed floating shelves on which she placed potted pothos plants with vines that spilled gracefully over the ledge. In a thrift store, she found framed prints: a palace garden vivid with yellow and crimson blooms, a sailboat on the verge of eclipsing a sunset, a clearing bathed in mellow rays piercing through the surrounding woods. Sophia hung these pictures in separate places to offset the randomness of her selections. She liked the clients to see something beautiful on the plain walls of the salon, happy and calming scenes. Not the usual salon posters of models with perfect hair.

All that remained from Olivia's days were the faded blue colour of the walls and the three stations: the two on the south side of the salon were hers, and Erica worked at the other side, behind the glass counter. Olivia also left behind her hair drying chair, which now stood next to the shampoo stations, rarely used. Parked between Sophia's two stations was a black salon trolley, another item she had purchased brand new.

Erica was perusing the appointment book. "Maggie's coming in for a touch-up."

Sophia glanced at the wall calendar. Maggie, one of her regulars, was getting married in two weeks. Light golden-brown hair. She chatted non-stop from wash to blow-dry. She had asked Sophia and Erica to come to her parents' house on the morning of her wedding, so they could style her and the bridesmaids. The wedding was on a Sunday, when the salon didn't open till the afternoon, so Sophia agreed. While it flattered her that Maggie had chosen her for the special occasion, she felt anxious as the date approached. Sophia imagined the harried and nervous pre-ceremony air, her salon supplies strewn around someone else's home, while a photographer documented their every movement. There were days when she wished she had turned down the gig; she could already imagine the chaos. But she loved Maggie and the salon could use a well-paying gig on a Sunday morning.

She made a quick inventory. For the wedding she had to fit her entire station into a kit or two. Hairspray, mousse, dry shampoo, and hair shiner. Capes, towels, combs, and brushes. Erica had said she would bring her own supplies, but Sophia felt safer bringing extras of everything in case one of them ran out. She scanned the workstations, searching for more items that she needed to add to her list and noticed the faint film of dust coating the row of light bulbs above the mirrors. There was the same powdery layer on the baseboard heater. She made a mental note to do some cleaning. Tonight wouldn't work; she needed to see Adrian right away. Perhaps tomorrow—Monday mornings were usually quiet—or after closing time. How sweet it would be, Sophia thought dreamily, to have an assistant who would clean the salon all the time. She envisioned Sophia's Hair Salon becoming an upscale boutique place, attracting the city's most stylish. Yet what she had right now was enough. She had arrived only a few minutes ago and her mood had already improved. The salon might be not as new, not as flashy, but it was hers and beautiful things happened in it.

Her reflection stood tall in the same mirror she used to clean for Olivia. She had been unprepared when she jumped at the opportunity to own a salon. How clueless she had been! Going over the salon's income, tallying it against monthly expenses, needed maintenance and upgrades, had been overwhelming. She waded through tiring paperwork and endless pans of grime and dirt. Even on her worst days, she had to put on her cheeriest mood for the clients. With everything she had gone through, Sophia thought she should be calmer, wiser, but she didn't feel these at all. Her eyes landed on her set of styling scissors. Glinting blades with sharp tips that could cut through skin. In the mirror, her face darkened. Back in Manila, Auntie Rosy was more careless than ever. Without Cine Star, how much support did she need from Sophia? Were Auntie Rosy's parents and siblings still relying on her? Could she get back on her feet after such a horrible mistake? She wanted to talk to Adrian—he would be calm and reasonable about this—but if something was bothering him, this didn't seem to be the right time.

"Erica, have you ever hurt a client with your scissors during a haircut?"

"Whoa! Why do you ask? Did you hurt someone?"

"No, no," Sophia said, laughing. "Just wondering."

Erica smoothed the tuft on her forehead. "I know stylists with arthritis that can still manage well. You have to be overly clumsy to hurt someone. Or vengeful." She playfully raised an eyebrow.

"True." Sophia smiled, inwardly battling worrying thoughts.

MAGGIE WAS ON TIME. SHE SAT ON SOPHIA'S CHAIR, TAPPING her foot, the top part of her hair gathered up with a sectioning clip.

"I was hoping to do the touch-up closer to the wedding. But my calendar's filling up fast. My girls want to whisk me away for a stagette God knows where."

"Two weeks before is still good." Sophia was stirring powdered lightener and peroxide developer in a tinting bowl. The mixture was too runny; it dripped from the brush when it needed to be more like a paste. She added a scoop of lightener.

"We went over the budget on flowers and Patrick's not happy about it. And, oh my God, the seamstress sent back the dress and it's still too long. After so many fittings at the shop."

The mixture was too dry now and Sophia poured in a little bit more of the peroxide. Then she realized that she was using 30 Volume, instead of 20 Volume. *Shit!* She would overbleach Maggie's highlights by a couple of shades.

"So, have you and Adrian started planning?"

"One sec." Sophia turned toward the bathroom and almost bumped into Erica's client who had just stepped out of the door. "Sorry!" Sophia said to the woman wearing a styling cape.

"You're such a bully!" Erica joked.

Sophia dumped the unused colouring in the bathroom sink and rinsed the tinting bowl. She exhaled a full pocket of air, collecting her bearings. When she returned to her station, Maggie was leaning forward, studying her face in the mirror. "I need a facial appointment too. I'm breaking out. Talk about bad timing."

"Take it easy. Everything will work out fine." Sophia had triple-checked her products and was mixing colouring again.

"Hey, so you guys found a venue?"

"They're going to get married right here in the salon," Erica said.

Maggie giggled.

"Not a bad idea." Sophia smiled as she began weaving the end of her pintail comb to pick up the highlights behind Maggie's right ear. With the blond lock secure in her fingers, Sophia took a piece of foil with her other hand, folded its top edge, and held it against Maggie's scalp right beneath the section she was holding. Releasing the strand, she could now clearly see the brown growth against the foil.

"We're still working on it," she told Maggie as she applied the colouring with her brush, the batter-like mixture clinging to the dark sections. The sight of the dye's perfect consistency relaxed Sophia.

"When are you guys getting married, again?" Erica asked.

"August 14." Sophia folded the piece of foil on top of the touched-up section and moved her comb toward the back of Maggie's head. It was the only solid detail about their wedding—and less than a year away, Sophia realized. Last April it had felt like they could plan things slowly.

The hum of Erica's hair dryer filled the salon, drowning out Maggie's voice right after she had said "to make it easier—" Sophia removed the clip on top of Maggie's head, releasing another layer of highlighted locks. She caught the tail of Maggie's sentence, "—it's all about the memories, you know?" Sophia nodded, eyes trained on her comb working through the highlights.

Then it was quiet and Erica was smoothing her client's new cut with her fingers. Maggie seemed oblivious to the noise level in the room. "I've learned not to be so picky about the little things. The important thing is that we make our way down the aisle. And back." She giggled. "But I swear, there are days when the stress makes me want to call the entire thing off."

4

P LEASE LET THE SITUATION BE UNDER CONTROL.
After closing the salon, Sophia had felt torn about what to do next: to chat with Erwin about Auntie Rosy or to see Adrian who had missed her earlier that day. Erwin had won out because of the difference in their time zones; it was morning in Manila now and he only had the late morning to early afternoon free before his commute to Makati for his graveyard shift.

There was a time when Sophia steadfastly believed that their friendship wouldn't change; it would weather tides brought about by time and distance. If their family hadn't moved to Canada, she would still be seeing Erwin, as well as visiting Cine Star frequently. But they rarely talked now, even if Sophia would catch him online on Skype. When one of them actually initiated a call, in which Sophia spoke of the stresses of managing her salon, while Erwin relayed some office scandal overheard in the break room, it seemed as if they were lukewarm acquaintances. They smiled politely while the other laughed, they sighed kindly when the other complained. They would talk about the neighbourhood, and if there wasn't anything juicy, they dipped into the past, a tired but reliable topic.

As she waited for him to go online on Skype, she hoped Auntie Rosy's situation was not as grim as her gut told her.

"Sofi, hello!"

"Thank God, Auntie Rosy's not with you," Sophia said, seeing only Erwin on the screen.

"Oh, no! She's actually right here next to me." Erwin started to adjust the webcam.

"Oh!"

"Joke lang, 'no!" Erwin laughed. "It's just me. She's on her way though."

"Putcha, Erwin!" Sophia relaxed. "Kumusta?"

"Just woke up, having breakfast." Erwin held up what looked like a homemade sandwich. "I don't know what to do with Auntie. No one will come to the salon now except for the ever-loyal Aling Soledad." Erwin twirled a forefinger pointing toward his temple.

"How's Auntie doing?"

"Last week she came to our place asking for rice— good thing my father wasn't home. I asked her how she's getting by, and she said her savings are running out. The accident happened two weeks ago. I don't think she has made any money since."

"Oh God," Sophia mumbled.

"That is why she asked me if I can get you to chat with her," he said sheepishly. "She's desperate."

"So, about the client, was it really an accident?"

"That's what she says. That she turned her head while she was cutting her hair. But Auntie's always going out with her usual drinking gang." Erwin looked troubled. "Those guys like having her around for fun. Sometimes Auntie would be too hungover the next day and open the salon late."

"Erwin, what do you think really happened?"

He shook his head. "I don't know. The client was a grown woman. I just can't imagine someone not sitting still during a haircut. I know Auntie drinks, but I like to believe she has some common sense."

"Maybe she's sick," Sophia mused. "With arthritis, or something."

"She's not that old."

"She doesn't have to be old. Aling Soledad is not old and she's lost her mind," Sophia pointed out.

Erwin sighed. "When I head out to work in the evenings, I sometimes see her hanging out at the stores. Even now that she's not making any money."

"How is she managing this?"

"I think her friends are treating her."

"If they are real friends, they would get her things that are useful. Like food, for instance." Sophia was annoyed. How could a failing business owner go out to drink at nights?

Erwin shrugged. "She's lonely."

"Right." Though she seethed at her friend's immaturity, Sophia was somewhat relieved that Auntie Rosy hadn't entirely lost her fiery spirit. What would have happened to her own life, if not for Auntie Rosy's gutsiness, her way of thinking that shuns the right way of doing things?

Years ago, when Erwin had gone to college and was no longer free in the afternoons, Sophia still showed up at Cine Star to watch Aling Helen and Auntie Rosy work. She wondered whether she would be able to find time to do this once she herself attended university.

At school, there was an exhilarating charge in the air that she was growing to hate. Her classmates talked only of two things, graduation and college. Everybody knew what they wanted to study, and they wore their plans proudly like a medal. A degree in education to become a teacher. Many girls were applying to nursing schools. Boys talked about attending maritime programs to earn a lot of money working aboard a ship. Even the dumbest kid in class had decided his major.

At home, her parents talked about moving to Canada. "This country is hopeless," her father lamented, and Sophia wondered whether all those miserable nights of doing homework on the dining table would amount to nothing if they stayed in the country. They heard stories as she and her family stood in endless, humid queues for passports and all other documents with complicated names. Relatives and friends abroad took on jobs that were much lower than their qualifications, like the engineer doing construction work, a high-school teacher cleaning houses. Sophia looked up Canada on the internet, the slow dial-up connection gradually unravelling landscapes with soaring pine trees, craggy mountains with icy peaks. Neighbourhoods with smooth, even lawns and no people in sight. It was hard to tell whether it was a place of freedom or her continuing captivity. "You and Samuel will have better lives." Her mother said this as if she knew for sure.

Sophia initially thought that this meant her choice of college program would matter less. Why bother if they were headed for a country that would strip them of their diplomas? But her parents pressed on about her plans after graduation, reminding her that their application to immigrate might get denied. They pushed Sophia to medical professions: nurses and doctors were leaving the country for foreign hospitals. She sullenly shook her head, explained she needed more time to think.

Her mother called her indecision laziness. Her father, surprisingly, had the kinder word—confusion. The annoyingly perky career counsellor who had given a talk to their class called it pressure, and her friends said Sophia was freaking out. Nothing they said gave Sophia answers, and only reinforced her belief that none of them knew what they were talking about.

"You can take the general courses and figure out your major later," her father suggested. He dutifully drove her to various campuses around Manila to take admission exams—each trip a tiresome litany of pep talk with a rundown of testing tips that made Sophia's head hurt even before she had read the first test question. After each test, her brain felt like porridge ready to spill out of her ears. She hardly cared about the results, only relieved that the test was over—for now. Months later, the universities sent their notifications in crisp white envelopes, all turning Sophia down for admission.

The rejection letters brought Sophia relief. Her parents

were growing anxious, but a rejection from a campus meant she had escaped another prison.

"Your grades aren't bad. How come you can't pass the exams?" Her father's patience was fraying.

Her mother was taking her turn to be the kind one. "She's just under pressure. You see, they don't make those tests easy."

The first acceptance letter she received was a blow, and Sophia resigned herself to having a respectable future. "Some mediocre college," her father had remarked, "but if your grades are good enough, you can transfer to a university."

It felt like a prison as Sophia had feared, made worse by the liveliness of the people around her. Many of her classmates were serious and driven, and those who slacked off were upbeat still, savouring a sense of freedom that Sophia didn't feel. Each day was a blur in which she slipped past cliques and sororities, greens and study halls, a tired shadow. Classes stretched for hours, and Sophia could only sketch so many faces and hairstyles. She always sat at the back, ignoring the lecturer at the front of the room.

By the end of the first term, it was as if the gripping air conditioner chill and stark fluorescent lights in the classrooms had snuffed out her soul. Sophia couldn't bear the thought of going through another semester. Her parents remained blissfully oblivious, calling her a late bloomer.

The day she was scheduled to register for the second term, Sophia left the line in the campus registrar's office. Her father's blank cheque for the tuition fee was folded in her clammy palm. She didn't want to go home, so she headed to Cine Star where Aling Helen, Auntie Rosy, and Erwin watched her weep.

"I want to run away and train as a stylist."

"You don't have to run away," Erwin said.

Aling Helen folded her arms. "It's not as easy as it looks. You think it's all about playing with hair and nodding to stories? You don't even know the crazy side of it, crunching numbers, not having holidays, and dealing with people's tempers."

"Diyos ko, Aling Helen, why do you have to be so negative!" Auntie Rosy threw up her hands. "Can't you see she needs some moral support?" She sat next to Sophia on the waiting bench. "It's a very rewarding job! You lift people's moods and give them a feeling of control over their lives by changing the way they look."

"Aba, Rosy!" Aling Helen planted her hands on her hips. "You don't know how much harder I work around here. She has to know this is not child's play."

"Ay, Ma'am, you need to take it easy. It wouldn't hurt to close the shop one day a week," Auntie Rosy said in a teasing voice.

"*Hmp!*" Aling Helen picked up the broom.

Sophia wiped her eyes, uneasy about this exchange. Erwin was looking outside, pretending to watch the children playing in the street. Then there was an arm around her back, Auntie Rosy holding her close. "Darling, we will get through this. Everything will be okay."

She had been yearning for this kind of sympathy. A chunk of the weight she carried for years melted, revealing a tiny kindling of hope. Sophia rested her head against

Auntie Rosy's chest. "I don't know what to do."

"Can't you tell them?" Auntie Rosy asked.

"It's impossible."

The salon was quiet now save for the children's squeals and the roar of vehicles motoring past. The familiar sense of isolation claimed Sophia again. She closed her eyes, the scent of peroxide from Auntie Rosy's fingers vaguely comforting her.

Gently, Auntie Rosy pulled away. "Sit here, dear. I'll go get us some snacks." She grabbed her wallet and left the salon.

Aling Helen's eyes followed Auntie Rosy with a look of annoyance. She swept the floor with short, quick strokes, hair and dust forming a pile at her feet. "Some assistant I picked. She acts like she's already made it big." The dirty mass ended up in a dustpan, and Aling Helen gestured with her broom toward Sophia. "Listen, if this is really what you want, tell them. They won't be happy at first, but you can't just cut off your family. You need to make an effort to be understood. When you become a stylist, you'll see that it's not the scissors, but the comb that we use for the tangles."

When you become a stylist! Sophia's eyes ached from crying, and her nose was runny. But where Auntie Rosy had left kindling, Aling Helen sparked a flame.

A client walked in. Erwin rubbed Sophia's back as she hurriedly wiped her wet cheeks and blew her nose with her handkerchief. Aling Helen led the woman to her chair. As she started working, another client arrived. "Rosy should be here any minute," Aling Helen said to her, holding back her irritation at being left alone again.

Erwin turned on the TV. A laundry soap ad filled the lazy afternoon. Then a jingle for a vitamin-enriched powdered milk for kids. Sophia now understood why some people found TV commercials annoying—they were too joyfully dumb. There was nothing that could help her difficult situation. Erwin nudged her shoulder, murmured something about a new three o'clock teleserye. She blew her nose again, the exertion hurting her head. Her despair was now turning into dread, her chest felt as if it housed thousands of flapping birds. Why was it so hard to tell the truth?

Aling Helen finished with the two women just when the angelic lead, playing a servant in the telenovela, found out she was made pregnant by the son of the rich family she was working for. Credits rolled, and a cheerful announcer asked them to stay tuned for the next episode. Erwin shook his head. "They'll make her get rid of it."

Aling Helen angrily pulled a chair. "Where is that Rosy?"

Sophia was wondering whether it would be easier to tell her parents she was pregnant when Auntie Rosy appeared at the door.

"Where have you been?" Aling Helen demanded.

Auntie Rosy placed a hand on Sophia's shoulder. She wore a calm, accomplished look. "Go home, Sophia. I talked to your parents. They know the truth now."

"What?" both Sophia and Erwin exclaimed.

Aling Helen looked suspicious. "You didn't create a scene there, did you?"

"No. They were quiet when I explained things to them." Auntie Rosy said simply. "They didn't believe me at first, but now they understand. They're not happy, of course, but it's all up to Sophia now. Sorry, I didn't bring any snacks."

Sophia walked home as slowly as she could. The birds in her chest were flapping harder now. She fought the urge to cry right there in the street. Her body felt encased in ice despite the hot and humid evening.

Her parents were waiting in the living room, still in their work clothes. Like they were expecting guests. A tide was making its way up Sophia's throat. Her head felt heavy and numb. Perhaps she really was only suited for mindless work. She wished she could just float, out of this situation, toward the night sky.

It was her father who spoke first. "We were told you don't want to go to school anymore." There was no accusation in the tone, just a cold statement of a fact. His elbows were resting on his knees, his chin perched on clasped fists. He looked like he was praying to her.

"I want to do something different."

"You want to be a beautician?" Her mother said this carefully, flinching a little. As if saying something hurtful.

Sophia nodded. Her father squinted at her as if studying a strange object, the lines on his forehead furrowing deeper. "You want to work with those women who do nothing all day but gossip and watch TV."

Her father's tone was that of a gathering storm, his words meant to slap her back into being the daughter he expected her to be. Sophia had never felt so alone in her life. "You don't have to send me to school. I'll support myself." Her voice splintered.

Her parents looked at each other with puzzled expressions. Her mother spoke with a reluctant kindness. "Rosy told us you were at the salon many times. Why do you go there?"

"They are my friends."

The angry slam of his father's palm on the wooden coffee table resounded in Sophia's chest, jolting her bones. "How many years did you lie to us? You should be home studying with Samuel instead of spending time with those stupid women!"

The corner of her eyes turned hot, she swallowed something bitter. Sophia stood, hearing herself breathe. True, she lied to them. Every single afternoon she spent in Cine Star was tinged with daughterly guilt. But what gave her father the right to speak like that of Aling Helen? Of Auntie Rosy?

"They're not stupid."

Her father chuckled in an angry way, something he did when he was exasperated beyond belief.

"What is your problem? Really, what?" Her voice had a surprising clarity and sharpness. A shard of broken glass. "You wouldn't understand the things they know even if they tried to teach you. You don't know them. And you don't know me. That is your problem!"

Her father attempted a response, but for some reason, wasn't able to say anything. She had stunned him speechless. This scared Sophia, but she stood still without averting her gaze. Had he demanded what they knew that he didn't know, or let out another furious outburst, she would have crumbled, weeping. After all, she was still filled with doubts. For many nights after she would still wonder whether she was truly throwing her future away. Whatever strange sense of certainty that had made her defy her father that evening couldn't be put in words, but it had enough weight to steady her during that moment.

From the wall of shell-shocked silence came a small voice, her mother's. "I can take her to the schools."

"You take her, Evelyn." Her father looked pained by his defeat. "And you, young lady, do whatever you want, but don't ever answer back like that again."

⋙

"SO COULD YOU HELP HER?" ERWIN LOOKED MEEK AND nervous on her laptop screen. "Look, she's not here yet. If you're still mad at her, I can say you're offline."

Did she want to hide from Auntie Rosy? Sophia felt bad for even considering this option. Years ago, it was Auntie Rosy who stood behind her, giving Sophia a voice at the time when it felt impossible to use her own. How could she let this woman go hungry?

"Hey, Auntie Rosy just walked in," Erwin said.

"Let me talk to her."

Erwin waved at someone not visible from her screen. "She's been drinking last night, so she's going to be weepy. Diyos ko, I could smell her," he managed to whisper, before standing up to offer his plastic chair to Auntie Rosy.

She was older and more frail. Sophia noticed the bulging crescents beneath the weathered eyes, which deepened into pools as Auntie Rosy started to cry.

"Sofi, darling, I thought I'll never see you again," she whimpered. "How are you?"

"Auntie, please don't cry."

Auntie Rosy wiped her tears with her forearm. "My head hurts so bad. But I really wanted to see you. Even when we stopped talking, I thought about you every day." She was steadying her voice, straightening her face, failing at both as she burst into another round of sobs. "I'm sorry that this has to happen for us to talk again."

A dash of unease shot through Sophia as she remembered the reason they had stopped speaking.

"How are you? Tell me how you've been. Erwin told me you're marrying a Canadian."

Sophia nodded. "Yes, Auntie. We've been together for more than two years."

"Is he a good man? Because if not, he'll get this." Auntie Rosy held up a bony fist.

"He's a very kind man." Sophia smiled. It felt good to glimpse Auntie Rosy's feistiness after all those years. "How are you doing?"

"I'm getting by with Erwin's help. Yesterday, he brought me sardines with rice." She patted Erwin who had pulled another chair beside her.

"Are you hungry?" he asked.

"I ate a little at home," Auntie Rosy said before turning to Sophia. "Darling, I just need some money so I can support myself until my clients come back. Whatever you can spare will help a lot. I can manage with very little."

How could she say no to this? "How much do you need, Auntie?"

Auntie Rosy looked really embarrassed now which made Sophia wish she had worded her question differently. "Just enough for food and bills. Until I can support myself again."

How long would it take for her to be independent again? Sophia thought, but she stashed this question away in her mind. She still needed to see Adrian tonight. "Auntie, I have to go somewhere. But I'll send you some money tomorrow, okay? Just to help tide you over."

"Ay, Sofi darling." Auntie Rosy clasped her hands. "Maraming salamat! You have a very good heart."

5

THERE WAS RELIEF TO HAVE MENDED THE RIFT WITH Auntie Rosy. The past three years, whenever Sophia had thought of Cine Star, she felt barred from the warmth of its memories. The reconciliation allowed her to reclaim her place in the beloved hangout. But after saying goodbye to her friends on Skype, the sense of unease had become heavier, more persistent. She wanted Adrian to allay her fears, to validate her decision. Wasn't she merely being kind by offering to send Auntie Rosy some money? Sophia couldn't shake the feeling that their bond was unravelling, entering a shaky territory. She remembered how Auntie Rosy looked tonight, the droop in her frame, the gauntness of her face. Eyes shining with undisguised pity for herself. This helpless beggar, profusely grateful for her generosity, seemed more daunting than the spirited and demanding woman who had angrily cut ties with Sophia three years ago.

"ELOPE? ARE YOU SERIOUS?"

Adrian didn't turn from the sink, but Sophia could see his shoulders tensing at the topic. Just a while ago, the scene had been peaceful, with her stretched out on the couch, enjoying the sight of her fiancé who had insisted on washing the dishes. After the Skype chat, Sophia drove straight to his apartment to find him engrossed in another video game. "Games again," she had called out, as she let herself in with her copy of his key, lacing her frustration with a playful voice. He had been playing for hours, it turned out, and he even forgot to make himself supper. The first-person shooter had a hold on him, gripping her fiancé in an intense shell of concentration that even Sophia found hard to penetrate. "How can you complain about having no time when you spend hours on these stupid games?" she had scolded while helping him whip up a late dinner of scrambled eggs.

Now Sophia felt a light wave of regret. Maybe, just maybe, she needed to pick her battles with this man who was caring, responsible, and had never been condescending the way her father could be toward her mother at times. When he recalled scenes of his boyhood mischief, Sophia was often in disbelief. Did he really, for instance, wrestle with his older brother? Kick over a slug so he could see what its belly looked like? It was a puzzle to her, the transformation she had never witnessed, and now she was the only person with whom he could share his playful side.

From the sight of him labouring at the sink, Sophia's eyes wandered to the polished kitchen counter and cupboard, the dining table adorned only with a potted plant she had given him, to the widescreen TV and speaker that were the only occupants of a glass media stand, their cables clinched together with a twist-tie. Shoes were promptly kicked into the coat closet by the door, and there was never a sight of a forgotten drinking glass or used socks on the floor. Instructional manuals, loose change, and leftover nuts and bolts from IKEA furniture had designated spots in this tidy space. Nothing floated out of place.

"If we elope, we could just go somewhere, sign papers, and tell people it's done. We could fly to Las Vegas next month and spare us all the hassle."

"I see." He turned off the tap and approached her, wiping his wet hands on his jeans. What happened to the kitchen towels she had bought him? Adrian knelt beside the couch, so their faces were at the same level. "Sofi, I know it's been hectic lately, but I don't think we need to hurry."

Whenever he stared at her like that, Sophia would get lost in the swirls of his blue-grey eyes, their honest, probing expression. Was he hurt because she wanted to make their wedding less special than planned?

She had come to talk about her decision to send money to Auntie Rosy. Maybe it wouldn't be much, but who knew how things would turn out? Either way, Sophia felt better Adrian knowing. She wanted their life together free from the fog of secrets. But a tired mood reigned tonight. Wanting some playfulness and ease, Sophia introduced the idea of elopement.

"There are just so many things to think about. It's kind of expensive too. Would be great to save money."

"There's no need to hurry," Adrian replied. "We actually need to take it easy."

"I'm not hurrying." She was getting this wrong so she tried a different tack. "Is something bothering you? Why did you come to the salon yesterday?"

She was surprised when Adrian dropped his gaze, caught off guard. "Nothing. It's nothing."

"I don't believe you. There must be something."

Adrian sighed. "Just feeling kind of overwhelmed. I was going to tell you I needed some time alone tonight."

Sophia's heart sank. "But you were playing video games. Don't tell me you have work tonight."

"I know." He squeezed Sophia's hand. "That's what I like about you. You're helping me focus on what's important."

She felt her disappointment in him melting, chased away by his guilty smile. Their relationship didn't need more pressure; it was time to take the edge off. Flashing a playful smile, Sophia grabbed his arm, pulling him. "Come here."

"Babe, the dishes ..."

"We're not married yet and you're already behaving like a wife," Sophia teased.

"Hmm ..." He untangled his arm. Then he was back at the sink, leaving Sophia to wonder if her joke had annoyed him. It had been months since he first brought up the transition happening at his work. A merger of two firms. Sophia had nodded sympathetically as Adrian broke the news that he was being transferred to a division specifically devoted to serving long-standing clients who had to be appeased about the changes in their financial management with quicker turnaround times. He was one of the hand-ful of junior financial officers who were recommended to assist in these complex time-sensitive accounts.

"You got this, babe." Sophia had kissed him, hav-ing sensed that he wanted her support. He had beamed, pleased and inspired.

Now it didn't feel right to complain about their lazy nights, or when Adrian's face would deflate whenever she suggested a movie they could go out to see. There was nothing to worry about. A lukewarm phase because of work stress was nothing compared to the bigger trials that awaited them as a married couple. Someday, they would have their share of *real problems*. Sophia hoped she would always be able to summon such patience and understand-ing even when she was alone with her own worries.

She walked over to Adrian at the kitchen sink, wrapped her hands around his waist. The water was running in a small, quiet stream. No wonder it was taking him forever to clean up. Sophia reached over to turn the tap. Adrian chuckled and scrubbed with his sponge a little harder.

When he finished, she was still clinging to his back. "Everything okay? You seem quiet," Sophia asked, her nose pressed against his spine.

"Just tired."

"Tired tired?" She slid her fingers under his shirt.

Adrian sighed. "Dead tired."

Sophia squeezed herself between Adrian and the sink, latching her fingers to the waistband of his jeans. His wet fingers were light against her back, almost not there, and she felt like a precious crystal in his hands.

"I think I overslept this morning."

Sophia tilted her head toward his bedroom. "You need a workout."

Adrian blinked, considering the invitation. Sophia kissed him on the lips—he looked handsome when baffled. By the time they landed on the bed, Adrian had come to life, seemingly ignited. Everywhere Sophia gripped him was warm, while Adrian's hands, still cold from the water, left swathes of moisture on her skin. In the tight clasp of their bodies, Sophia could feel tensions shrinking, their muscles loosening. The sunset casting rays from Adrian's window blended their shadows together as one.

THERE WAS A TIME WHEN AFTER MAKING LOVE, SHE AND Adrian would talk in a heady, gleeful mood before falling into a luxurious nap. But tonight, he kissed Sophia on the cheek and turned his back to her. She reached over and rubbed the knots on his upper back—he used to do this for her. Though he was quiet and still, Sophia could tell he was awake. Then he muttered, "Are you okay?" as if it was her who had been acting differently.

"I'm fine."

He stood up and put on his clothes with surprising vigour. Then he sat at his computer desk where the screen brightened with a spreadsheet listing long strings of numbers. Sophia stayed in bed, her bare skin soaking in the fading warmth left by Adrian's body. It was enough, she could fall asleep in it. Being in that bedroom always made her carefree and light. But she resisted the familiar sensation of surrender. She rose, walked over to her fiancé. "Something's happened back home."

Adrian didn't take his eyes from the screen. "What happened?"

"Auntie Rosy, she needs my help."

He looked up, still gripping the mouse. She had interrupted his work but he was ready to listen. "Who is Auntie Rosy again?"

"My friend." Then she remembered she had told him they stopped being friends. "We were friends, but she was also my mentor." But the word mentor was at once inadequate and excessive. Auntie Rosy taught her everything and taught her nothing.

Adrian's face turned quizzical once he remembered. "You haven't talked for a long time. Didn't you have a fight or something?"

"I know. But she's in a really bad place. Financially." Sophia decided not to talk about the accident. "She hasn't been getting any clients."

"Is this the reason you wanted to elope?"

"Yes. Wait, no!" Had he misunderstood her? Did Adrian think he was being enlisted to shoulder Auntie Rosy's financial hardship? "It's about saving money, that's all. I will be responsible for her. It's only until she can support herself again."

"I know you're not asking me to get involved. But do you think this is a good idea? You were just telling me the other week that you're too slow in paying down your line of credit. And the bank loan. You were also worried about slow days in the fall."

"I can't say no. It doesn't feel right."

"If that's what you want."

Sophia stood there, not feeling reassured. How would she make him understand? The image Adrian had of Auntie Rosy could only have been formed by how Sophia related what happened. They had started dating shortly after the falling-out.

That she and Auntie Rosy became salon owners in the same year convinced Sophia of their special bond. But Auntie Rosy had come first. Sophia could still remember receiving news of Aling Helen's death from Erwin. It was a particularly long day—she had stayed with Olivia after closing time to rearrange the furniture in the salon, which naturally entailed a thorough cleaning, so she was redolent with the sickening mix of hairspray and Lysol. In the shower she turned the water to the hottest setting. The feverish droplets created a cocoon in which she let tears flow and allowed herself child-like sobs. She emerged from the bathroom with red eyes.

This was the occasion that introduced her to Skype. Erwin sent an invitation. The two friends saw each other's faces for the first time in years. He still appeared stunned. "She had an asthma attack. We think it's the salon and traffic fumes."

It came rushing back, that laboured, whistling sound that they would hear in Cine Star from time to time. It was heard only during the rare times when it was quiet in the salon, as if Aling Helen had been concealing her sickness.

She never talked about it. But Sophia and Erwin knew to look at the skin on the hollow of her neck, frail and heaving like a kite in the wind. She would surreptitiously go into the bathroom, its walls unable to conceal the spate of thick coughs. Cine Star was closed when Aling Helen was sick—she didn't want Auntie Rosy running the salon on her own. To Sophia, it meant boring afternoons with Samuel after school.

"Auntie Rosy won't stop crying."

And she was still crying a few days later when Erwin brought her to the internet café. Sophia almost didn't recognize her. All she could make out in the dim video reception was a woman wearing black, with sunken rings around her eyes and thin shoulders, hunched miserably. "I can't believe she's gone. She was a generous lady. I don't know what I'll do without her!" Auntie Rosy wailed, fervent even in grief.

Erwin put his arm around her shoulders. "Don't worry, Auntie. I'll help out in every way I can."

Sophia's eyes welled, remembering the afternoons at Cine Star, the women she watched transform, the stories they shared along with the sugared bananas and pastries, the TV shows. And at the centre of all these idyllic memories was Aling Helen, with her gentle but firm recommendations and the sure glide of her combs and blades, gifting women with a lighter heart and step, a new beginning in their ordinary lives. Now she was gone, their merry gang one person short. Sophia was far, far away in this rainy city, closer to richer and greater possibilities. But back in dusty, sweltering Manila, she had lost someone dear.

"If there's anything I can do to help, please let me know," she said to her sorrowful friends on the screen.

Auntie Rosy had a keen ear. And, Sophia learned in time, no business sense. In the weeks that followed, Erwin would tell Sophia stories from Cine Star of overdue bills, broken equipment, and supplies running out without being replenished in time. "One time, she had to run out to buy shampoo when the client's hair was already soaked!"

"Is she doing okay? Maybe she's not ready for this," Sophia said.

"She always says everything's fine whenever I ask," Erwin said. "She's even talking about opening up branches."

Auntie Rosy's requests had been small at first. "Sophia, darling, the salon's lost all its good combs and the scissors are getting dull. Would you be able to send money for new ones?" Auntie Rosy would wring her hands. Then she would gush, "God bless you, anak," once Sophia promised to see what she could do. "Maybe you can throw in some extra cash to replace the chairs? Aling Helen was so thrifty she didn't care that things looked so old."

Sophia dutifully, even happily, sent cash. There was a tremendous feeling of satisfaction in being able to support the business where she had spent the best parts of her childhood. One evening, while browsing around London Drugs, she was struck with an inspiration. She armed herself with a shopping cart and headed to the hair care aisle where she grabbed litre bottles of TRESemmé and L'Oréal's professional-grade products infused with avocado, aloe vera, and tea tree oil. Nourishing conditioners, anti-frizz balms, hair shiners, moisturizing blends with botanicals. There were shampoos, conditioners, and other salon products back home of course, but they were sold in diminutive bottles stamped with incredibly steep prices. Sophia paused at the end of the aisle, realizing that of course, she didn't have enough to fill a balikbayan box. The packages sent by her mother to Auntie Mila usually took time to stuff, the gigantic cardboard box sitting in their living room for days, its humble, brown interior gradually growing festive and cozy with chocolates and stationery, jumbo packs of toiletries from Costco, pairs of Naturalizer pumps and Nike runners still in their boxes, all of them cushioned by folded clothes, some new, some her mother's hand-me-downs. Auntie Mila was employed and didn't have dependents, but how happy she was when she received these gifts.

Sophia's idea was to send her own balikbayan box to lift Auntie Rosy's spirit, breathe vitality into Cine Star. It was a much-needed support after Aling Helen's death. Her parents would surely say demeaning things about her lavishing Auntie Rosy with her hard-earned dollars, so the entire operation would have to be in her bedroom. She stashed away the hair products, the brush and comb sets, the towels, and finally the chocolates. She brought the box last, only when she had enough products, sealed and labelled it late at night. The only time the box left Sophia's bedroom was during the pickup date, which she had scheduled during her day off and while her parents were at work. Then she waited for its month-long journey to Manila to complete.

"Salamat—the rollers and towels are so beautiful—everything's so new in the salon now." Auntie Rosy was ecstatic the next time they chatted.

"She had to get a new shelf for all the products," Erwin quipped.

Then the request for favours got bigger. Once, Auntie Rosy needed money to repaint the entire salon. A few weeks later, she mentioned that the old TV was bad for the clients' eyes—a high-definition widescreen would be better.

"I'll have to see." This was the beginning of unease, Sophia realizing that she might have been too generous. Later she asked Erwin, "Is the salon not breaking even?"

"It's tough with Aling Helen gone." Erwin shook his head. "But she seems to have enough for drinking at nights."

Sophia was irritated. "Tell her to be more careful. With money, with herself."

"Careful?" Erwin said. "I remind her every time I drop by. But you know our Auntie Rosy."

At work, Olivia had started to depend on her more. Olivia of perpetual frown and sharp joints. Two years ago, Sophia had been intimidated by her, but now she was used to her acerbic expression and swift gait, recognizing efficiency and experience where she once saw panic and brusqueness. Between them, the favourite topic was family. "They hold you down, hold you together." Even with her veiny arms acting out a gesture of being burdened by a huge rock, Sophia understood that she was conveying something like a blessing. Over mugs of tea on slow days, she showed photos of her grown-up children, grandchildren, nieces and nephews. Sophia didn't have photos to show, but she talked about having grown up at Cine Star and making lifelong friends there.

"She must be special to you." Olivia sipped her tea after Sophia talked about the package she had sent Auntie Rosy. They were savouring the lull after a hectic morning. "It must be hard for you to be away from her."

Sophia tilted her mug, almost empty save for the drenched tea bag remaining in the dregs of the strong tea. It was one of those instances again when words were failing her thoughts. The seed of ambivalence had taken root at this point: she wanted to make Olivia understand that while she didn't regret sending money and the balikbayan box, she wanted to distance herself from Auntie Rosy. This new direction of thought was uncomfortable: avoiding the person whom she had talked about so fondly.

Olivia herself seemed preoccupied. Her worried gaze bore through Sophia, daytime glare highlighting the lines on her face. From time to time, Sophia had to work alone and for longer hours because Olivia had to see her mother in Abbotsford who was frequently ill. Sophia didn't mind—she could always use the extra cash. There were always upgrade courses. Her parents had bought a house and living with them meant contributing to the mortgage payments. Thankfully Olivia always chose a weekday for her trips, not wanting to leave Sophia alone during the busiest days. At times, she had to stave off boredom by reading magazines and counting the number of people who strolled by outside. But other days, Sophia found herself fielding a burst of walk-ins who seemed to have conspired amongst themselves to arrive within the same hour. Before closing up in the evenings, she wrote detailed notes to bring Olivia up to speed on the clients who had asked about her availability, phone calls from suppliers and property manager, and the day-to-day earnings. Being alone was tough, but it felt great to be trusted.

Olivia was morosely rubbing her chin. "I need to be away again. This weekend."

"This weekend?" Sophia swallowed. "You have appointments on Friday. And Angie's coming in on Saturday."

"I'll call them to ask if they're willing to reschedule." Olivia reached for her phone. "My mother was hospital-ized again. She'll probably get out soon, but she'll need someone at home. Every movement causes her pain. My sister's freaking out."

It turned out that Angie couldn't be rescheduled— Olivia had forgotten that she was attending a nephew's wedding that evening. On Saturday morning, Sophia brought out the bendable rods, which would be less severe on Angie's treated hair. As she wound up the curls, a young girl walked in for a haircut. Sophia indicated the other chair and handed her the styling magazines.

While waiting for Angie's style to set, Sophia turned her focus to the new girl. Square-jawed with thick chest-nut hair. She wanted to try bangs. After their consultation, Sophia gave her a mid-length cut, finished with a shattered perimeter that lent a textured backdrop to the sharp edges of the girl's face. By the time she finished the look with a full fringe skimming right above the eyes, there were two other walk-ins. And Amber was scheduled to arrive in less than an hour.

"I'll be with you right away." Sophia handed them the magazines. She tried not to hurry as she released and smoothed Angie's curls.

By the end of the three days, her shoulders were throbbing with hot, stiff pain, which she also felt coursing from her shins to the bottoms of her feet. As Sophia feverishly wrote her notes for Olivia, she comforted herself with the thought that there hadn't been any catastrophes. Sure, there were clients who had seemed displeased when Sophia made them wait or were offered later sessions. At one point, she was working three chairs at once, which made her panic a little. But she had survived.

On the day Olivia came back, Sophia busied herself with cleaning and organizing—chores she hadn't found time for when she had been alone. During a break in the afternoon, Olivia asked her to sit down. "I need to tell you something."

Sophia, noticing Olivia's tired and thoughtful face, anticipated another few days of working solo. She felt stressed about the idea.

"It's getting clear that my mother needs me more than ever. She's having a hard time moving around, taking care of herself. My sister, as you know, has young children."

The heaviness Sophia was feeling lightened, turned into a floating cloud of uncertain sentiment—somewhere between dread and excitement. Her gut sensed a bigger change.

Olivia dropped the bomb. "I'm thinking of selling you the salon."

"Oh my God!"

Olivia pressed her arm. "I know you want to run your own place. I need to move right away and it feels right to ask you first before seeking other buyers."

Sophia thought about her modest savings. "I'm not sure I'm the right person to sell a business to."

"I'll lower the price for you. It will be a turnkey business—you will get everything. Look into a small business loan. If you have good credit, things should work out."

During the commute going home, Sophia's lips kept pushing up into a smile. Owning a salon had been a distant dream and now here was the opportunity. The modest, sensible side of her told her she wasn't ready, that she had more to learn. The day she had arrived in Canada, when she and her family wheeled their belongings through the exit of the YVR airport as the wintry air blew on their weary, jet-lagged faces, was still a vivid memory. But who could truly say that she didn't have it in her? Those days of looking to other people to push her toward her desire were long gone.

"That's exciting!" Erwin said after Sophia shared the news. "But are you ready? You said you don't have a lot saved up."

"I know it will be a gamble," Sophia said. "But can't you see I have nothing to lose? My heart's about to burst!"

"Auntie Rosy's going to be so happy," Erwin said. "Next time I'll bring her to chat with you."

Once the loan was approved, Olivia agreed that Sophia would take over by October. Only three months away! On top of her usual salon hours, Sophia had an endless list of things to do. Olivia turned over her store membership accounts, but Sophia wanted to see if there were better places to get merchandise and products. She reviewed the lease agreement, pored over utility bills. The business licence and signage had to be changed. She signed up for evening upgrade courses.

"Darling, that's very good news!" Auntie Rosy exclaimed during a Skype chat. "I'm proud of you!"

And Sophia felt the glow of pride within her.

"But who's helping you out there? You need an assistant."

"I wouldn't be able to afford it at the beginning," Sophia replied. "I'll probably hire one when I can manage."

Auntie Rosy leaned closer to the screen. "Sofi, have you lost your mind? Why hire someone you don't know when I'm here? I have twenty years of experience of being the all-around person—styling, makeup, cleaning, and fixing things—you name it. Wasn't I your mentor?"

Sophia wished that the internet connection would fail right at that moment. Here she was, bleeding funds to start a business, and Auntie Rosy was trying to wring a Canadian visa out of her. She remembered Erwin's stories about Auntie Rosy's troubles managing Cine Star.

"Auntie, I don't think I can afford an assistant right now—especially someone from overseas." Sophia laced her voice with laughter.

"It'll be worth it, darling! I know the documents are going to take forever. Just the reason for you to get the process started right away. You'll be overwhelmed, but once I'm there, things will be a lot easier. And you don't have to pay me for the first year." Auntie Rosy's words were still reasoning, persuading, but her tone had the finality of a smart decision already made.

She imagined Auntie Rosy working in her new salon, telling her how things should be done, and taking breaks whenever she liked so she could explore her new Canadian neighbourhood. She loved Auntie Rosy, but there was no way she would run a business with her.

In the weeks that followed, Auntie Rosy talked to Sophia about how difficult it would be for her, a young lady in a foreign land, to run her own business. It only made sense to hire an experienced and reliable right hand. Sophia waited for Auntie Rosy to sense her hesitation, throwing a wordless plea at Erwin who sat beside her, equally helpless. She finally felt the cold now-or-never sensation when Auntie Rosy said she was excited to be working with blonds and redheads.

"Auntie, listen," Sophia began, nervously, "I never agreed to sponsor you to Canada as my assistant. I can't afford it."

Silence. Sophia shrank at the sight of Auntie Rosy whose mouth was still half-open in an interrupted sentence.

"The visa and other documents, they're too expensive, and it would take time ..." Sophia finished the reasoning in her head: *and I want to choose the person I'm going to work with.*

Auntie Rosy scowled and murmured something about Sophia changing her mind someday. In the next chat with Erwin, Sophia learned that Auntie Rosy had been telling some of her clients that she was going to Canada.

"That's ridiculous. I never promised her anything!"

"I tried to tell her, but she really believes you need her."

"Tell her to stop saying things that are just not true!" Sophia was furious. "What was she thinking anyway?"

The message was passed on. Auntie Rosy stopped joining their chats. When Sophia asked about her, Erwin said Auntie Rosy no longer considered her as a friend. "She was really mad."

6

OVER THE PHONE, ADRIAN SOUNDED HESITANT. He was behind on his work, he needed to stay late as usual. Sophia was feeling bad about insisting on having lunch together, but she really wanted to talk. As a concession, she offered to drive to the Greek restaurant right below his office. He finally relented.

Now she was driving along West Broadway, scanning the shop windows advertising hip workout clothes, bright banners boasting fusion cuisine, cavernous lobbies of greying commercial buildings. She was able to spot a Western Union branch two doors down from the taverna. But Adrian had sent Sophia a text—he was already waiting inside. Even their kiss was hurried, dry pecks on each other's cheeks. Before they could even open the menus, Sophia started talking about Auntie Rosy's accident and how she was going to need financial support for an indefinite period of time. She reminded him of how special

Cine Star was to her, how she looked forward to the final bell as a schoolgirl to hang out with Auntie Rosy. She had ultimately helped Sophia become the person she wanted to become. It was true that they hadn't spoken for a long time, but her situation was desperate.

Across the table Adrian was quiet the entire time. Then he finally shrugged, offering no protest. The restaurant had wooden chairs and small tables with rounded edges as if made for children; the diners looked odd in their crisp shirts and jackets, even Adrian, in his plaid, button-down shirt, seemed out of place. It was different when they had dined here in the evenings, the shadows thrown by the tea lights hiding the incongruities, and there were only their smiling eyes and the hearty aroma rising from their plates.

"I wanted to let you know because the last time we talked, I don't know, you seemed negative about it."

"No. I meant it when I said it's up to you." He looked at her as if asking if she had anything else to say. His fingers drummed on the tablecloth, pale against the Mediterranean blue. Sophia hadn't expected this lack of reaction. But she realized she needed neither his permission, nor his tolerance. She wanted her future husband to support her decision because he *understood.*

"Life there is different," she pressed on. "Eating out like this is a rare treat for someone like her. We do it a few times a week. My family eats at a Chinese restaurant every Sunday. And do you know that a few dollars here can cover a month's worth of bills over there? She really needs my help. But I am torn because she's the type to take your arm when you lend a hand. I have to guard against going overboard." She smiled. "I'm sure you'll see to it that I won't."

Adrian toyed with his serviette. "I really don't mind you helping her. Just do whatever feels right for you."

"Thanks. I'm glad you understand."

The weight was melting off Sophia's shoulder—she couldn't believe this conversation had made her anxious. But she also couldn't believe Adrian's lack of reaction. At times, he had acted as her voice of reason when it came to expenses, from salon upgrades to presents to her family. "Is your budget ready to take that on?" or "You're over-compensating again, Sofi. I'm sure it's not about the price." He would have a tenderly indulgent smile during these instances.

The server set two glasses of water on their table.

"Oh shoot," Adrian mumbled.

"What's the matter?"

"I left my wallet at home today." He felt the pockets of his pants and front of his shirt, holding out his palms after not finding anything. "Sorry, Sofi. Been kind of absent-minded lately."

"No, no, it's okay. I got it." Sophia reached out to smooth his hair. He rubbed his eyes, but they still looked troubled after a few blinks. She stroked his hair more, pro-gressing to a gentle massage. "Hey, if it's slow at work this afternoon, I'll look for restaurants, start making inquiries for wedding venues."

"Okay." Adrian was still pressing his eyelids with his thumb and forefinger. Sophia, who had expected him to be grateful for taking on the wedding planning, felt a little wounded. They each ordered a full roast lamb meal. In one of their earlier dates in the same restaurant, Adrian had gaped when Sophia finished the dish. "Goodness, I can't believe a tiny girl like you can eat that much!"

"I had a long day," Sophia had shrugged. "Don't you find yourself needing fuel after working hard?"

Today, she felt like she could once again finish a gigantic meal. As they pried roasted flesh from bones, Sophia studied her fiancé. One side of his face was illuminated by the window. There were faint lines on the skin at the side of his eyes—ones Sophia couldn't remember being there before—that made her wonder what other changes had taken place.

※》》

HAD IT REALLY BEEN TWO-AND-A-HALF YEARS? SOPHIA'S Hair Salon was a fledgling business then, feebly reaching its first spring. During the winter, Sophia had had to endure her parents' endless questions about how her salon was doing financially. They were waiting for her to buckle and admit to having made the wrong career move. But the brighter days brought in new faces, adding to the regulars who had been trickling in after Olivia's departure. There was actual income in April. As the deadline for filing taxes approached, Sophia had begun searching around for an accountant. Her father usually filed their tax returns, but she wasn't going to let him see how badly she had done those first months.

"There are some guys from my work who do income

tax filing on the side." The lady whom Sophia was giving a trim worked as a temporary receptionist for a newly founded accounting firm. "I can take your card and get you connected to this guy I have in mind who's really cool. Cute too."

Sophia could still remember waiting for Adrian at a café, how she had waved when the door was opened by a clean-cut guy with a kind, searching face. When he nodded at her from across the tables, Sophia suddenly realized that she had acknowledged him without knowing what he actually looked like.

"Hey. Are you Sophia?" He had the tired but obliging posture of someone who had just finished a long day and just wanted to get this meeting done with. He took off his jacket to reveal a cleanly pressed shirt. "How did you know...?"

"I don't know. Jane said you're a good-looking guy." The ends of Sophia's lips curved up, her cheeks throbbed as she stifled an embarrassed laugh. Had she come across as too forward? As he bought himself a drink, Sophia debated whether she should follow him to the counter and offer to buy. He was, after all, working for her. She decided to stay put and look through her paperwork, fixing a businesslike expression on her face.

Some frenzied piano tune was playing in the café, and Sophia wondered if Adrian could concentrate as he went over her receipts, invoices from suppliers, and the lease agreement. She nervously sipped her tea, watching his expression for signs of disapproval. It occurred to her that he was looking at figures she had never shown to anyone before. Papers that chronicled risky decisions that hadn't paid off so far.

"You keep a good record of your expenses. That will help a great deal." There was a tinge of consolation in his voice.

"Oh, I try my best. I'm afraid I had a rough start."

"Pretty normal for new businesses." He was still looking at the papers.

"I still live with my parents." She regretted offering this information right away. But Adrian raised his eyebrows, in an amiable, even congratulatory manner. "Good for you."

Sophia had expected tough questions, with pointers about debt management and expenses. But Adrian had a manner that made him seem apologetic about his skill and knowledge. When he said, "There might be deductibles that you don't know about," it seemed to Sophia that he was blaming himself for her ignorance.

"I can work on this myself, if that's easier. Some people are completely comfortable doing it on their own, and they just want me to show them how it's done."

"I'm really not in a place to learn that for now. It's better if you do it." There was something about him that made it easy for Sophia to reveal herself, but now she worried that she was sounding like an idiot. "I would like to learn how to do this on my own someday," she added.

There were a few moments when their tiny table shook, making her wonder if her nerves were showing through. She couldn't wait to tell Erwin about this cute guy. Then she realized that it was Adrian's foot that was making the table shake. His black leather shoe was drumming against its single thick leg. At times he would stop, only to continue tapping after a moment. A crease emerged between his brows from time to time, as if he were getting a drastic haircut that was too late to prevent.

"Excuse me, Adrian. Is everything okay?"

He blinked at her. "Pardon me?"

"It's just that you seem distracted."

"Oh." Adrian straightened, looking taken aback. Sophia wondered whether she had come across as intrusive. Crossed the line of Canadian politeness.

"I'm sorry." Adrian laughed a little. "Just kind of stressed today."

"Oh, I could meet another time."

"No, no, it's all good. I've just been jumpy today. My younger sister in the Yukon is giving birth to her first baby."

"Oh, that's wonderful!"

"Yeah." Adrian now allowed himself a quick a peek at his cell phone. "She went into labour last night, and we've just been a bit worried because it might be a complicated birth. But, anyway ..." His voice levelled to a professional tone again. "Uh, if you let me work on this, I'll be able to finish it before the end of next week. Hopefully. I will call if I have questions."

"Maybe that's better." Sophia watched as Adrian gathered the documents and carefully placed them back into the manila envelope. "I hope everything goes well for your sister."

"Thanks. My folks are up there." He stuffed Sophia's envelope in a big mailman-style bag, which she noticed contained thick sheaves of documents and a laptop in a separate compartment. He seemed to be in a hurry.

"So, I'll go over these during the week, and I'll be in touch if needed." He looked up and Sophia decided to ignore the fact that he was repeating himself.

"Sounds good." They put on their jackets. Sophia wanted to get away fast, to be in a quiet space where she could replay their encounter and convince herself that the things she had said didn't make her seem too weird. Tomorrow this nice guy would be talking to his buddies about his crazy side client.

Adrian's phone, which was still on the table, beeped. A text message.

"It's my dad." He grinned after reading the message. "My sister had a boy and they're both doing well. Whew!"

"Wow, congratulations!" Sophia only then loosened her shoulders, which had been stiff the entire time.

"Thank you. And sorry for being out of it today."

"That's fine. I'm used to people just randomly talking about their lives." Sophia cringed. She couldn't seem to stop embarrassing herself.

A flush passed over Adrian's face. "That's good then."

Outside the café, she tried to remedy her faux pas. "I'm really happy for your sister. Please congratulate her for me."

"I will. Thank you." He beamed. "Oh, hey, don't I need your number?"

It was endearing, the way Adrian had waited until after her tax filing before asking her out. For many weeks the memory of their first meeting buoyed her mood. Sophia imagined him growing intrigued whenever she had opened her mouth, those times when she had feared she was talking too much and saying the wrong things.

He picked her up at the salon on their first date. "Where would you like to eat?"

The bright signs from the restaurants reflected on the dark car window as Sophia pondered the choices. She worried that a simple selection would betray the plainness behind the initial impression she had made.

"I'm not picky," she told him.

Adrian scanned the places, the car easing along the early evening traffic. Sophia wondered how he would feel about her not knowing how to drive, just planning to take lessons later that year.

"Come on, what do you want?" he coaxed kindly, excitedly. She sensed his eagerness to please her.

They ended up in a Japanese restaurant. When she had gotten a grip on her nerves, she studied Adrian's face, lit by the soft glow of paper lanterns.

"What do you do for fun?" he asked.

"My work is fun. I spend most of my time in my salon. It's not an easy job, though. People ask for a certain style, expecting to look a certain way. But hair has a will of its own. Working with it is a challenge I enjoy. It also feels great to be able to transform people, make them feel good about themselves." Sophia no longer felt insecure about explaining herself. "When I was young I used to hang out at a hair salon after school. Parents never found out until the damage was done. They really wanted me to get a university degree."

She noticed Adrian's thoughtful gaze.

"I'm sorry. I could go on and on. How about you?"

Adrian set his plate aside, placed his elbow on the table so he could lean forward. "When I first saw you, and your finances, I thought, 'Oh, another one of those passionate but inexperienced entrepreneur types.' Those who use their parents' money to follow their dreams. I did returns for people like that when I was in college. I could always tell those who wouldn't be in it for the long haul." He was revealing the shrewd and practical side of himself, but Adrian quickly put Sophia at ease with his next words. "But you're different. I can't figure out why I think that. Maybe there was something about the way you were at the coffee shop. I somehow sensed you were alone in your decision. But you seemed at peace. Truly happy despite all the difficulties. You took risks and I could tell you had a rough time, but I can tell you will manage. You just came across as a confident, self-assured person. I admire that quality. I said to myself, I will take a chance too and ask her out."

It was as if Adrian had seen through her, aimed a spotlight on her every desire and struggle and thought her to be extraordinary. Later that night, after he had dropped her off, Sophia ran her fingertips along her lips, the spot where his careful kiss had landed, which gave her the physical sensation of belonging after what seemed like a very long time.

They met after work, trading stories about their days. With spring gifting them with longer sunsets, they strolled along the seawall, gazing at the sleepy forms of distant ships. He smiled goofily when Sophia pointed out how serious he was most of the time. At the cinema, they snickered during the melodramatic parts of the plot, their stomachs aching with the effort not to laugh out loud in the darkness. They went for brisk walks on forest trails where they took turns hiding from one another. When one of them had a particularly hectic day, they relaxed at Adrian's place, lying with their legs coiled around each other's, waiting for the doorbell ring that signalled the arrival of the pizza or Chinese takeout.

In the fall, her mother asked Sophia to invite Adrian home for dinner. "Your father and I would like to see this man you're spending most of your evenings with." She could barely conceal her excitement.

On the way to their house, Adrian asked Sophia, "Do you have any tips for me?"

"Hmm, I really don't know," she said casually. "They're suddenly taking an interest in me now that Samuel's in college and spending more time on campus."

"Well, you're their only daughter too."

Her family was already seated at their round dining table when they arrived. *Jeopardy!* was on TV. Only Sophia's mother stood up. "Hi, Adrian. My name's Evelyn."

"Nice to meet you, Evelyn." They shook hands.

Sophia's father quickly glanced at Adrian. "Welcome to our home, Adrian." He then turned to the TV again. "What is Mexico?"

"What is Mexico," a contestant echoed. "Correct," Alex Trebek said.

Her mother pulled out the single chair that wasn't facing the TV. "Have a seat, Adrian." Sophia sat down next to him. Beside Adrian, on his right, Samuel introduced himself.

"How are you doing?" Adrian asked.

Samuel looked down at his plate. "Not bad."

Sophia's father blurted another question-response to the show. A contestant echoed him and the beep for error was heard. "Bwiset! Biglang malas." He took a gulp of water.

"Vincent!" Sophia's mother tilted her head, not very discreetly, toward Adrian.

"Di niya naintindihan." He didn't understand. Her father lifted the platter of rice. "Help yourself to some rice, Adrian."

"Can we turn the TV off?" Sophia eyed the remote control next to her father's plate.

Her father looked at Sophia, surprised. He then aimed the remote control at the TV.

"Oh, no, I really don't mind. I actually like *Jeopardy!*" Adrian placed a hand on Sophia's under the table.

Her father put down the device. There was a commercial break. "I'm Vincent, by the way." He extended his hand across the table to Adrian.

It seemed to Sophia that they were celebrating a special occasion. Her mother had prepared beef caldereta—the beef and carrots were simmered to tenderness and the potatoes were baked separately before they were put into the stew. She wondered how her mother found the time to do all of this when she had also made eggplant salad and pork chops.

"I heard you're an accountant," her father said to Adrian. He looked skeptical, as if he couldn't comprehend that a person like him could actually be spending time with his daughter.

"Actually, I assist senior accountants at our firm, but I'm working toward a CGA. Sophia told me you work in a bank."

"There are some young finance specialists at work who have absolutely no clue about numbers. They use calculators for even the simplest calculations, and have the nerve to tell me I'm doing things wrong," her father sneered. "I was a mathematics professor back home."

"One of the country's best," Sophia's mother chimed in.

Jeopardy! was back on. Alex Trebek was interviewing the contestants. "Maybe we should switch seats," Sophia's mother said to Adrian. "That way you can see the TV too."

"Oh, no. I'm good here."

"Come on, sit over here," Sophia's father said. "It's not the same if you can't read the questions." Her mother and Adrian switched seats. Sophia was glad they had left the TV on.

AFTER LUNCH, SOPHIA FOUND ERICA AT THE COUNTER, receiving payment from a well-dressed old lady. The air was heavy with the harsh odour of perm solution. Sophia held the door open as she wedged in a doorstop with her foot.

"How's the impatient fiancé?"

"Worked to death. You should go get something to eat."

"I was about to do a coffee run, but Lily walked in. Peroxide made me feel less hungry."

Sophia laughed. "Don't get addicted to it. It's not cheap."

"I know you only get the best. Well, now I'm gonna head to the deli and try to get myself a sweetheart." Erica winked. "So someone will treat me for lunch, too. Bye!"

"I paid for lunch!" Sophia called out after her.

As she had predicted, the afternoon was quiet. Sophia found the list of restaurants and venues for the wedding she had started months ago, right after Adrian had proposed. She was surprised to reach a booking manager who could meet with them that coming Saturday. A Pan-Asian bistro that had a ballroom on-site. Appointment at eleven. Finally, some progress. Sophia's excitement bubbled to a height she hadn't felt for some time.

That night, a message from Erwin popped on her laptop. "Auntie's here. She wants to chat if you have a moment."

Auntie Rosy started talking even before her face became visible on the screen. "Darling, I got the money. Thank you so much. It's a huge help."

"It's okay, Auntie." Sophia said. "Hope you got yourself some groceries."

"*Ay*, of course! I haven't had a decent meal for a long time! But I set aside some of it. I will now take matters into my hands."

Sophia thought that could mean something really good, or not. She tried to read a clue off Erwin's face. "What do you mean, Auntie?"

"That stupid woman spun her head while I was giving her layers, and now she's spreading lies in the neighbourhood about me being drunk on the job. Leche! No one comes to Cine Star now just because people see me drinking some nights. Aba, don't I have the right to enjoy myself once in a while?"

"I really think we need to wait it out," Erwin cut in.

Auntie Rosy turned to him. "I grew up in poverty, iho, so I don't mind eating the same stuff every day, if that's what you're worried about. What I can't live with is a ruined reputation. Sofi, I'm going to use your money to file a lawsuit."

Sophia's ears burned. "Ha? On what grounds?"

"Libel. Just like what movie stars do when tabloids write lies about them."

"The accident was in the papers?"

"No! But she was telling everyone. The damage to my business is up to thousands of pesos now."

"Auntie," Sophia sighed, "you sue someone for libel when someone writes something about you. Yours is more like slander, because it's by word-of-mouth." She suddenly felt stupid for bothering to explain this distinction. "Naman, Auntie, she got hurt in your business premises."

"Because she was an idiot!"

"It's your responsibility to ensure her safety in your salon."

"Why are you taking her side?" Auntie Rosy demanded. "Don't you believe me? I was careful the whole time. I have been styling for thirty years!"

"What you're trying to do doesn't make any sense, Auntie! Look, I want to help you with your basic needs, but there is no way I will fund your lawsuit."

Auntie Rosy looked hurt, but her forehead was still

knitted in rage. "Is that how lowly you think of me? Do you think I'm happy to get by through your generosity? I'm choosing to stand up for myself."

Sophia sat tall and gripped the side of her seat. "First of all, I have no plans to support you for life. Second, blaming a client isn't going to help you get your business back. This is ridiculous!" She was shaking out of nervousness, not anger. She had never raised her voice at Auntie Rosy before.

"You don't understand!" Auntie Rosy's voice splintered, her fortitude making way for despair. "I shouldn't have to admit to a mistake that's not mine. Well, now that you're getting married, you probably don't care for me as much!"

"That's not true!" A separate wave of anger engulfed Sophia. *What had marrying Adrian got to do with this?*

"I can live with hunger. I don't need your support to fight for my salon and for my name!" Somehow, Auntie Rosy figured out how to hang up the video call, ending their conversation with the dramatic abruptness of a telenovela episode.

The woman was not right in the head. Sophia wanted to bolt out of the house, drive to a Western Union branch, and demand that they return her money, even though Auntie Rosy had already received it. She settled for sending a quick note to Erwin:

Erwin,

I'm fed up with this—I've done what I can. She can do whatever she wants, but I'm not helping her sue a client. If she needs more money for food, etc., tell her to get another job. I don't want to waste any money on her stupidity.

Sofi

7

ON SATURDAY MORNING, SOPHIA FLUNG THE blanket away as soon as she opened her eyes, and rose so quickly that the room spun around her. She steadied herself, then pulled and smoothed the covers, humming a tune. She had asked Erica to work alone that day so she and Adrian could go to their restaurant appointment and spend the afternoon visiting party stores, florists, and confectionaries. She had stayed up late the night before creating an elaborate itinerary, which she knew was impossible to squeeze into a day, but she wanted to accomplish a lot on this day off. They would have fun too.

Her chat with Auntie Rosy a few nights earlier had left her with that familiar but unnameable feeling, somewhere between incensed and relieved, dismayed and liberated. Today she was tilted toward the happier end, feeling relieved and liberated. Sophia couldn't be responsible for the choices of a woman who refused to be sensible. She had done everything she could to help.

The rich and salty aroma wafting from the kitchen reminded her that she would be leaving this household soon, making her feel sentimental. If there was one enduring thing she loved about the family, it was Saturday breakfast of fried cured meats, scrambled eggs, and fried rice. Heading downstairs, she paused to study the framed photographs on the wall along the stairway. There was Sophia as a little girl with that unimaginative apple cut, wearing a radiant, toothy smile; she couldn't remember being *that* happy. The next photo was of Samuel, back when he still had flesh on his cheeks. He was grinning too. The last frame at the foot of the stairs was a family portrait: a coloured print that was now mostly yellows and browns. Sophia was sitting between her parents, her mother holding baby Samuel on her lap. She recognized the rattan sofa, the dark tawny curtains.

What happened to their lives after these cheery memories? There must be more photos upstairs, from graduations, birthdays, and other milestones that warranted stiff poses and frozen smiles. Sophia recalled Auntie Mila taking a photo of their family in front of the NAIA airport, posing beside a trolley piled with suitcases and boxes. Her mother would wave her pocket digital camera whenever the family was out to some forest park in Squamish or Hope. Funny how she remembered the capturing of such moments and not see them displayed.

There weren't any other photos around the house. The walls of their living room were plain. Their windows were shaded with blinds that came with the house; her mother had not bothered with curtains. The sofa was of rock-coloured corduroy, facing the widescreen TV on a low table made of thin slabs of wood and glass. Beside this was a frail-looking metal bookshelf holding a few paperbacks, unopened mail, loose change, and bundled keys. It was hard to believe that their living room in Manila had an entire wall devoted to books. Various novels and anthologies her mother read. Textbooks her father used for teaching, hefty volumes he had perused during graduate school. Sets of encyclopedias through which Sophia and Samuel were to learn about the world. Sophia wondered briefly about this stripped-down look. True, she had heard her father speak against clutter, her mother dismissing candle holders, vases, and other knick-knacks as gaudy objects that would merely gather dust. But the result wasn't an intentionally minimalistic look, but rather one that shied away from any semblance of taste and individuality. Only the pictures along the stairway spoke of the people who lived in this house.

In the kitchen, her mother was getting coffee started at the counter. She had been up early. Sophia could tell by the spread on the table and the lingering sharp smell of the all-purpose cleaner that made the stove and the surrounding kitchen surfaces shimmer.

"Where are they?" Sophia asked, wanting to eat right away.

Her mother tilted her chin toward the ceiling. "Your father's having the usual talk about the future with your brother. You know how he is."

"Really?" Sophia did not hide the sarcasm in her voice,

but her mother, who was now playing compassionate parent didn't seem to notice. Wasn't she the one who had echoed her father's constant badgering about her career decisions? She mentally stashed away this sentiment. Nothing could darken this day.

"Day off today, right?" her mother said. "Have you chosen a venue?"

"We're looking at this restaurant in Yaletown. Might be pricey, but it's nice."

"Are you excited to marry him?"

Sophia thought this was a strange question. "Very excited. Why?"

"That's very good. I'm happy to hear that."

They could hear her father upstairs, his words obscured by the closed door, but their seriousness resounding in the morning's silence. Once in a while there was a short response from Samuel.

"Your father is the smartest man I know. I was excited to marry him."

Sophia fought the urge to roll her eyes. Were they having a heart-to-heart talk now? The dreaded string of relationship tips usually followed such remarks. She could recall one time when her mother had asked what she and Adrian usually talked about. When Sophia answered truthfully that she told Adrian stories about her clients, her mother cautioned her against giving him the impression that her head was mostly filled with womanly gossip. Sophia had been stunned by the comment, and for many days constructed clever retorts in her head, in case the same kind of exchange occurred again. But she always found herself unprepared. There was no antidote to well-intentioned advice that happened to arrive with unintentional insults. Just like the time when Sophia had mentioned that Adrian was giving her advice about managing her salon expenses. Her mother's eyes had widened. "Don't tell him about your biggest losses. He might think you're careless with money. No man wants that."

Her mother sat down across the table, her face pensive as she sipped her coffee. "I knew I would go places with him. Achieve a lot of things. But, Diyos ko, he's never happy. Poor Samuel."

Sophia had to admit that she felt a little bad for her brother. But why make a huge deal about it on such a happy day? Besides, there was no way Samuel could disappoint them more than she already had.

"Ever since your brother started university, your father has been hovering over him a lot. You kids are all grown up. It's time for us to reward ourselves with a trip, 'no?"

"Wow! Where do you want to go, Ma?" Sophia asked, genuinely curious.

"But no, he thinks all those holidays are a waste of money. You know, I used to think I'm much better than my co-workers who were born here. I always tell myself I have the advantage of being raised and having worked in a different country. What do they know about dealing with rude clients? All they know to do is nod and smile, kill them with kindness. Me? I know when to bare my fangs to put certain people in place."

Sophia didn't know where this speech was going so

she looked at the kitchen drawers, imagining the cooking gadgets her mother purchased on a whim. A spiralizer. Pasta maker. Flower-shaped egg rings. Her mother who rarely cooked when they had lived in Manila now used her stentorian voice to remind her father to put things back where they belonged in the kitchen, and to wipe off the splatters he left around the sink.

"But then at lunch, they talk about places they have visited. London and Paris. Lima. Saigon. And I feel small, like I have seen so little of the world. I realized most of the things I know are from books. And that's because of your father." Her mother took another sip from her mug, wincing at the bitterness of her brew. "When I was about to marry him, everybody told me that he would change over the years. I was ready for that—I reminded myself to love him despite any change. What nobody warned me about was that he will never change."

Putting her personal grudges aside, Sophia had always been proud of her parents' solid union. They would go out for movies and the occasional concert from time to time. She wondered if years down the road, she would seek her mother's counsel, and they would forge a bond with their experiences as wives. Would she find herself lamenting about Adrian's shortcomings someday? She thought of the lines near his eyes. His face would always be kind. And handsome. She attempted a candid inventory of his faults. He worked long hours, making him feel entitled to a weekend's bingeing on junk food and hours of video games. When he wasn't working, he was a sluggish homebody. The flaws seemed trivial, hard to magnify.

Heavy footsteps on the stairs disrupted her thoughts. Then her father and Samuel were downstairs.

SOPHIA DROVE INTO THE PARKING SPACE OF THE BISTRO HALF an hour before the appointment. She could have asked Adrian to pick her up so they would arrive together, but that would have meant sitting at home, waiting for him. Instead, she texted him that she would bring her car and he could walk as he lived close to the restaurant. She was so excited like they were heading out on a holiday.

The shops around the area lured her with lavish displays. A window showed neon-coloured paper lanterns printed with cherry blossoms, suspended above matching leather sofas and futons. Sophia jogged toward the entrance, deciding to browse while waiting for Adrian. The thick smell of lavender embraced her, as if a wreath of it had been placed around her neck. Near the entrance was a cushioned patio set. Sophia traced her fingers along the polished surfaces. Once she and Adrian were married, next on her list was to make them a beautiful home. Her head was filling with design ideas, soft lines, warm colours, and matching prints. Adrian still ate on mismatched plates, and he didn't differentiate between a hand towel and a kitchen towel. Only his bedroom, which functioned as his home office, showed signs of adulthood: a double bed, computer desk, and some filing cabinets, since he took his work home.

There's a lot of upgrading to be done, Sophia thought with gleeful pretend misery.

"Can I help you find anything?" The sales clerk wore her shiny black hair in a ballerina bun and was smiling with perfect teeth. Sophia wanted to ask her about setting up a bridal registry, but it was lower on her to-do list. "I'm good, thanks." The sales clerk turned back to folding silk serviettes.

The Dutch ovens were priced at three hundred dollars. Sophia gazed at her reflection on the yellow glazed ceramic. She was mulling over closing the salon earlier in the evening once they were married, when her phone buzzed. A message from Adrian.

He was in a café a few doors down. Sophia guessed he hadn't bothered to make breakfast at home. Typical. She took a quick glance at the shiny frying pans, perfect for pancakes, before leaving the store.

Adrian was sitting at a table next to the window, hands around a small paper cup. Sophia was a little miffed that he hadn't bothered to ask if she wanted anything. "You slept in?" she asked as she kissed his cheek. "I guess we can be a little bit late."

"Sofi, I'm not sure I can do this."

She immediately knew what he meant. It landed on her like an ominous web, its cold, shattering truth settling without being wholly taken in.

"You're not sure about getting married?" Sophia sat down, without registering the cushion, the floor, or the table before her.

Adrian nodded, sliding the cardboard sleeve around his coffee up and down.

"Why?"

He glanced at the street outside, the brightness making him squint. Sophia wanted to fill in the pause, but her mouth had become dry. He continued fiddling with the sleeve.

"Please say something."

"I guess I'm not so sure if I'm doing it for the right reasons."

"What?"

"I thought ..." Adrian took a deep breath, blowing away what he first wanted to say. "You're great, Sophia. I care about you deeply. But I'm just not sure if I want to get married."

"We can move the date." She reached for his hand but he drew it back, hid it under the table.

"The thing is, I don't know if I'll ever want it. I've been thinking about this for a while. Maybe I'm not ready to become a husband. I tried to talk to you about this last Sunday, so I drove to your salon. But Erica was there and you weren't. I know this sounds stupid, but I took it as a sign that maybe this conversation was a bad idea. Or, I don't know, maybe I'm being nervous for no good reason. But I thought about it more this week and my feelings haven't changed. Or I guess, for you they have changed—"

"What's going on?"

"Actually, I'm not sure if my feelings for you have changed." There was a tone of helplessness in his voice that softened Sophia a little. "But I don't feel like settling down."

Sophia swallowed. "Why not?"

"I'm sorry. I ... I'm looking at my brothers and sisters—they were already married when I met you, and some had been parents for a while. I thought I wanted to be like them.

"And now you don't?" Sophia looked at Adrian, his face no longer a face, just a cold mask of moving features.

"I'm not sure. Sorry—"

"Why are you not sure?" She leaned on the table and it rocked to one side. She remembered the shaky table they had shared when they first met in a café, the memory gutting her.

"I guess I'm not excited about it anymore. I'm so sorry."

"Stop saying sorry! Tell me what's wrong."

"I'm thinking of the years ahead. I'm sorry, Sophia—"

"God, if you say sorry again—"

"—but for now, I don't see myself being married. That future that we planned together, for some reason, I don't want it anymore."

"What kind of future do you want?" There was a tiny flagging hope in her that she could still be a part of the life Adrian was visualizing for himself. He just needed to realize that whatever it was that he wanted, she would want it for him too. A wedding wasn't necessary, anyway. What truly mattered was they would stay together.

"I'm still figuring things out. I just don't want to drag you into this fog."

"We need to cancel the appointment." Sophia recognized the futility of this concern, but a bigger part of her was thrashing about, desperate to regain the blissful normalcy of that morning. "Is it the wedding? Really, we don't need to have it."

"It's not just that." Adrian practically whispered.

"Maybe we've been too busy lately." She didn't recognize her own voice. "We've forgotten how we felt. We just need to spend more time together."

"I thought about that too." He was looking down as Sophia absorbed this merciful possibility. "But whenever we spend time together, I've been feeling ... kind of a weight."

"I'm not the only one who's been moody."

"It hit me when we were talking about your friend." Adrian finally met her eyes. Sophia was surprised by the emotion brimming in them. "I realized we will need to decide on things together."

"Auntie Rosy? So you don't want me to help her."

"No, you don't understand. I don't care whether you help or not. But talking about her stressed me out. I had no idea she was that close to you."

"I've been telling you stories about her. That is if you've been listening."

Adrian shook his head. "I remember, Sophia. I swear it's not about money or anything like that. It's just that it hit me that we will make many decisions together. Huge ones. For the rest of our lives."

Sophia's hands folded into hot fists. "We have made so many decisions together. Like getting married."

"I know—"

"I was only trying to be considerate."

"I know. I get it. Thank you, Sophia." The renewed firmness of his voice made her bristle. He proceeded with a softer tone. "But it really struck me that our lives, our future will become one and the same. I'm not sure if that's a good direction for both of us to take. I think it's best for me to ... to be on my own for a while."

"Are you breaking up with me?" Her voice was louder than she had intended. The guy at the next table looked up from his laptop.

"I ... I don't know. If you want to."

"Why don't you just tell me what you want?"

"Because I don't know. All I know is that I'm feeling unsure about getting married. I wish my thoughts were more clear. I wish I knew what to tell you about myself. But I need to think, and I thought I should tell you now."

Her body remembered to breathe, the intake of air bringing tears to her eyes. Sophia blinked them away, turning to the window. The day was white, a car was gliding away from a parking meter, a dowdy-looking woman was passing by, pulling a shopping cart filled with plastic bottles. Everything in sight, storefronts and their displays, clothes and traffic signs, seemed to pale, their colours bleeding out. Her chest was a hollow cave.

"This hurts really bad," she said quietly.

"I'm sorry for hurting you. Sorry I can't say anything that makes sense right now."

She wanted to grab him, turn him onto his head like a bottle, and shake out every last bit of his inscrutable reasons. But Adrian looked at her with hard, crystal-clear eyes and Sophia knew she had run into a wall. She suddenly couldn't stand the sight of him. Or the idea that she was sitting there, pleading for him to give back her happiness. She stood up. He didn't look up. She wanted to slap him hard across the face for not trying to keep her from leaving. She became aware of rage bubbling wildly within. Before her was a coward who had just proven his extraordinary capacity to deceive her.

"Talk to me when you have something to say." She left the café, clumsily bumping into chairs and tables along the way.

The daylight was stark, the noontime sun searing her forehead. Sophia strode down the block, unsure where she wanted to go. She paused by the restaurant where they were supposed to talk about reserving a date, number of guests, table arrangements, and menu. The manager had to be told that the appointment was cancelled, but Sophia didn't have the strength to walk in.

At the end of the block, people were waiting to cross the street. She felt like she was standing on the edge of a cliff, that if she crossed she would plummet to a different life, a life without Adrian in it. The pedestrian sign flashed, people moved past her. She turned around. Maybe Adrian was still at the coffee shop, regretting what he had just said. Maybe he was waiting for her to come back. Sophia jogged toward the café, past their potential wedding venue again. They could be a little late for their appointment. Soon the glass window was at her side, and the tables in view were all unoccupied, except for the one at the very end where an old man was working on a crossword puzzle. She whirled around, scanning every face coming down the road, the passersby across the street. Adrian had disappeared from her life. A sob escaped her throat.

As she slowly made her way back to the car, the rage resurfaced. He hadn't said anything when she made that restaurant appointment. How long had he been unsure?

How many weeks had he been putting on this loving fiancé act for her? Why had he even proposed?

There was nobody home, her parents both working on Saturdays and who knew where Samuel was? Sophia wasn't sure whether she welcomed the solitude or not. She was bursting with the painful news, but also didn't want to have to say it aloud because that would make it real, something everybody else would have to come to terms with. Along the stairway, patches of faint sunlight hovered on the glass surface of the picture frames. As Sophia approached, her sorrowful face reflected against the smiles frozen from a long time ago.

In her bedroom she looked down at her bed, the quilt laid out neatly, smoothly sloping over her pillows. Just this morning she was in such a jolly mood. She let her stupid self fall forward, sprawled on her stomach. Shutting her eyes, she let the heaviness within churn violent currents as she wept loudly.

⋙

WHEN IT COULD HAVE STARTED, HIS CHANGE OF HEART?

Last May, Sophia had gone out with some of her friends from the hairstyling program. They were eight girls all in all, meeting up for Sunday brunch at a place a block away from their former school. It was Carmen, the loudest one in their class, sporting a silvery purple bob, who had noticed the ring. "Gorgeous!" She had grabbed Sophia's hand from across the table, inspected her ring over plates of eggs Benedict and whole-grain bagels. For the rest of the morning, Sophia could feel envying looks from around the table.

That night, she kissed Adrian and thanked him for picking such a delicately exquisite ring. Those were Carmen's words, and though she was not a jewellery expert, Sophia agreed with the compliment.

He merely shrugged. "I was nervous about picking one to surprise you. But they all looked the same to me."

Good going, Sophia had thought glumly. Why did he have to be so self-deprecating? But she had let it slide. It was the intention, the feelings, that mattered.

She was basking in the excitement of those first weeks and didn't put much thought into wedding planning. Life went on; they were both busy at work. Sophia fielded her mother's constant inquiries about the wedding date with the vague "Sometime next year."

Summer came along with the realization that while Adrian had made the engagement happen, it fell on Sophia to make the wedding take place. On Canada Day, when they had managed to set aside a whole day to be together, they went to English Bay in the morning. Sprawled on beach towels and surrounded with the quickly growing holiday crowd, Sophia decided it was an excellent time to talk about the event.

"I'm thinking of just a small party. We'll invite some relatives, our closest friends. My parents would probably invite a few co-workers."

Adrian lazily turned his head toward her. His bare torso glinted against the sun. "Sounds good to me."

"Do you have any ideas how you want it? Do you

want it outdoors or indoors? Do you have a theme in mind?"

"I don't care that much." He was facing the sun again. "I've been to my brothers' weddings. They seemed like a lot of work, so a simple one suits me just fine. But if you have any ideas ..."

"Adrian, I need you to be on board with this."

"I *am* on board. That's what I'm trying to say. I'm fine with whatever you want."

Sophia perked up at the hint of irritation in his voice. She had been lying on her stomach beneath an umbrella—she didn't want a tan—and she raised her head so that he could see, despite their sunglasses, that she was glaring at him. Adrian sighed and rolled beneath the shade to be beside her.

"I'm sorry, babe. I'm just tired." He reached out for an embrace, kissed her on the cheek. "I want to hear your ideas."

What ideas did she have? She wanted her wedding in a cozy, indoor venue, sheltered from any chance of rain. She wanted a hearty feast of rice, stews, and vegetables, not platters of bite-sized meats and sweets. She wanted her hair up in a lush, stylishly messy updo and a bell-shaped dress. It was all coming together in her head but she was falling asleep. The sun was making her drowsy. Adrian was rubbing her back, still trying to appease. She drifted off without asking him to stop.

For the rest of the summer, she had browsed articles online, read reviews about catering companies, listing venues considered reasonably priced. She archived wedding blog posts about creative favours, centrepieces, event planning tips. She asked Erica for any photographers and musicians she might know. From time to time she thought about presenting to Adrian the options she had compiled, but Sophia couldn't imagine Adrian fussing over those kinds of details. When they discussed the wedding, he had nodded respectfully to her suggestions, only reminding her to keep within their budget. Fair enough. Sophia had thought then that the arrangement wasn't so bad at all.

⇒⟫⟩

IT WAS LATE AFTERNOON WHEN SOPHIA LIFTED HER HEAD, listened for voices in the house. Had she really fallen asleep? Her last memory was her own unrecognizable cries and a terrible yearning for the phone to ring, a sound of rescue from her heartache. But when she checked, Adrian had never called; the device only showed that the hours marched on without care.

Just that morning she had had thoughts about no longer being a part of that household, and now as she made her way to the kitchen, the familiar smells and fixtures seemed to mock her. The clean stack of dishes they had used that morning. House slippers sitting in a careless row by the front door. A copy of the *The Province* folded at the dining table next to two bananas that had contaminated each other with brown freckles. The mosaic of receipts, notes, flyers, and magnets on the refrigerator. How was it that everything appeared unchanged when her life had practically fallen apart? When she no longer knew the person she had trusted the most?

She felt weak all over but Sophia decided to be useful by making her family supper. In the freezer she found a bag of chicken. She checked for ginger and vegetables. Spinach could be used in place of malunggay. Her mind was wrapped in a cloud, but a part of it operated like a blinking store sign, reminding her how to wash, slice, and cook.

Thaw chicken pieces.

The frozen lump of pink flesh revolved in the yellow glow of the microwave oven. She wished that she, too, was a frozen piece of chicken. Icy and rock-hard, she wouldn't feel anything. A few minutes into the thaw, she ran back upstairs for her phone. Still no message or missed call from Adrian.

Samuel was the first to come home. "Hey," he said, unusually friendly when he spotted her in the kitchen. "Did you see Adrian today? I wanted to tell him—"

"Go tell him yourself!" Sophia snapped angrily.

"Oh." Samuel drew back as if Sophia had hurled a spider at his face.

Sauté ginger. Footsteps thundered up the stairs. *Brown chicken pieces.*

Oil sizzled and splattered against her wrist. Sophia ignored the hot pinpricks on her skin. Everything was sticking to the bottom of the pot. She silenced the sizzle with some water. At the counter, she plucked the spinach leaves from the stems. The dish wouldn't need the entire bunch. But Adrian was a sweet and caring man. They were happy most of the time. But the spinach would go bad if she didn't use the entire bunch.

Her father arrived next. He paused at the kitchen. "You're home early."

"Just making us supper."

"Why are you crying?"

Sophia wiped her eyes with her knuckles. "Just the onions."

His father, ever observant, studied the remnants of the ingredients on the counter. She hadn't used any onions. "Onions?"

"Adrian's not sure if he wants to marry me."

"What? Why?" He approached her. "What's the problem?"

Sophia steadied her voice. "I don't know." The pot hissed, the chicken smelled too salty. She couldn't remember putting in any salt.

"Do you want me to talk to him?" There was a steely tone to her father's voice.

"No."

"What did he say?"

"He said he's not sure. He's not sure what he wants."

A robust huff came from his father. He was leaning with both his palms on the counter, puzzling over her news. "There has to be a reason."

"I told you, I don't know."

"How could you not know?" he demanded.

Sophia stifled a sob. "He can't even explain himself."

"Stupid boy."

With this remark they were allies again. Sophia stirred the pot so she wouldn't lose her composure, which would make her father lose his. The broth had turned thick and fatty. The rising steam stung her eyes, which were already smarting from rubbing them with ginger-moist fingers. She couldn't decide whether she was feeling spent or relieved for having told someone what had happened.

Her father started making rice. "Your mother would like to eat as soon as she gets home."

He was avoiding her eyes, focusing on the pot in which he measured the water soaking the grains with his fingers. Sophia caught a glimpse of his grim expression, and it hurt her that he was as crestfallen as she was. She wanted to collapse in his arms, but a wall made up of disappointment after disappointment she had heaped upon him prevented her.

At dinner, she stared at her empty plate as she numbly answered her parents' questions.

"Did you have a fight?" her mother asked. "Maybe you just need time to cool off."

"There was no fight, Ma."

"Then what happened?"

"That man is not true to his word," Sophia's father declared as he piled his plate for a second serving. "If he ever tries to reach you, tell him he has to speak with me first."

Sophia imagined Adrian begging for her forgiveness, a wispy flame of hope lighting in her. Was it possible? The whole thing felt like a huge error waiting to be corrected.

"And you," her father turned to Samuel, "if he talks to you, ignore him."

Samuel, who had not said a word at the table, nodded sombrely.

II
THE WAYS
OF WATER

8

ERICA HAD COVERED FOR SOPHIA THROUGH SUNDAY and left the salon immaculate. Sophia, who arrived an hour before opening that Monday, was vaguely disappointed to not find anything to do.

She had driven to work on an empty stomach. Its grumbling could be heard in the silent morning. With her thumb, she soothed the bare strip of flesh where her engagement ring used to be; taking it off last night had felt like wrenching her heart from her chest. Perched on a stylist's chair, she gazed at the window, hugging her knees tight. On the couch, a part of her painted name on the glass reflected—squiggly shadows of flipped letters S, O, and P—the rest of her moniker disappearing on the shadowed floor. Despite the cramped surroundings, the salon felt bare. Like something was missing.

Sophia visualized pedicure stations lined up along the space occupied by the couch. She stood up, somehow spurred by the idea of expanding her salon's services, and squatted on the floor, inches from the couch. If the couch were taken out, three stations could fit in the space. But those pedicure chairs with built-in sinks she had seen in nail bars would be too costly and ridiculously out of place. Perhaps she could keep the couch and purchase some porcelain washbasins, manicure kits, and a whole line of nail polish. She could probably hire a manicurist. Or learn it herself. She would need to ask for an additional loan. Sophia sighed, dreading the idea of taking on more debt.

The glass counter was only a few steps to her left. If she were giving someone a pedicure, she would have to stand up to let clients in past the counter. If she edged to the other end of the couch, her back would be very close to her styling chair. There was very little space.

Still on her haunches, Sophia turned her head to the rear of the salon, eyeing the tiny space next to the bathroom door. She wondered if she could fit in a facial bed, then shook her head at the silly idea. Nobody would want a glimpse of the toilet in the middle of a deep cleanse. She stared at the walls, as if willing them to draw back and lend a few more square metres. The place had felt big and overwhelming when she had taken over. She had inspected every nook and cranny, brushing away the slightest trace of dirt, fixing every defect. It was ownership that made her notice the empty light bulb sockets above the mirrors, the unsightly stains on the walls, the parts of the floor that were sticky with unwashed dirt underneath the heavy furniture. Now everything seemed faded, the surroundings not entirely reflecting how much she had learned, the many things she could offer. The wall's light blue colour had been appealing to her when she had taken over, but now it seemed too plain. A more vibrant shade would lend a fresher atmosphere. Sophia imagined the walls in cherry red. Then lavender or emerald. Too dark. Too dramatic. Too much.

"Too much, my dear. Sobra naman." Aling Helen had clucked her tongue at a client who had asked to have all her hair dyed red. "Listen, what do you think about highlights?"

Behind them, Sophia and Erwin had traded sly smiles. The woman wanted her thick curly hair bright red—she would have looked like Ronald McDonald. She had stubbornly pointed out that her fair complexion would suit any hair colour. Aling Helen, in her usual persuasive way, explained that it was more than just the skin tone; she talked about lustre and undertones, things Sophia didn't understand at that time. They even looked at pictures of women in the magazines. Just as Aling Helen was about to lose patience, the woman agreed that the look she envisioned might just be too weird for her co-workers. Aling Helen, nodding along with her client's line of thought, made a remark that many people were not receptive to original and bold looks. She left a few hours later, her still-black hair glistening with coppery streaks.

Aling Helen had wielded a comb at Auntie Rosy after the client left. "No one is leaving this salon looking like a clown, you understand?"

Sophia was giggling now as she and Erwin had that day long, long ago. Her lips turning up at the corners felt weird after a weekend of crying. She laughed some more, even though she was no longer thinking of the woman who wanted to be a redhead. It felt good to hear herself happy, filling the empty salon with hollow cheer.

"What's so funny?" Erica was at the door.

"Hey!" Sophia's face turned hot. She was still wearing a mid-laughter grin. "Umm, what do you think about set-ting up a nail station?"

"We don't have space for that." Erica sat on the couch, looking concerned. "I got your text about Adrian. Are you okay?"

"I'm fine." Sophia stood up, hardening her still-tingling jaw. "Not the best weekend, obviously." She wanted to keep things in, to not expose herself. Aside from the endless weeping, the other thing she had gotten sick of the past two days was pity. On Saturday night, when her mother was on Skype with Auntie Mila, their voices had been soft and serious. There was no doubt that Sophia was the topic of their conversation. The wedding was can-celled. There was no prized son-in-law. Reason was not clear. Between them, these sad specifics took on flesh and limbs. From her bedroom, Sophia couldn't hear the words being exchanged, but noted that their chat was longer than usual. She curled under the covers as if guarding herself from things being said about her downstairs. Imagined Auntie Mila extolling on the advantages of singlehood, of new beginnings, a time for reclamation. For the first time, Sophia didn't feel like being in her corner. Her mother would think back to the recent months, search-ing for missed signs. Over the weekend, she knocked at

Sophia's door many times, asking if she was all right. Then there was her father, stoically wordless. Sophia resented his stance that their relationship didn't deserve a second chance. Samuel avoided her gaze; he looked as if he was the one who was heartbroken.

"Kinda gives you a chance to think things over too," Erica remarked.

The comment had the deceivingly comforting connotation that she controlled things. But the painful truth rested on her stomach, weighing her down as she stood up to turn the door sign to Open. Adrian was thinking of leaving her.

But there was still hope. He could still choose her. The past two years must be worth something.

Erica, who sensed the need for a fresh topic, started talking about the nearby café that had a Facebook page. Sophia should open one for the salon too. "Yes, I should," she muttered. Erica went on about the shop's overpriced coffee and pastries, but Sophia was no longer paying attention. She imagined Adrian waiting across the street. They would spot each other, his pleading eyes holding her blazing stare. When the road was clear, he would run across, as if it were raining hard and he was desperate for cover. But beyond the cars driving past, there was only an empty sidewalk.

Two doors up, a woman with long chestnut hair was approaching, stranger's eyes instead catching Sophia's. "Are you open?"

"You bet we are."

She was a new face. Sophia quickly glanced at Erica

who, by the split-second tilt of her head, indicated that she didn't know the woman either. They had agreed to keep their clients separate, and that new ones would be taken on by whoever was available. If both of them were free, Sophia would take the job.

But she didn't feel like working. Her eyes were still on the quiet street, willing an apparition between the trees. Sophia kept half an eye to the window as the woman took time with the styling magazines.

Her fingers were jolted by the water as she washed the woman's thick hair. When Sophia grabbed a towel, it felt coarse against her palm, as if she had slipped into a papery kind of skin that barely held the rest of her crumbling self together. And her mind was scattered. During the haircut Sophia had asked the woman a question without being really aware of it. Whatever it was, the client replied that she was a mom who had just dropped off her toddler at the daycare for the first time.

"That's fantastic. You'll have some free time."

"Tomorrow I'm starting my first full-time job in ages. I sure hope the daycare works out. And the job. I couldn't keep one without the other."

New life, Sophia thought, combing the wet hair. "Have you ever tried having bangs?"

"Uh, I don't think I'd look good with bangs."

"It might be worth a try." Sophia's efforts to sound enthusiastic rang false even to her own ears. "To surprise someone special, maybe?"

"Oh no, not necessary, really." The woman laughed dryly. "We're going through a divorce."

"Oh!" Sophia wanted to slap herself. "I'm so sorry."

"Oh, trust me, it's for the best."

For dropping off a kid at a daycare and stopping by a hair salon, the woman on her chair had picked out a cream-coloured cardigan, sequined aquamarine tank top, and shiny black pants. The polished armour of heartbreak. Sophia wanted her to open up, talk of the many nights she had wept, the anger that gripped her at random times throughout the day. Of missed clues, discarded vows, caring gestures that never really had much weight. But the woman on her chair was talking about a man who was completely unbearable. He had criticized everything she did, taunted her with demeaning names during their fights. Accused her of cheating, when he had been straying himself. "Then it's good, that you're rid of him," Sophia offered mechanically, a little disappointed that her client's ex-husband was nothing like Adrian.

The woman went on about borrowing from her RRSP to hire a lawyer. "He turned all my accusations around, made it seem like I was the hostile one." There was no end to this man's faults. Lifting sections and trimming layers, Sophia quietly wondered whether there was something about herself that drove a kind, harmless man away. *Snip. Snip. Snip.* Locks fell at Sophia's feet. She loved the sound of sharp blades cutting through wet hair. She looked up to see her client's questioning face in the mirror. She hadn't been paying attention. Sophia shook her head as if outraged at what she had heard so far, and this seemed to satisfy the woman.

By the time she was finished, there were two other clients waiting on the couch. Erica was also busy. Sophia squared her shoulders. She only needed that first job to get her into the swing of the workday. The young Asian lady with long, thin hair falling limply past her shoulders, pointed to a picture of a short-haired Charlize Theron in the magazine. It was a soft convex cut, falling evenly like a helmet along the chin. *An expertly used straightener did the trick here*, Sophia thought. The cut would look its best if the girl would take the time to style it. "Do you use a hair iron?" Sophia asked.

"Just a hair dryer."

Sophia had an idea. She would cut a jagged bob at the back and feathery ends at the front. It would be as short as well, but the shape would keep for a longer time, with less effort.

"What if I give you a different style?" Sophia said, flipping the pages to a smiling Katie Holmes centrefold. "It'll be shorter at the back. The layers at the front will bring out your cheekbones. It'll be easier for you to manage too."

The girl was surprised and flattered by the selection. "Sure, I guess I could try that."

When they finished, the client leaned toward the mirror, riffling through her new hairstyle. Sophia had rolled the front ends of the haircut with a large barrel brush during blow-dry, demonstrating how to play up the volume.

"Thank you so much." The girl tipped almost half of the fee.

A warm hopeful energy coursed through Sophia as she swept away the clumps of hair on the floor. Life could go on without Adrian. He could spend years and years finding himself, but Sophia knew exactly where she belonged.

She wanted to laugh aloud, just like she did that morning, at his stupid speech about needing to be on his own and going into a fog. He would soon find out that being with her was the happiest he had ever been. Did he really think the universe would give him answers as he spent his days at work and wasted his free time on video games?

It had been a while since she had attended upgrade courses—it was time to learn new cuts and improve her foiling. There were new trends in colouring too.

A wedding would just be an unnecessary expense.

IN THE SHOWER, SOPHIA NOTICED THAT HER RIB CAGE HAD started to press through her skin, her belly sinking inward. It was ironic that she was going to achieve the trimmed figure she had coveted now that she might not need to look for a wedding dress. She had missed supper four nights in a row, mostly spending the evenings working on her Facebook account. It surprised her that she managed to get things done with so little nourishment.

Adrian had not deleted their photos on his profile. What to make of that? Sophia was not sure, but she didn't feel too comforted. Though he kept an account, he never cared so much about social media.

Their sweaty and triumphant grins after a daylong hike. A restaurant photo with some of Sophia's friends from the styling school—his arm was draped around her shoulder possessively. Deleting these and unfriending him had felt like demolishing an old beloved building. Sophia replaced them with photos taken of her salon.

Tonight, she decided to join her family for supper. She stepped into the dining room, interrupting her father's disgruntled account of yet another colleague overstepping his boundaries. "He said I was explaining the loaning options in a complicated way, when all I've been trying to do was to clarify how they work. Not everyone wants to be treated like they're dumb!" He noticed Sophia and raised his eyebrows meaningfully. "O, how have you been?"

"I'm fine." Sophia smiled widely. "Adrian and I have not spoken for almost a week now; I bet he's missing me terribly."

Her parents and Samuel regarded her as if she was afflicted with a strange disease. Her father cleared his throat. "Anak, have you ever thought of going back to school?"

"Vincent," her mother said, "can't we let her have a bite first?"

He ignored her. "I know how much you'd like to move on." Sophia noticed that his voice was gentler than usual. "We were just thinking you might like a change, and your mother and I can help you."

"I'm thinking of master classes. But they cost money."

"Masters? Like an MBA?"

From the corner of her eye, Sophia noticed Samuel squirm.

"No, Pa, master styling classes. To refresh or learn new hairstyling techniques."

"Oh." Her father gave a slow nod. "Sounds like money-making scams to me."

It was astounding, his father's ability to be caring and condescending at once. Sophia urged affection in her voice. "Dad, every decent stylist takes them."

Surprisingly, there was no further comment from him, nor from her mother. Sophia was grateful for the topic to pass, but she had the sense of something being left hanging, the weight of an unfinished discussion. Whatever it was, they had all silently agreed it was a matter better deferred for another day.

That night she dreamt that she was working for Olivia once again.

The salon was still as busy but everything was in disarray. Supplies and debris strewn on the floor. Construction noise ringing in her ears. The workstations were dusty and cluttered. Oliva was making the rounds through all the stations, fussing over Sophia's client, whose face she couldn't see because the mirrors had blurry patches on them. She somehow surmised, in a way dreams conveyed things without direct explanation, that the salon was being renovated. Outside, it was raining hard; the droplets beating against the window made noises like a wok on fire. Sophia was looking around, trying to figure out how to make things look cleaner, more organized. Was Olivia not bothered by this? She was now talking to her about her clients moving away to far places and that in order for the business to survive, they would have to move their location. Sophia was being asked if she was willing to leave her family behind.

"Where are we moving to?" Sophia was hopeful that it wouldn't be somewhere far. But Olivia's response was muffled by the rain.

Sophia mulled over the idea of uprooting herself once again. A fresh start, away from the city that reminded her of Adrian, was appealing. She could imagine him driving by their salon, seeing it closed down. He would wonder where she had gone and feel the void of her absence.

The dream ended just as she was remembering she hadn't known Adrian when she was working for Olivia. Heartbreak in her waking life claimed Sophia the moment she opened her eyes. She blinked, trying to reclaim the details, but all that came to focus was the loneliness of those struggling years. Daylong dusting and sweeping, greeting clients that ignored her, then coming home to their poorly heated basement suite, curling up in her bedroom as she visualized a more glamorous workday, staring at the low ceiling mapped with mildew. Though she now lay in a newer home and no longer worked for anyone, it felt as if she had been tossed back into that depressing period of her life.

There had been other men before Adrian. There was Tino, who also wanted to be a stylist. He had envisioned himself running an edgy unisex shop, claiming that men would come in for his talent and the man-cave inspired interiors, while the women would flock in for his good looks. It was true that he turned heads with a lush crown of black curls and playful eyes. His physique made up in verve and quickness what it lacked in brawn. They drank and danced with other friends at nightclubs downtown. He blamed Sophia for not being available other evenings for the lack of variety in their date nights. Right from the beginning, she had known it wouldn't last. Sophia wanted someone more grounded, who could appreciate the fact that she had to work at the food court after class hours. But on Friday nights, the Top 40 hits blaring from the speakers drowned the obvious truth that they were merely using one another. To this day, Sophia marvelled at how they had carried on until the end of the program.

And there was Mon, who humbly listened to all her complaints from the sidelines. Though his face was partially concealed by the logoed cap they were all required to wear while piling cold cuts and vegetables on slices of bread, Sophia could read his jealousy. When Tino disappeared during her exam preparations, he had gallantly stepped into the void, promising respect and devotion. He was Filipino too, and being surrounded by other immigrant co-workers, he had called Tagalog their love language. If Sophia hadn't been contending with her upcoming styling tests and the long lineups at the front counter, she would have pointed out how corny this was. But Mon proved himself a consummate suitor, staying in the food court past his hours so he could help Sophia with the closing tasks. He was, after all, done with the schooling thing; he had sympathized with Sophia's tales of being bored during that one semester she had attended university in Manila. Mon believed sheer dedication would take him places; he was eyeing the supervisor position in the very same sandwich place they were working in. "Really?" Sophia had looked at him, stunned. "Is that all you want?" This reaction of hers told them all they needed to know. It was over even before Sophia handed in her resignation.

Adrian was perfect. Adrian was just right. He had

walked into her life at a time when she had a whole self to offer and nothing left to prove. But the hope that they would get back together was receding like the final reach of the sunset on the edge of a high mountain. How had she gone from the captivating woman, the one he had admired for her ambition and independence, to someone whom he had to get rid of like useless baggage? His abruptness was the cruellest part, how underhanded he was, how sneaky. Was there something she could have done to salvage their future together? It was obsessive, this futile task of rehashing their last conversations. It was like standing in front of a wide panel with many different switches, with Sophia flicking each one, or perhaps a combination of them, to find out what it would take to make the machine perform its lovely work once again.

The night before his gutting confession, she had told Adrian over the phone about the renewed discord with Auntie Rosy. "Can you believe it? She wanted to bring the poor woman to court!" Sophia had laughed off her exasperation and now she was being punished for her heartlessness. Adrian had been mostly quiet, saying cursory yeahs here and there. She had stupidly chalked it up to the usual tiredness, even asking if he had eaten a proper dinner and wished him sweet dreams.

Sophia closed her eyes, drifting into the morning without another dream.

9

EVEN ERICA HAD BEEN ACTING DIFFERENT. FROM TIME to time, Sophia would catch her with a wary look, which would be quickly averted once detected. At least she didn't ask a lot of questions like her parents did.

It was the salon that was keeping her sane. The snug feel of the scissors around her fingers and the arresting scent of shampoo and styling solutions created a zone that hinted there were things to look forward to in life. Sophia willingly immersed herself into any topic her clients offered. "Change jobs," she had told a woman who worked in a pharmacy managed by a man with a leering smile. She gave Amber her blessing to purchase a five-hundred-dollar Coach purse. A budding travel blogger was contemplating getting a tattoo, and Sophia, who never wanted one, urged her to select a design as adventurous and vibrant as she was.

Erica was free to stare as much as she wished.

"I'm famished. I'm gonna get myself one of those

gigantic subs for lunch," she was telling Sophia now, while putting on her jacket. She sounded like a caregiver leaving a ward. "Do you want me to get you one?"

"Yes, please," Sophia said. She had been hungry too, her stomach finally expressing the pangs of an appetite. But a new client with overgrown light blond curls had just walked in.

"Are you thinking of a particular cut?" Sophia asked her.

"I haven't cut my hair in ages. I'm really busy and want something simple and manageable," the woman said, her eyes shifting shyly. She was flipping through a magazine. "Like this one. But not that short."

A heaviness gathered in Sophia's chest as she washed the woman's hair. Flaxen blond with ashy undertones. So much like Adrian's hair. She forced herself to focus. The curls were thick with residue of unrinsed conditioner. After the wash, Sophia carefully scrunched the dripping tresses and wrapped a towel around them.

At the chair, she held the thinner side of her styling comb so that its thicker-toothed side combed through the wet hair. The hair now appeared straight, with very faint waves rippling down the lengths. She glided her comb carefully, not wanting to overextend the curls and cut the hair shorter than she should. Her fingers worked through some wet tangles. Her client, clearly not a talker, was engrossed in an issue of *Vanity Fair* from last year. Sophia gingerly guided the client's chin toward the other side, to prevent the hair framing her cheeks from resting on the shoulder. After trimming off the split ends, Sophia gathered the top layer with a clip and parted the lengths at the back of the head.

There was that one night when she and Adrian were slouched on his couch, their legs stretched on his coffee table. It was January, Sophia remembered, because they had been talking about New Year's resolutions, following a related news story on TV. Adrian was telling her that it was the week when people buckle and start giving up their unrealistic goals. The starvation diet, the overly frugal budget, the resolve to be a better person overall. "Change is difficult," Adrian had said. "An ambitious goal becomes less and less of a motivation when the novelty of a new beginning starts to wear off."

Sophia had poked the crumpled wrappers of burgers and fries on the table with her foot. "So much for healthy eating, huh?"

"We didn't make resolutions to eat healthier," Adrian mused smugly.

They had been a *we* back then. Sophia had glanced at his profile, admired the delicate line running from his brow, down to his cheekbones to his chin. That lovely contrast between smooth features and rumpled hair. Struck with an inspiration, Sophia sprang from the couch, went to the bathroom, and came back with his styling gel and a comb.

Adrian sat up, curious. "What are you up to?"

"Sit still." Sophia combed his hair. Adrian always cut his hair short, preferring a clean-cut look. But he had been too busy with work to drop by at the barbershop. Sophia playfully tousled his hair.

"Hmmm, that feels good."

His hair was feathery in her fingers, his scalp had a warm, manly smell. Her hands sticky with styling gel, Sophia pulled up his hair to create rock star-style tufts. When she had finished, Adrian looked at his reflection. "I look cooler than I actually am."

"That's your new look," Sophia said.

She hadn't expected him to take her seriously, so she was surprised to see him when they went out for lunch a few days later, wearing a lazier version of the same hairstyle. Crowning his boyish face and the usual sweater over polo shirt attire, the hairstyle gave Adrian an uncharacteristic rebellious look. Sophia was delighted. "Hey, sexy!"

Adrian grinned. "My co-workers said I look like a model."

"But I knew that already."

The style stayed for a few more days, then Adrian got a haircut. When he didn't style his hair after it had grown back, Sophia didn't mind. He was fine the way he was.

The resurfacing of this memory drained the energy from Sophia's hands. It was taking more effort to control the woman's curls. Her blades had their own spirit, lopping off the uneven ends. In the mirror, Sophia glimpsed that her eyes were glistening. She blinked and sniffled. The woman was looking down at her magazine. Sophia gently propped her chin upward.

By the time she had diffused the curls, Sophia's stomach was rumbling so loudly she was sure both of them could hear it.

"What do you think?"

The woman studied her reflection, not saying anything.

"Do you like it?" Sophia was suddenly nervous.

"It's kind of ... different."

"You look younger," she offered. "Sometimes it takes time to get used to a new look."

"I guess." The woman took out a credit card. Sophia felt relieved when she noted the tip in the receipt.

When she was alone, Sophia stood by the door. Clouds were sailing along the crisp sky. Dead leaves covered the pavement. Her hands clenched and unclenched, ridding themselves of the clinging memory of styling gel.

⋙

SKYPE REGISTERED FOUR MISSED CALLS FROM ERWIN, THE last one only a few minutes ago. When Sophia called back, both Erwin and Auntie Rosy were waiting for her at the other end, their faces grim and tired.

"Hey," Sophia said. She wondered briefly whether she should tell them about Adrian, but decided against it. Spreading the news might drown what was left of her belief that he would return to her. She clung even to the silliest superstitions these days.

"Sofi, dear." Auntie Rosy seemed to have forgotten how their last conversation had ended. "I really need your help this time. Sorry na, my darling. This is different."

"What happened?" Sophia looked at Erwin.

"You haven't heard of Ondoy?" Erwin asked.

"Who?"

"The typhoon, darling!" Auntie Rosy's voice shook. "It

poured non-stop for more than a day. The water reached the salon. I nearly died!"

"Hala! What happened?" She now vaguely remembered her mother mentioning a strong typhoon that hit the Philippines a few days ago. But Sophia had been too self-centred to pay attention. Back home, typhoons happened every year.

"I took a nap on Saturday," Auntie Rosy said. "I don't remember how long I'd been sleeping when I felt cold water on my back. I stood up quickly, picked up my pillows, and folded the banig. It's the first time I've seen the flood reach Cine Star."

"Why are you sleeping at the salon?" Sophia asked.

"I gave up the apartment the other week. I'd rather keep the salon." There was pride in Auntie Rosy's voice. "More water came in. It was brown and came with garbage. Kadiri! Soon it was up to my knees. It was a blessing that there hadn't been clients lately; everything in the salon was unplugged. But I had to go on top of the chair and sit on the narrow counter. My buttocks still hurt!"

"Oh, my God!" Sophia's hand went to her mouth. "How did you—"

"I found her just like that," Erwin said. "I was coming home from my shift. The traffic wasn't moving at all, so I got off the bus and waded in the flood along the highway. I thought we lived on a higher place, so it wouldn't be as bad out here. But you know, the closer I got to home, the deeper the water became. Diyos ko, Sofi, I was so afraid. I could have fallen into an open manhole. A lot of people were trying to make their way home, too. Cine Star was on the way, so I went to check on Auntie Rosy. When we got home, some of our stuff was floating. My parents and brothers were all sitting on top of the table."

Sophia recalled cozy days when classes were suspended because of a typhoon, and she and Samuel had stayed home eating chocolate rice porridge. But she had no memory of their neighbourhood being hit by such a deluge. "Thank God you're all okay."

"News reported we got a month's worth of rain in twenty-four hours," Erwin said.

"His father kept wanting to throw me out!" Auntie Rosy thundered. Then she softened her voice. "Listen, darling. I want to be back on my feet again. I will use your money so that I can reopen Cine Star. I will clean it up. The water might have destroyed some things." Auntie Rosy paused, and then sighed heavily. "But the worst is my last sack of rice. I'm sure it's spoiled now."

"Auntie, don't worry about the rice. I'm going to give you some. But maybe you want to think about going back to your family," Erwin said gently.

"Erwin!" Auntie Rosy brusquely shook her head. "No matter what happens, I'm not going to abandon Cine Star. There's a reason I didn't die. The salon is not meant to close down." She slid her chair forward, drawing her face so close to the screen that Sophia could spot the silver patches near her temples. "I was doing some thinking, Sofi. You were right. Filing a lawsuit against that woman is a waste of time. I just need to show people that Cine Star is still here for them. If they see that it can open its doors after this calamity, they will come back."

Sophia's heart was swelling. "Auntie, I will send more money right away."

"Dear, maraming, maraming salamat!" Auntie Rosy brightened with relief. "Adrian is a lucky man."

Erwin had to go to work. Auntie Rosy had to clean up at the salon. Before logging off, Erwin told Sophia quickly, "I sent you an email earlier."

Sophia had been avoiding her email, hoping that doing so for extended periods would somehow invite a message from Adrian. Another one of her silly but comforting superstitions. But there was only that one message from Erwin, which had come in that afternoon.

> Sofi,
>
> Kumusta na? I've been calling you but you're offline. Auntie Rosy's family is asking her to come home to Bicol. You probably heard of Ondoy. This is our chance to get her to give up Cine Star. Help me convince her.
>
> Erwin

10

CINE STAR HAD BEEN CLOSED FOR TWO WEEKS AND Auntie Rosy was running out of money. And because bad luck wasn't through with her, her salon where she had been living, was flooded. Money, a lot of it, would be needed for some repairs, the chairs would have to be replaced, all of the electronics were probably damaged by water, and many tools unusable because of the dirt. And worst of all, Auntie Rosy was nearly killed. But her spirit was intact, she was more determined than ever. Sophia envied Auntie Rosy's unshakable resolve. It would be heartless to take back her offer.

Could Sophia refuse her friend who had fought so hard? Could she let Cine Star close down?

As a child she had suffered during the summers when school was out and she couldn't visit the salon. At eleven, Sophia was still deemed too young to leave the house on her own. Their home was so quiet that Samuel's squeals and

Ate Liza's demands for him to behave echoed throughout. The windows were closed off with curtains. Her mother's favourites were the ones with deep dark colours. Viridian. Burgundy. Indigo. She favoured the colours that blocked the sight of their lowly neighbourhood. To Sophia, it felt like living in a cave.

"I need a haircut," Sophia would tell her mother, holding up the ends of her hair. "I feel hot with this long hair." When her mother nodded and promised a visit to Cine Star that weekend, Sophia counted the days.

"She likes going to the salon, this one." Her mother meant it to be an amusing remark during dinner. "Like me."

But this prompted a stern look from her father. "I don't want her growing up vain, just thinking about her looks."

She slipped into her parents' bedroom one day and sat at her mother's dresser. There was a neat row of fragrances and ointments, along which sat a hairbrush with a carved shiny handle. That such things existed in the same room where her father slept was somehow comforting.

Before school opened that year, her mother bought Sophia her first training bras, sanitary pads, nylons, but she was not to tell her father. When she stepped into Cine Star after the first class of the term, Auntie Rosy blinked, loudly remarking how tall she had grown. It was also during that year that Auntie Rosy started talking about her lovers, and Sophia had a hard time keeping track of their names and the streets where they lived. Maximo from Kamiyas Street. Elmer with thick eyebrows from Cabral Avenue. Rey, the tricycle driver, whose address was still a mystery by the time Auntie Rosy decided to dump him because a wide portion of his gums showed whenever he laughed. Auntie Rosy made their names sound melodious, like incantations from her lips. She would spit out the same names in disgust whenever the affairs ended.

"Is it true that Liza eloped with Badong?" Auntie Rosy asked Sophia as she put on her lipstick that evening. It was called Valentine Rush. After smacking her lips, she passed the tube to Sophia, holding it between two fingers like a cigarette. Feeling womanly, Sophia took it and made careful dabs on her lips. In the mirror, she could see Erwin watching her enviously. He wore his hair spiky, hardened by a generous amount of styling gel, the style sported by the same boys who made fun of him at school. He had tried on some makeup earlier, but had washed it off as it was almost time to go home.

"That's what Mama thinks. Last summer, I would watch them necking at the back of the house," Sophia said in a voice that was bored with the spectacle. "He came to the house every day."

"If only we could be as lucky," Auntie Rosy sighed.

"Spending the night with jobless drunkards," Aling Helen remarked as she combed her thin hair. Sophia glimpsed the pale scalp beneath the tight curls. "You won't find love. Just a big, ugly mess."

These words made Auntie Rosy hurry, checking her reflection one last time before flying through the door. Sophia and Erwin scrambled to put on their backpacks and followed. They had barely reached the end of the block when Auntie Rosy hissed, "She's so old, love is dead to her."

Sophia turned back to see Aling Helen pulling the

metal railing that barricaded Cine Star's entrance at night. Her scrawny arms bulged with the effort; her silver hair caught light from a nearby storefront. The sight of this old woman exerting heavy force made her feel bad, but she remembered that Auntie Rosy had offered to perform this task in the past and Aling Helen, who took home the key, insisted it was her job and nobody else's. They crossed the street. Sophia had to make her steps bigger because Auntie Rosy was walking fast. She wore an irritated look on her face and didn't acknowledge the bystanders who joked and whistled to catch her attention. Erwin was looking down, unable to restore their group's jolly mood. It was one of those awkward situations. Auntie Rosy was their friend, their champion. But deep down it was Aling Helen they admired. It was her work that they enjoyed watching. She and Erwin secretly agreed that women flocked to Cine Star because of Aling Helen.

"What am I supposed to do? Leave Soledad alone?" Auntie Rosy's voice quivered. "My friend just got her heart broken and that miserable hag wants me to stop seeing her. But she relies on me, you know?" She looked back at Sophia and Erwin, as if searching their faces for signs of agreement. "She doesn't have anyone, not since the congressman lost the elections. I don't believe in abandoning people you care about."

They strolled through another block wordlessly.

"I want to be like you when I grow up," Sophia blurted. She had to change the topic. "I will style women the whole day, go out at nights."

"Come work with us." Auntie Rosy brightened. "Do

you want me to tell Aling Helen? I can train you."

Sophia paused, as if caught in a lie. It was true: she would love to work at Cine Star. Each client represented a transformation, a new beginning. She observed this in the sprightly step of a plain, mousy woman after a perm, or in the surprising elegance of a tomboyish debutante after her hair had been curled and adorned with a jewel-encrusted tiara. During the quiet times at the salon, Auntie Rosy would teach Sophia simple things. "Remember, ears are not necessarily even, don't use them as a guide for haircuts." She took Sophia's hand. "This is how you hold the scissors, thumb goes here, your ring finger in the other hole. Your hands are small, you'll need shorter blades. Relax, your fingers are too tensed."

"Rosy, don't have her playing with our things," Aling Helen would say.

"But look, she's learning."

Sophia would manoeuvre the blades in the air, imagined them slicing through thick tresses, forming stylish cuts. She wanted to go home, show her parents the scissors latched to her hand like a natural extension of her fingers and say to them, "This feels good. This is what I want to do for the rest of my life."

And they would gape at her, horrified at the idea of their eldest child without a degree.

A tricycle rushed by, hurting Sophia's ears. She watched the figures lurking in the dusk, the people Auntie Rosy mingled with after work. If she opened a hair salon in a nicer area where nobody drank in the streets, would her parents approve? The place wouldn't make a difference, she realized.

They wanted her to use what she learned in school, to make the best use of her great mind. Her father had this speech about the amount of money they were spending so she and Samuel could get a decent education in a country where everything was substandard or downright rotten. Her eyes wandered to the cinder-block walls bearing graffiti, the rusty corrugated roofs weighed down by rubber tires. She imagined her brain corroding like these structures, becoming poor and useless, if she didn't attend college. Would she really end up with men who also drank at nights?

Auntie Rosy seemed to sense something in her silence. She nudged Erwin. "How about you? Do you want to work with us?"

He shook his head vigorously as if the question had insulted him. "Everybody thinks I want to be a beautician. I will get a degree and find work. Away from here."

But Erwin was still there. Unable to get away.

There was a pulsing ache around Sophia's eyes. How in the world was her friend managing this situation? He was within reach to deal with everything that could happen out of Auntie Rosy's carelessness as long as she stayed in town and struggled with Cine Star. Surely he had other things to worry about. She hadn't been asking him about what was going on with his life. In the past, he had told her stories about difficult people he had assisted on his job as a call centre agent, his struggles with various unreasonable requests and curses he received that needed no translations. He had started as a telemarketer, earning a commission for every client who would agree to receive an information package for some phone and internet deal or insurance policy, and quickly became an expert on mimicking accents.

"We don't need any insurance, fuck off!"

"While I have you on the line, is there any way you can connect me to my boyfriend in Barbados?"

He was powered by coffee breaks at a nearby Starbucks and 7-Eleven. Naps in the breakout room and yearning glances at the cubicle where his crush battled the same onslaught of frustrated complaints with scripted remedies. The company he worked for now was more bearable, dealing with software troubleshooting. "At least, people are happy to hear from me," Erwin had said, "though not all of them show appreciation."

"Don't you want to look for another job?" Sophia had asked once.

"I don't know what else is out there for me. Besides, I like not being home during the evenings when my father's home. To him, I'm just someone invisible contributing to the bills."

She would be so tired in the morning. But Sophia rose and sat before her laptop.

Hi Erwin,

Sending Auntie Rosy back to Bicol is a
good idea. Sorry, sorry, sorry, I didn't see
your email right away. How did you find
out? I'll send her some money and then
let's try to persuade her to leave Manila.

Let's chat sometime.

Sofi

She felt a little lighter when she went back to bed. But even as she tried to push away the troubling thoughts, they kept coming back, claiming space in surges like flood-water. Just how was she going to take back her word? She missed having someone like Adrian who would listen to her rant about annoying situations like this.

What were the chances that he was losing sleep as well? Did he also miss her? Was he still undecided? He must notice the empty spaces she used to occupy in his life. The patch of night sky outside the window stared with dull, untwinkling stars. Wasn't there a song about lovers sharing the sky? Could he see what she could see, think the same thoughts? Remember the same memories? But Adrian was probably too preoccupied with finishing yet another level of a newly downloaded game.

In the quiet she became aware of clicking sounds coming from somewhere in the house. Samuel was still up, playing video games. It strangely comforted Sophia that she wasn't the only person awake at that hour.

Samuel and Adrian used to play video games together.

She found herself getting out of bed. It was like an out-of-body experience, a separate consciousness carrying her down the hall. She quietly knocked on Samuel's door. "Sam?"

The clicking continued. Sophia was mortified. Was her brother ignoring her? Standing there in the dark, she struggled to remember the last time they had talked. When Sophia was a girl whom Auntie Rosy had to walk home following an afternoon at Cine Star, she would see Samuel in the living room, fresh from the noontime nap, glancing up at her with curious eyes. She had pitied him for being Ate Liza's lone captive, but as they grew up, Sophia developed a benign resentment toward her brother. Samuel always mastered his school lessons and finished his homework faster; he took home high grades. Their parents always raved about the glowing comments he received from his teachers, the same ones who once had Sophia in their classes but never really noticed her. He was not the type to brag; they were too indifferent toward each other to compete. But the past year, it seemed to Sophia that his eyes had taken on a barely concealed haughtiness. She had even confided to Adrian about their non-existent bond as siblings. "Everything Samuel does with his life I only know through my parents. And we live in the same house still. Someday when we have our own families, I probably won't hear from him for years."

"A lot of families are like that," Adrian replied. "But your brother's a lot like you. Focused and smart. You guys should talk more."

Sophia knocked louder, hoping their parents were sleeping too soundly to hear the noise. To her relief, Samuel opened the door.

"Ate?"

"Can I come in?"

"Sure." Samuel looked reluctant as he let her in, revealing his bed where clothes and a comforter made a hill that smelled of fabric softener and sweat. A UBC hoodie was draped over his chair. His open backpack lay on the floor; thick textbooks and some papers were spilling out on the carpet. On the walls around them were posters of *Final Fantasy* characters and of other mystical-looking creatures from anime shows that Sophia thought her brother had outgrown a long time ago. They reminded her of young girls who came to her salon for neon or metallic-hued highlights.

On the desk sat a widescreen monitor showing a hazy desert-like landscape. Sophia noticed the headphones resting on the seat, somewhat relieved that her brother hadn't been ignoring her at all. Next to the monitor was the latest PlayStation console. Sophia knew this because Adrian had been planning to get one of those for himself.

"Uh, what's up?" Samuel was gaping at her.

"You can continue playing. I'll watch." Sophia sat down at the corner of the bed. The mess, the soaring bright-eyed characters on the wall, and the mixed odours around her began to feel comforting. It assured her that Samuel was just an ordinary young man, not as exceptional as she had always believed. "I couldn't sleep," she said. "And I don't feel like being alone."

"'Kay." Samuel unplugged the headphones. Sophia was touched that he wanted her to hear the sound effects. Then he slid the mouse. The world on the screen came to life with ominous background music. Creatures with shrivelled heads and eight legs howled as they emerged from the blur. Samuel, with the barrel of his firearm jutting from the bottom centre of the screen, shot the monsters, whose bodies spurted with blood before falling to the ground.

Zombies surrounded by buzzing flies were also advancing toward him. They took longer to annihilate.

"Where did you get the money to buy these?" Sophia asked.

Samuel glanced at her warily, as if deciding whether she could be trusted with a secret. "I saved up from my summer job. I buy things open-box so there's a discount."

She nodded, feeling embarrassed that she didn't even know where her brother worked during the summer. On the screen, a shadow appeared from behind a patch of trees. "There's another one coming at you!" Sophia pointed out.

"Shit! I'm out of ammo." Her brother gripped the mouse as he fled from the approaching threat, finding a shack that seemed to have appeared out of nowhere. Its door creaked as Samuel nudged it open. Inside there were dilapidated-looking shelves draped with cobwebs. Sophia watched as Samuel searched the room, clicking on the jars and boxes on the shelves. Everything looked so grimly realistic. No wonder it was hard to pry Adrian away from his games. Sophia leaned forward, finding herself drawn to Samuel's exploration. He had gone to another place. A foggy lake. There was a sign covered with moss. *No Swimming.*

"Would you die if you go into the water?"

"I'm looking for stray ammo."

"Did Adrian play this game?"

A row of bullets flashed at the bottom of the screen, indicating Samuel's ammunition was replenished. "Yeah."

"Did you guys talk about me at all?"

"Sometimes."

"What did he say about me?"

Samuel glanced at Sophia, then back at the monitor. In the game, he had left the lake and was trudging into the field again. "Not much. He used to say he'll invite me over for games when you guys are married."

Sophia's heart raced. "When was that?"

"Months ago."

It occurred to Sophia how uncomfortable this conversation must be for her brother. He probably didn't enjoy being mined for details of his sister's failed relationship. But she had been so good at holding herself back from calling Adrian. The least she deserved were some answers.

Some misshapen blob of flesh was rolling toward Samuel, who promptly fired at it.

Ping! Ping! Ping!

Whatever it was used up a lot of bullets. It spun circles around Samuel. There were red, lightning-like flashes on the screen, and Sophia understood he was in trouble. She felt a little guilty for distracting her brother. The monster eventually collapsed into a bloody pulp. There were no other creatures in sight. Samuel exhaled and his shoulders sagged. He headed into a distant forest.

Sophia decided to take advantage of the lull. "Did he tell you anything about me the last few times you guys talked?"

"No. We didn't talk much recently." Samuel's voice was laced with reluctance. "I was kinda busy with school."

"I see." Sophia's voice was calm though she was feeling

defeated. She realized she had come to her brother for answers he didn't have.

In the woods, Samuel reached a railroad that led to a tunnel in the distance. As he advanced toward the opening, the background music quickened to a march. Sophia tensed as she wondered what waited in the darkness. The screen froze when he reached the mouth of the tunnel. Samuel had paused the game and tuned to Sophia.

"What?" she asked.

"Ate, this part might be scary. I just don't want you to scream and wake them up." He tilted his head toward the wall, on the other side of which their parents slept.

"What am I, four? I'm not going to scream." But when her brother continued the game, Sophia grabbed a pillow and held it close. It smelled like it hadn't been washed for months, but she rested her chin on it anyway. Samuel entered the tunnel and then nothing was visible except for the dark blue outline of his drawn firearm. He was pushing the mouse forward slowly and intermittently, taking small steps.

"Have you talked to him since we, um, stopped talking?" Sophia asked.

"Dad said I shouldn't talk to him." He sounded annoyed at having to state the obvious. "I already unfriended him."

"But did he try to get in touch?"

"Wait lang, Ate!" Samuel leaned forward, bracing for an attack.

"Did he say anything about me recently? Did you know he had doubts?"

Samuel glanced at her. "He sent me a message couple of days after you guys split up."

The shock passed through Sophia like a gigantic cannonball. "We didn't split up! Did he really say that?"

"Fuck!" Samuel jumped from his seat. A bloodstained face, half-concealed by the darkness, had emerged on the screen. He frantically fired at it, the tiny flares revealing the rocky walls of the cave. The face, or the creature that owned it, had disappeared. Sophia watched the encounter without a feeling in her body aside from her raging heartbeat. Time seemed to stop until Samuel paused the game again and turned to Sophia.

"His message was really quick. He said he's sorry that he wouldn't be able to talk anymore because you guys were through."

"Did he say anything else?"

"Ate, naman. Of course he didn't go into details with me."

"Are you serious?" Sophia's voice broke. "That's not what he told me."

Samuel frowned. "What do you mean?"

Sophia felt like screaming and hurling objects. The lateness of the hour and their parents sleeping across the wall constrained her urges like the straps of a straitjacket. Now that she had the brutal truth, she wished she hadn't come to Samuel. There had been hope before that moment that Adrian would somehow turn around, tell her that he couldn't stand being without her. All this time, he was out there believing they had nothing to do with each other anymore. Her brother was staring at her tensely. Sophia knew there was one thing she needed to do. She rose to leave.

"Be careful with the door," Samuel said.

11

I N THE EARLY MONTHS OF DATING ADRIAN, SOPHIA HAD
responded to a Craigslist ad for hairstylists to assist in
a student fashion show. They had very little budget but
she had just opened her hair salon and thought it was a
good opportunity to promote her business. It was an
eco-fashion show, and they wanted her to design nature-
themed styles and use as little chemical on the models'
hair as possible.

The event was to be held on a Thursday night and
Sophia only mentioned it to Adrian in passing. She didn't
think a fashion show was interesting to him, and it wasn't
the kind of activity they would enjoy together, with her
slated to be backstage, working with about a dozen nervous teens tottering in dresses made of beverage cups and
straws, wrapped in skin-tight suits of weaved food wrappers and shopping bags. During the actual event, Sophia
found herself wondering if their materials were really

LEAH RANADA

discarded trash salvaged from the landfill or newly bought from dollar stores.

They didn't even have a proper dressing room, what with the fashion show being held in a kitschy daytime-only restaurant. A week before the event, Sophia was still unclear whether the prep would be held at the actual venue, where they were faced with the problem of space, or at the campus, which meant that the models would have to be styled and already dressed in their first numbers before heading to the restaurant. Whenever Sophia raised this question, the event organizer had sounded annoyed, repeating that she was trying her best to make things happen. She swore never to work with student productions again.

In the end, the restaurant manager agreed to open up a rear dining room for their use. Sophia, armed with organic hairsprays and gels, did what she could in a dimly lit room and her models' desk mirrors. They were all impatient for their turns; a few asked if she was the only stylist. Fortunately, she only had to style each model once; they would keep the same hairstyle even when they changed outfits. So she did have the chance to step out of the backroom before the actual show began, and was surprised to spot Adrian, sitting in the first row by the makeshift catwalk, an ostentatious bouquet on his lap.

Sophia could feel herself tearing up—she had only then realized how frustrating the entire experience was. When their eyes met, Adrian stood up to approach her. She shook her head, *stay where you are.* God, she didn't want the attention: the audience was there to see the dresses, not the haggard-looking hairstylist emerging from the sidelines. She quickened her pace. "Keep your seat," she called out when she was within his earshot. The booming music went down a few notches, the emcee's mic squealed. The show was about to start. But in the first row, people were looking at Sophia and Adrian, embracing. She wiped her eyes the way she would a perspiring temple, using the back of her forearm. Why was she being emotional? People might think she was running the show.

⁂

IT WASN'T EVEN SEVEN IN THE MORNING BUT SOPHIA WAS already at the salon. The coffee she had grabbed on the way made her fingers tremble as she dabbed the dark rings around her eyes with liquid concealer. Its pigment shimmered under the glare of light bulbs.

After leaving Samuel's bedroom last night, she had sent Adrian a text message: *I need to talk. See me at the salon. 7:30 am. Won't be long.*

Sleep never came that night.

Sophia took a sip of coffee and blinked at her reflection. The skin around her eyes felt cakey. She glimpsed the box of facial tissues on her counter and vowed not to cry in front of Adrian. Her shaking hands searched her purse for the eye pencil. When she picked it up, it fell through her fingers, nearly falling into her coffee, and clattered onto the floor.

Jesus, get a grip on yourself!

She was still staring at the mirror when Adrian tapped on the glass door.

Half of Sophia wanted to rush to him, hold him close

and feel the solidness of his body. The other half remembered the conversation with Samuel mere hours ago, which made it tempting to fling the rest of her still-hot coffee on his face. She couldn't believe that he had somehow broken up with her through her brother. It was cowardly beyond belief.

"How are you?" Adrian was newly showered. The whiff of his cologne made Sophia weak, not because it was familiar and it brought memories, but because it was a new scent. A new life. Surely this wasn't a dress-up, cologne-splashing occasion. Was he headed somewhere after their meeting? A date on a Saturday morning? Sophia was falling apart on the inside. She steadied herself by sitting on the chair, watching Adrian through the mirror. She wasn't going to make time for pleasantries.

"So, I understand we've split up."

A confused expression momentarily passed over Adrian's face, before turning serious. "The last time we talked, I guess I wasn't clear."

"That you wanted to break up?"

"I wasn't sure what I wanted. That's what it was. You walked out on me, so I thought we had broken up."

"We never agreed on anything!"

Adrian nodded mutely. She was getting tired of his vacant expression, his vague explanations. She wished that for once he would offer something clear and straightforward. No matter what it meant. Or how painful it was.

"All I remember," Sophia said coldly, "is that you were afraid to make a decision. You were talking about needing to take some time to figure yourself out. Blah, blah, blah."

Adrian was looking down on the glass counter. "There is something I didn't tell you," he said, slowly. "There was this girl at work. Her name is Gretchen."

What an ugly name, Sophia thought. She said the name aloud. Its sound made her think of things splitting apart, tearing to pieces. Gret-chen.

"Our firm bought this new tax software and she was the software specialist." Adrian mustered the courage to look at her. His voice had gotten lower, his eyes shining with turmoil. "My boss had her coming in every day for like a couple of weeks so that we could all become familiar."

"With Gretchen?"

"With the software."

Sophia picked up her scissors, cutting the air with its blade. "Did you sleep with her?"

"No." Adrian was watchful of the scissors. "We just went out a few times. Coffee and sandwiches. I'm sorry, Sophia." He took a couple of steps closer, edging past the counter.

Sophia put down the scissors and whirled away from Adrian's reflection to Adrian in the flesh. "When was that?"

"A ... a while ago. We'd gone out for group lunches before, but one time when I had to work late, we grabbed dinner together. Sophia, I didn't think much of it, but while we were having dinner ..."

"Where did you go?"

"We flirted a bit. I'd never flirted much before." He released a heavy sigh, slipping Sophia an evasive look. "Not with a girl I didn't know. I can't say I didn't enjoy it, but I didn't really think much about her. But when she asked me for coffee the next day, just by myself, I said yes and started to feel guilty."

Sophia felt cold. "What else happened?"

"I knew I was doing something that would hurt you." Adrian's voice became strangely businesslike. It was just so fake; she much preferred him sounding troubled. "But I remember feeling excited to be with her."

"You like her so you want to end things with me?"

"I started feeling funny about things."

Adrian kept dodging her questions. This revelation that something had been threatening their relationship without her being aware enraged her. Her hand reached for the counter behind her for something to throw; her fingers wrapped around a slender, hard object. Sophia had meant to hit the floor, but her arm flung the weapon in Adrian's direction. Only when it was mid-air did she realize that she had thrown her scissors. Adrian ducked, the blades narrowly missing the side of his head. The scissors bounced on the wall, then landed next to his feet.

"Are you out of your mind?" He was suddenly livid.

Sophia stood up. "I didn't mean that." She wanted to say more but she was breathing hard. "I ... I'm sorry."

Adrian edged further away along the counter. "Look, I get that you're angry, but jeez—"

"I need you to tell me everything!" Sophia knew he wanted to leave. But she couldn't let him go when there were more things she needed to know. "Stop lying to me!"

"I don't have feelings for her, Sophia. I never had." Adrian sounded exhausted. "But I guess I enjoyed her company. I never experienced getting that much attention from a girl I hardly knew. And that made me think hard about whether I wanted to be in a committed relationship at this point."

"What does she look like?"

"Brown hair, brown eyes."

"Is she pretty?" Sophia immediately regretted asking the question. It made her feel small. Beauty was her work, her cause; she helped people see it within themselves. Beauty wasn't supposed to be her enemy. Never once had she felt the need to guard her relationship with Adrian. What they had together was a solid rock of trust, affection, and bright promises.

That rock was shattered by a dinner invitation.

"She's okay."

She decided not to press further. "You lied to me."

"I never wanted to hurt you." Adrian knelt down and Sophia thought for a moment he was going to ask for forgiveness, beg her to take him back. But he only picked up the scissors, holding them so delicately that Sophia was reminded of his tenderness.

"Adrian, don't you love me anymore?"

"I care about you, Sophia. But you have a clearer view of what you want for your future." His tone, once again empty of any feeling, seemed to create a greater distance than the past days they hadn't talked. "If you think I could no longer make you feel as loved and secure, we could go on our separate ways."

"Do you want your ring back?" There was the first sign of whimper in her voice.

"It's up to you."

"You're such a coward. You're going to make this my decision?"

Adrian rubbed the back of his head. "I wasn't sure when we last talked. To be honest, I'm still not sure now."

The day was getting brighter. Sophia willed away the desire to know Adrian's plans for the day. She noticed how well-dressed he was, like he was going to work. He used to come here, wait right there where he was standing now, as Sophia finished cleaning and locking up the place. It felt as if she were inventing those memories, they never really happened. Years from now, she wouldn't feel any-thing when she remembered every lovely moment they had shared. The problem was Adrian had gotten to that place mere months after he had proposed. Sophia wanted to ask him how he did it, but she knew better than to seek solace from his limp denials and hurtful revelations. Those eyes no longer adored her and she could no longer seek warmth in his arms. She wanted him gone; his presence would leave a stain of painful memory in her salon. But once he stepped out of the door, their day, and the rest of their lives, would cleave into separate paths.

"Fine, then." Sophia could hear her voice, weak and distant. "Go away."

"Goodbye, Sophia." Adrian headed out into the morn-ing, leaving her scissors on the glass counter.

12

THE WEDDING WAS TO BE HELD IN A VENUE ON Burnaby Mountain. Maggie's parents lived in a hilly neighbourhood that had a partial view of the Burrard Inlet. Sophia drove by imposing porches with stately columns, winding driveways, gated yards with storybook grass and stone pathways. Instead of pulling in front of the address Maggie had given her, she stopped a few houses down to collect herself. The water and the mountains basked in the light of the morning. A flock of seagulls cast graceful shadows on the blue surface of the inlet.

The meeting with Adrian the day before had left her reeling with fresh unrelenting pain. The rest of the day, busier than the usual Saturday, passed in a blur. There were moments when she wanted to drop whatever she was doing and weep. She didn't do that of course. Sophia waited until she was alone in the salon, packing her kits for today's event.

All she wanted for today was for things to go smoothly.

The wedding party had emailed in their hairstyles. She had done a trial with Maggie a few weeks ago, and she had approved the look. Erica had been enlisted to help. Sophia rang the doorbell, wondering if she had arrived.

A woman wearing heavy makeup and a lilac-coloured sheath dress opened the door. Sophia tried to hide her disappointment. She had much preferred that the makeup be done after the hair.

"Good morning. I'm Sophia, the stylist."

"Come in. I'm Claudia, maid of honour." She hollered into the house, "Mags, Sophia's here!"

Sophia was inwardly going through her list of items, hoping she hadn't forgotten to pack anything. Beyond the marble foyer, the sunlight streamed through a row of tall windows, illuminating enormous chintz sofas and armchairs, porcelain vessels crammed with flowers, and rugs with deep colours and ornate prints. This opulent and somewhat imposing sight was framed by the dark balustrade of a sweeping staircase leading to an overhead hallway where Sophia spied more doors. There was no one in immediate sight, but there was an excited buzz—cheery voices, clinking dishes, and the hurried clattering of high heels—emanating from the rear chambers of that great house. "Where's Maggie?" she asked.

Claudia led her to an adjacent room. "She's right here."

"Hey, Maggie said you're also getting married?" Another bridesmaid was coming down the stairs, wearing fake eyelashes. Sophia pretended not to hear her.

She entered a cozy living room with a brick fireplace above which there was a display of tastefully arranged framed photographs in various degrees of fadedness. There were two other lilac-coloured ladies both hovering over Maggie, who was sitting tensely on an ottoman in her bathrobe. Even she was wearing makeup.

"Sophia, hi." She rose and gave her a tight hug. "I'm freaking out."

"You're going to be fine." Sophia swallowed, tasting something bitter. Envy had an actual physical taste.

Maggie let go. "I keep thinking of catastrophic scenarios. I stayed up last night reading things online. Embarrassing speeches, drunken fights. I thought if I imagine every single bad thing that could happen, it'll prevent them from happening."

A bridesmaid whom Sophia didn't know shook her head. "You're being paranoid."

"Maggie, you have to relax." Claudia spoke with the authority befitting the maid of honour. "The worse that could happen is for Patrick to call everything off. But as of last night he was still pretty excited."

"It'll all work out. Just relax," Sophia added.

Maggie smiled at her, then her eyes widened, remembering something. "Ladies, listen!" She waved for everyone in the living room to be quiet. "Sophia here is about to get married too. Woo hoo!" She rose as she clapped. The room was suddenly filled with cheers. Sophia's chest brimmed with horror. All eyes in that beautiful room were looking at her like she was swathed in gold.

"Congratulations!"

"When is the wedding?"

"It's kind of on hold ..."

"Sounds familiar." Maggie waved a freshly manicured hand. "This was a hundred years in the making."

"Once you pick a date, it's gonna go by like that." A bridesmaid snapped her fingers.

Sophia frantically looked around the unfamiliar house, past the eager faces, searching for an exit. "I need to use the washroom."

"Oh, the closest one is beside the kitchen." Maggie started to get up. The bridesmaid with falling eyelashes gently pushed her down. "Sit pretty, Mags. I'll show her."

Sophia followed the lilac lady through the kitchen, where she met Maggie's parents and a few other relatives crowded around the granite island strewn with plates of croissants, coffee mugs, and leather clutches. She recoiled at the mix of smells, heavy perfume, corsages, lipstick being dabbed after sipping coffee. In the bathroom, she found the light switch and was confronted by her frightened face on the mirror. It was a long and narrow washroom. The vanity that occupied the entire length of the space had about twenty drawers. Sophia wished she were small enough to crawl inside one and hide there for the rest of the day.

Erica didn't pick up when she called. Fearing that she could be heard through the door, Sophia lowered her voice as she left a message. "Where are you? Hope you're on your way and didn't forget about Maggie's wedding." She was capable of styling everyone on her own, but today it felt impossible to function alone.

She washed her hands with hot water and took deep breaths before returning to the living room.

Erica had arrived. Thank God! Her back was turned to

the archway leading to the living room where Maggie and the bridesmaids were gathered. She was quietly talking to the group, who was crouched around her rapt and serious. One of them cried out in alarm, the others started talking in low careful voices. Sophia overheard Erica as she approached.

"... but she's excited about this wedding, so I'm sure she'll be fine overall."

Seeing Maggie's horrified face, Sophia realized what just happened. Maggie stood up. "Sofi, Erica just told us ..."

Erica turned around. "Oh, you're here. Where's your car?"

"What happened?" One bridesmaid had somehow missed the news.

"Is there something wrong?" An older woman in the kitchen called out.

Sophia glared at Erica, who quickly flashed an apologetic look.

Maggie and her bridal party were looking at Sophia now. She felt her skin crawl. "Adrian and I have called off the engagement." She kept her voice as composed as possible. "We needed to figure some things out."

"Are you okay?" Maggie's eyes shone with tears.

"Of course. Jeez." This came out sharper than intended so Sophia softened her voice. "Don't worry."

"Sorry about that dear," one of Maggie's aunts chimed in from the kitchen.

The confession strangely relaxed Sophia as if something inside her had exploded, with remnants that now floated light and harmless. But around her were Maggie's bridesmaids, their dolled-up faces severe despite their sympathetic expressions, their matching dresses making them a united force poised to contain her miserable presence on this occasion.

Sophia cleared her throat. "Shall we get started?"

They trooped upstairs to Maggie's bedroom. The room was of decent size made cramped by old, bulky furniture, a stark contrast to the sprawling spaces downstairs. The wedding gown and accessories were artfully arranged on the bed, waiting for the photographer. The only mirror in the room was installed on a miniature dresser that Maggie might have owned when she was seven. Sophia half-heartedly set her kits down next to it. Erica and the bridesmaids would have to find themselves another mirror.

Maggie carefully sat down on the chair that was so low that if Sophia were standing up, she wouldn't be able to see the top of Maggie's head in the mirror. She sat at the foot of the bed, right behind Maggie, and wondered whose stupid idea it was for all of them to do their hair and makeup in a little girl's bedroom.

Two middle-aged men, probably Maggie's relatives, carried a full-length mirror into the bedroom. Erica was directing them toward the other side of the bed. Sophia wished she and Maggie had that mirror instead, but the four bridesmaids were already cramming themselves in front of the newly provided fixture, smoothing their hair, giggling among themselves.

"Where is the groom?" Sophia asked Maggie.

Maggie moistened her lips. "At his parents' house."

She was not used to Maggie being so quiet. She was

gripping the arms of the chair, pale knuckles jutting through paper-like skin.

"Are you okay?"

Maggie turned to her. Up close, Sophia could see redness at the corner of her eyes. "Sophia, I'm so sorry. I should have kept my mouth shut. I'm always so excited when people get married. I feel terrible."

It was Erica who should have kept her mouth shut, Sophia thought. "Don't worry about it. It's all for the best. And look, this is your day. Just focus on having a wonderful time."

"I'm glad you're here, though. Really. You're the only one I can trust with my hair."

Maggie had chosen a Grecian-style arrangement: loose braids running from her temples to the back of her head, their ends joined, with thick, lustrous waves to rest on one shoulder. She had ordered a wire garland of silver and white flowers that would finish the look. On the dresser, it caught the sun from the window and seemed to glimmer with joy. Sophia opened her kit. Her brushes and combs were arranged neatly on one side. First things needed were the bobby pins. Where were they? Sophia couldn't see the half-pound box she had ordered. An absolute must for today. How was she supposed to start?

She scrambled for her other kit, the one with the hairspray, mousse, and leave-on conditioner. No bobby pins. It wouldn't fit there with all the bulky bottles.

Sophia glanced at Erica who was putting up Claudia's hair in a ballerina bun. She looked longingly at her open kit, thought about asking Erica for some of her bobby pins. But she wanted to confront her about announcing the split later. She turned to Maggie, her brown wavy hair, loose and unadorned. She frantically rummaged through the first kit again. To her relief, she found the box of pins buried at the very bottom. Cold sweat broke over Sophia's forehead as she took out the rest of her supplies.

In a year she would have been in Maggie's place now, the fussed-over queen for the day, celebrating a new beginning with the love of her life. In Cine Star years ago, she had seen brides beaming on their chairs, their faces all sweetness and hope as Aling Helen carefully tended to them. She had no interest in boys then, but Sophia felt envious of all the pampering, the excitement evident in their eyes. The happiest day of a woman's life, Auntie Rosy had called it. She had told Sophia that it would happen for her too when she grew up.

Sophia glanced up, noticed the dark expression on her face. Someone downstairs announced that the photographer had arrived. "Send her up here!" Maggie called back. She was in a cheery mood now. The women, who were nestled at the sides of the bed, sat up, straightened their shoulders, inspected their faces. Sophia weaved Maggie's hair, reminding herself not to draw the braid too tightly. Then there was another person in the bedroom. From the corner of her eye, Sophia could see a tripod being set up, someone clad in black somehow finding space for lights and umbrellas on stands. "Just ignore me," the photographer said. Then she was going around the room. Camera clicks joined in the laughter and jolly conversations. Everything would be documented, possibly printed, surely to be posted online.

Sophia arranged her face in what she hoped to be a calm expression. She kept her eyes on the beautiful hair and the wonderful pins doing their job.

⁂

SOPHIA FOUND HER CHANCE TO TALK TO ERICA DURING A bathroom break, when they passed each other in the hall-way. Erica paused, expectant.

"What was that about? Why did you have to tell them?" Sophia kept her voice low.

Erica looked down and sighed. "Sophia, I'm sorry. You're right, I shouldn't have said anything."

"Oh yeah?"

"We have to get back. Mariette and Shauna are wait-ing."

She found it irritating that Erica knew the names of the other bridesmaids while she herself didn't. For the last two hours, everyone was having fun, trading inside jokes and humiliating experiences. Sophia had heard the names of Maggie's former boyfriends. But whenever she joined the conversation, there was a hesitant pause, everyone feeling unsure how to respond to her. Then Maggie would politely revive the conversation. She blocked Erica who was trying to walk past. "What made you think it was a good idea in the first place?"

"I was worried about you today." Erica actually looked troubled. "You've been kind of ... off the past few days."

"I know, okay? It hasn't been great. But you don't have to announce it to the whole world."

"Sophia, I haven't had the chance to tell you this. But one of your clients complained."

Sophia felt cold. "Who?"

Erica had a hand on her hips, the other one rubbing her nape. "Remember the woman with curly hair? She said you cut her hair pretty short."

Sophia tried to remember.

"Lunchtime. Light blond. About three days ago, I think."

The lady who had the same blond shade as Adrian. "She didn't say anything to me."

"She tried to like what you did. She also said you went too far, like you got carried away or something. It was kind of uneven too, I could tell. I offered to fix it for her, but she didn't want her hair to get even shorter."

Sophia wanted to fall through a hole in that carpeted hallway that would plunge her deep into the earth. How could she have been so careless? Where was her head that day? Erica was studying her, perhaps thinking she was on the verge of some meltdown. Sophia hated her for seeing through her stoic facade, and for having to resort to damage prevention on her behalf. "I planned to arrive earlier so I could tell Maggie not to bring up anything about the wedding," Erica was saying. "She was a huge fan of you and Adrian, and I worried about you breaking down. I didn't see your car when I arrived. Sorry things got a bit out of hand."

"Hey, there you are." The photographer was standing by Maggie's bedroom door. Her name was Martina. A huge grin was plastered on her face as she held up her camera. "The beauticians. Say cheese!"

Sophia turned a bit sideways, distancing herself from Erica and allowing a tight-lipped smile.

"Another one," Martina chirped, adjusting the lens.

"I have to get back." Erica headed toward the room.

Sophia turned to the bathroom, not bothering to explain. Returning to work, she was quiet when she styled the last bridesmaid. The air in the room had turned more frantic with phone calls being made to groomsmen running late, the venue coordinator who misplaced the signage, the bartender making a wine brand substitution. She noticed Maggie was studying her reflection in the little mirror, turning her head sideways. Sophia, who had finished working, held up a hand mirror at the back of Maggie's head to help her see better.

"Do you like it?" she asked.

"It's gorgeous." Maggie smiled up at her. "Thank you, Sophia."

On the mirror, the bride's face was radiant with delight. But Sophia couldn't shake the feeling of disappointment, the desire to turn back the time so that she could do a better job with that curly blond.

THEY FINISHED WITH THE BRIDAL PARTY AROUND NOON. Sophia was glad all of it was over. She and Erica drove to separate places to grab lunch before opening the salon at one. It turned out to be one of those busy Sundays. They didn't have the time to talk all afternoon.

The exhaustion she felt when she got home made her

feel like she was walking underwater. From somewhere in the kitchen, garlic and onions were sweating out their flavours, and her father was calling out about something he had left in her bedroom. Sophia absorbed the smells and the voice, but her head was too heavy to care. These days, being tired from work was her drug; it blocked all other unpleasant feelings.

In the bedroom, Sophia changed in the dark and lay down. There was something on the bed that didn't belong. Papers, smooth and stiff, magazines? She rolled to the other side of the bed to face the wall, her eyes shutting out the horizontal slices of twilight seeping through the blinds. Before drifting off, she recalled that she had planned to send money to Auntie Rosy. It had been two nights since she had chatted with them. Sophia hoped that Auntie Rosy didn't need the money badly. The day had been too long. How delightful the dark, how welcoming the softness.

There was a knock on the door. Sophia groaned. Her father needed to give her a break. But the bedroom door creaked; the sound she had made was somehow taken as an invitation to come in. A vertical bar of light appeared on the wall. "Sorry, are you sleeping?"

It was Samuel's voice.

She must be dreaming. Her brother never talked to her. Sophia tried to say, "What's up?" but it came out as another sleepy groan.

"Ate, I'm going to a gamer's con next week. It's like a huge event for gamers."

"What?" she mumbled.

"There's a cosplay. People come in costumes."

What is a cosplay? Sophia wondered.

"Can you help me with my hair and makeup?"

The column of light on the wall was hurting her eyes. She was ready to snap at him, but she couldn't even muster the energy. "Okay, we'll talk later."

"You can come too, if you want. But Adrian might be there."

Then it was dark again. Sophia's eyelids flew open. Had she just heard Samuel talking about seeing Adrian? She turned toward the door—it was closed and her brother wasn't there.

She edged toward the other side of her bed to flick on the bedside lamp, sensing the magazines or whatever they were beneath her body. The yellow glare almost blinded her. Once her vision had adjusted, she could see the catalogues for community colleges and universities, a flyer for an online MBA degree. Glowing, youthful faces in academic gowns, holding rolled-up diplomas. A woman with glasses wearing a black suit, arms folded, businesslike. A bunch of young girls in the pastel scrubs of health care workers. If there was something Sophia and her father had in common, it was stubbornness.

13

THERE HAD BEEN TIMES WHEN SOPHIA STOOD NEXT to Adrian playing video games, arms on hips, on the verge of a tirade. He would look at her warily and shake his head. "Just a minute. Let me finish this level." In Adrian's eyes, she had morphed into a joyless, demanding woman, the type who only came to life when conversations and activities were focused around her. Now, Sophia slapped a hand across her forehead. She never wanted to be that kind of partner.

A scenario played out in her head: Adrian noticing her in a gamer's event. She appeared to be enjoying herself, applauding as Samuel paraded in his costume. He'd realize there was a cool, fun side to her. He'd like to approach, but then he'd remember what a jerk he had been the last time they spoke. He would ache for her until she picked up his calls.

The glare from the bedside lamp brought her back to

reality. It was ridiculous to count on some geeky convention to help her win Adrian back. But it felt good to be hopeful, to be inspired even by the frailest of chances. All Sophia needed to do was to be a good big sister and help Samuel win a costume contest.

MONDAY MORNING DRAGGED ON WITHOUT A SINGLE CLIENT. Sophia took her time with the task of reorganizing her tools and supplies from Maggie's wedding, which she hadn't had time to do the day before. Erica was doing the same. Aside from the quick hellos they exchanged in the morning, they hadn't said much to one another. After their tasks, they settled on their chairs, scrolling their phones. Last night, Maggie sent a thank-you email, mentioning that they were flying to Brazil for their honeymoon. Her writing seemed too stiff, making Sophia wonder if Maggie had had second thoughts about her work. Where were the exclamation marks?

By noon, all their supplies had been organized and they still hadn't had any walk-ins. Sophia stole a glance at Erica who was flipping through the newest styling magazine. It was unusual for them to be so quiet during a lazy stretch. "Do you want to go for lunch?"

"Nah, I'm not hungry. You can go if you want."

It felt good to step out of the quiet salon. Sophia walked a few blocks, remembering the lulls in Cine Star. The TV kept them entertained, with Aling Helen making remarks about TV personalities with a loathing that seemed borne out of familiarity. She and Erwin always tried to figure out why she gave up that star-studded lifestyle to run a salon in a plain dingy neighbourhood. Now that it had been years, Sophia guessed that Aling Helen had gotten tired of the stars who were accustomed to being adored and worshipped, taking her services for granted. She created Cine Star to recapture her passion for her craft, offering her skills to ordinary people. In a way, she had created her own sanctuary.

These days Cine Star was deserted, with Auntie Rosy holed up inside, desperate yet resolutely hoping for the clients to come back. Normally, she'd be watching TV to pass time, but the typhoon had cut the power in the salon. Sophia paused, noticing a Middle Eastern market across the street with a sign advertising money-remittance service. She would send Auntie Rosy much needed funds. Then she would grab a light lunch and hurry back to work.

Erica was getting ready to step out when she returned. "Hey, I was meaning to ask you something."

"What's up?"

"Was your family back home affected by the typhoon? I know you're in touch with some people in Manila."

Sophia's mother had mentioned that Auntie Mila's apartment was flooded. Only up to the knees, which was considered less severe compared to other areas in Metro Manila. Then there were Erwin and Auntie Rosy, who waded through waist-deep water to reach safety. It had been more than a week since the calamity. Sophia was feeling embarrassed that she hadn't even bothered to read the news, too self-absorbed in her heartbreak.

"My family and friends are okay. Thanks for asking."

Sophia smiled at Erica, glad that the ice between them had been broken.

"Oh, that's good. Though I read that relief efforts are really slow. Things look bad out there."

Even when clients showed up in the afternoon, the hours crawled by. At home, she logged into Skype. Erwin was offline so Sophia left him a message to let Auntie Rosy know that the money was ready. Then she looked up news stories about Typhoon Ondoy.

Photos were all over the internet. Sophia clicked on a slideshow. A man in swollen water up to his chest, a child sitting on his shoulders. In the next slide, people in the streets were submerged up to their necks, and carrying bundles over their heads. Above them, a man was balancing himself on an electric cable, holding onto a wooden pole and a higher cable for support. Sophia shivered, imagining herself plunging into dirty water or being electrocuted by an exposed wire.

All the children in the photos wore blank stares, whether they were safe and dry by a high window or sitting in an inflated raft in the middle of the flooded road. The aftermath showed uprooted trees, remnants of homes, cars collided against one another like giant toys on the highway, a sidewalk littered with dirty furniture and other debris. Thick mud reigned everywhere, coating the bloated remains of a man near a rice field and the tiny legs of children lying covered with newspapers. The weeping man standing by them had no shoes.

Heavy floods, they became worse year after year, claiming more lives each time. The resulting destruction so great it appeared otherworldly.

Years ago, Sophia had surprised herself by longing for Manila. It didn't offer up tidy streets for a mindless stroll, nor pockets of sanctuary in swathes of shady forests. Rather, it was decidedly abrasive and careless, a city that grabbed one by the collar. Such a distorted level of nostalgia could only be reached after cold weeks of slate-coloured skies, the sight of puddles that never dried up. When the chill seeped through four layers of clothing and there was only warmth in another mug of pale tea. As she and Olivia waited for another client to break the afternoon lull, Sophia looked out to the window, remembering the city's pulsating air, the unapologetic frankness of an environment that necessitated alertness as she followed that handsome college guy in a crisp uniform with her eyes while she held on to her purse tightly against thieves. Pop songs in the frenzied air, cloying lyrics of a lover from a jeepney radio weaving in with the jilted rapper blaring from an old but trusty stereo player. Merry colours of cheap dresses and rubber slippers in the stalls screamed alongside the sheen of ripening fruits and vegetables. The streets buzzed with the harried energy of people running to catch the next air-conditioned bus, hailing that one rare vacant taxicab in the slow procession of rush hour traffic. Weathered buildings and neglected landmarks sat dusty but dignified, lording over the sweaty masses and the new crop of reckless developments that robbed the city of an identifiable skyline that could adorn key chains and souvenir mugs. There was always an air of danger and destination, causes and enterprise. The commute between the neighbouring cities took hours—a great deal of one's day was spent staring out into this bustling and sweltering scene.

Everyone complained about the poverty and despair, the dirt and humidity, the hard life, but people continued to pour in from the countryside. Auntie Rosy had been one of those, dreaming of a better life. How long had it been since she left her family behind? How long had she been struggling alone?

Many years ago, Sophia and Erwin had arrived at Cine Star to find Auntie Rosy weeping quietly in the corner.

"You're finally giving thought to consequences, aren't you?" Aling Helen was standing by, arms crossed at her chest. She turned to them wearily. "Both of you should go home early today."

With the school bus gone and Auntie Rosy too upset to go anywhere, Erwin offered to walk Sophia home.

"Why is Auntie Rosy crying?" Sophia kicked a stone. It bounced dejectedly on the pavement.

"I'll try to find out and let you know tomorrow," Erwin said. He lived closer to Cine Star and could stop by on his way back to his house.

During the bus ride to school the following day, Erwin whispered the news to Sophia. "She's pregnant!"

Sophia tried to recall who Auntie Rosy's boyfriend was. But all she could remember was the name of her lipstick. *Valentine Rush*. "Is it with Dino?"

"Naman." Erwin had that amused look that Sophia disliked. "She was through with him weeks ago."

"Who is it then?"

Erwin shrugged. "She would have told me if she knew."

They were allowed to stay at Cine Star that afternoon. It was as if nothing had happened the day before. Auntie Rosy was her usual lively self, joking with the clients and sulky during the telenovelas. Aling Helen tight-lipped as usual. But that evening, Auntie Rosy said, "Erwin, can you walk Sophia home from now on?"

The tightness of her voice left no room for questions. Unlike the other nights, Auntie Rosy wasn't getting ready for a night out.

"I guess she has to stay home now that she's having a baby," Sophia mused after they left Cine Star.

"True. But it's Aling Helen's idea, her not going out." Erwin had the proud tone of someone who could read much more into the situation. "She doesn't want Auntie Rosy getting into more trouble."

"Trouble like what? Can't she see Aling Soledad just because she's carrying a baby?"

"Of course not!" Erwin sounded a little exasperated. "How do you think they spend their nights together? Polishing their nails while watching TV?"

"I know they drink and meet men," Sophia retorted. "But they can do other things too, right?"

"It's not that simple."

For some time, it seemed as if the baby only existed in Sophia's imagination. When they were all at Cine Star, nobody mentioned the pregnancy. Auntie Rosy didn't act excited as her mother had years ago before Samuel was born. Sophia and Erwin took turns making fun of each other, hoping Auntie Rosy would join in, but she only laughed quietly and turned to her romance paperback.

One afternoon, Sophia got the chance to be alone with Auntie Rosy when they went out for snacks. Once they were in the street, Auntie Rosy placed Sophia's hand on her stomach. "I can feel her. Here."

She didn't feel anything aside from the smooth curve of her belly. When she looked up, Auntie Rosy's eyes were gleaming.

"I'll have someone to love and someone who will love me back."

Instead of standing in line at the next-door bakery, Auntie Rosy led her to the public market a few blocks away. "They sell baby clothes there."

"Aling Helen will be mad if we take long."

"Don't mind her. She's too busy to get mad at us."

Despite the growing life in her stomach, Auntie Rosy walked fast, greeting people on the way. At the store, she inspected tiny shirts and shorts, traced her fingers over the floral and cartoon character prints. "So expensive!" she complained after turning the price tag. Sophia was dying to ask who the father of the baby was, but she silenced the question in her head. It was great to see Auntie Rosy being her fun and noisy self once again.

A few weeks later, Erwin told Sophia that they couldn't go to Cine Star that afternoon. Auntie Rosy had been taken to the hospital the night before.

"What happened?" Sophia asked.

"She lost the baby."

Sophia was too stunned to speak. She felt her stomach and tried to imagine Auntie Rosy's pain.

"We shouldn't go to Cine Star," Erwin said. "Let's wait a bit."

Years later, Sophia could still not recall how they had arrived at that decision. But it was clear that she and Erwin didn't want to see Auntie Rosy right after the miscarriage. A situation where they would be consoling their proud, indomitable friend was unbearable. They skipped their afternoon visits to Cine Star and exchanged sheepish looks at school. They couldn't stay away for too long. When their combined curiosity and guilt mounted, Sophia and Erwin met after class and braved a return. Auntie Rosy beamed and spread her arms upon seeing them. Wrapped in her eager embrace, it seemed to Sophia that she had lost more than the baby, because she could feel her rib cage through her dress. Her voice shook as if she was about to weep but she was smiling wide. "You're finally back! Where have you been all this time? I better get us some snacks!"

THE SKYPE RINGING TONE JOLTED SOPHIA OUT OF HER reverie. Clicking the video icon, she saw Auntie Rosy sitting next to Erwin. They both had anxious faces.

"Darling, have you sent the money? It's really needed na kasi."

"It's ready, Auntie." Sophia steadied herself as she made a disturbing connection between the images she had seen on the news and her moneyless friend on the screen.

"Salamat, Sofi. Maraming salamat." Auntie Rosy

bowed her head, hands pressed together in front of her nose and lips.

"There should be more than enough for necessities. Maybe get yourself new clothes. Anything else that got wet in the salon."

"Oh, I've been doing a lot of cleaning." The mention of Cine Star seemed to give Auntie Rosy life. "I scrubbed the floors, the walls, washed all the things that could still be used. In a few days, I could reopen."

Sophia caught Erwin's shifty eyes. His expression said it was time. The plan made perfect sense in Sophia's head, but now that she was face to face with Auntie Rosy, who was still bowing and praising her, the task felt impossible. Did they really have to do this now?

"Auntie, Erwin mentioned that your family wants you back in Bicol. Have you thought about going back?"

"Sophia, naman! Don't worry about me. I'm not that old yet, you know." Auntie Rosy was chuckling. "Aling Helen ran the salon into her eighties."

"You've been through a very difficult time." Sophia's shoulders had turned rigid. "Aren't you tired of working so hard? Maybe it's time for you to lead a more relaxed life."

Erwin touched Auntie Rosy's arm. "We were thinking maybe it's time for you to give up Cine Star. After everything that's happened."

Auntie Rosy stared at Erwin and then looked back at Sophia. Her eyes grew vacant, her smile collapsing into open-mouthed disbelief. The exact same reaction when Sophia had said that she didn't need her in Canada. Another rejection.

"Oh, I can see now. You talked about this. You are teaming up against me."

"Auntie, we don't think people will come to the salon anymore." Sophia could hear that her voice had taken a fearful, pleading tone, but she didn't care as long as the words kept coming out. "Maybe you could try to open for a month or so, but you have to be prepared in case nobody comes. After all, you have family back home and maybe you can ..."

"Is this why you brought me here?" Auntie Rosy slapped the desk hard. Erwin scrambled to pick up the mouse that had fallen to the floor. "What are you saying? You think I can't work anymore? You think I don't have it in me to run the salon? You know that what happened with that woman was her fault!"

"Just think about it, Auntie." Erwin placed the mouse back on the desk. "Think of your health, the money ..."

"My mind's made up," Auntie Rosy snapped at Erwin. Then she turned to the screen. "You are not the only one with ambitions, Sophia."

"Auntie, Erwin is having a hard time helping you. I can't support you for life, either," Sophia said. "If Cine Star continues to lose money, it would be impractical to keep it open."

"Is that right?" Auntie Rosy turned toward Erwin who was looking down. "I know I've been a burden the past weeks. That's what I am, your source of problems."

Sophia and Erwin remained quiet.

"We've known each other a long time. I look at you as the children I never had."

"We just want what's good for you." Erwin was almost inaudible.

Auntie Rosy looked crushed but this didn't give Sophia relief. The fort she had built within herself was crumbling wall by wall, her courage draining into a pool of guilt in her stomach.

"So this is how it goes." Auntie Rosy's voice was hateful. "Both of you will go and live your lives. Decide my fate at this one and only time of my life I need your help."

Erwin rubbed a corner of his eye. Sophia pressed on. "Auntie, can't you see we've been helping you?"

Auntie Rosy stood up, planted her hands on her hips. Sophia could only see the faded pattern on her dress, the tiny folds of skin on her fingers. She knew Auntie Rosy could still see her face on the screen.

"Keep your money, Sophia darling. I don't need it." Auntie Rosy stepped aside and was gone from view, leaving Erwin in front of the screen.

He craned his neck to the direction she had gone. "You think I should follow her?"

Sophia sighed. "That was tough."

Erwin was still looking away, hiding his red eyes from Sophia. "Maybe she'll come around. You know, like with that lawsuit?"

Sophia wanted to believe it was possible, but her gut resisted this optimistic scenario. Dreams and desires had claws and teeth, especially Auntie Rosy's. "Maybe we were too callous."

"No, Sofi. We did the right thing. I mean for you, it's just a matter of sending money. You don't need to see her, have her knocking at your place, asking for food. Or to use the bathroom."

"Hey, I'm doing what I can."

He was quiet for a moment. "I know. Sorry."

She debated whether she should tell him about Adrian, feeling the urge to balance his perception of their miseries. But what if they got back together? Maybe things would still work out.

"Erwin, I will resend the money and make it out to your name. Take it in case Auntie Rosy comes by again."

14

B Y THURSDAY EVENING, SAMUEL STILL HADN'T mentioned the convention. Sophia was starting to wonder if she had only dreamt of him talking to her last Sunday. She totally understood that it wasn't something he would bring up at the dinner table, but any other time they were both home Samuel stayed in his bedroom.

So she found herself rising immediately after Samuel left the dining table. He usually said that he had a paper to work on or an exam the next day. In their household, that passed for a good enough reason to leave one's barely touched supper, while their parents were still working on their plates. His consistently good grades and the scholarships he maintained gave him credibility. Sophia, who now knew he wasn't spending the entire night achieving academic excellence, appreciated her brother's tactic.

She followed him up the stairs. "Hey, Sam."

He looked surprised when he turned to her from the

top of the stairs. Sophia felt a little embarrassed. "Did you still want me to go to that convention with you?"

"*Shh!*" Samuel stealthily took a couple of steps down. "I told them I'm studying with my friends the whole day. But the costume contest is not until 2:30."

Sophia shrugged to demonstrate she didn't care about this. "When is it?"

"This Sunday."

"It's this Sunday?" Sophia stepped up to meet her brother in the middle of the stairway. "Why didn't you tell me?"

"I dunno. I thought you weren't interested. I was gonna work on my costume myself."

"I told you I'll help. Do you want to come to the salon in the morning?" She kept her voice steady, not wanting to betray how eager she was to get involved. "I can skip church and lunch, too. Tell them I have an early appointment."

Samuel looked pleased. "Do you know *Wielding Wizards*? I got myself a cape like Daiki's."

"Who's that?" Sophia almost chuckled. He sounded like a little boy.

"What's going on here?"

Their father was at the foot of the stairs. Sophia suddenly became aware how weird it was that they were all in the stairway. "Sophia, your mother and I wanted to talk to you."

"About what?"

"Anak, listen." Her father had one arm stretched pleadingly toward her as if she were aiming a loaded firearm. "I think your mother and I have been thinking of ways to ... to help you. We have this idea, if you could just think about it."

"What's going on?" Sophia asked.

"Just listen. For a moment." Her mother's shaky voice came from the dining room. Then she was behind Sophia's father, looking up at her.

Her father spoke. "We're thinking you could take a break. You deserve it. You work hard. Perhaps close the salon for a while. Stay at home, do some thinking. If you want, you can take courses."

"Short ones," her mother added.

Sophia could feel her ears turn hot; they picked up the small noises of Samuel's retreating steps and the latching of his bedroom door lock. She was aware that they were trying a different tactic, something more conciliatory, inviting even. They were treating her like a child to be cajoled. "I'm not going back to school."

Her father took a couple of steps up and sat down. "I want you to understand that this is not just another ploy to make you get a degree. If you do end up changing careers, it would be up to you, not to us. But the past years, you've been working so hard."

"Right," her mother chimed in. "When we first arrived here, you started working right away and went to those styling courses at night. I guess we didn't really appreciate how hard you've been working to help us and get what you wanted, too."

Their new plan of attack was slightly intriguing, but Sophia could already tell she didn't like where this was going. They were really trying everything to bend her to their will. "I'm going to my room."

"Sofi, just listen please." Her mother cowered at the foot of the stairs. Was she really that scary?

"If you just take some time, maybe you'll discover more things about yourself. Something beyond what's comfortable and familiar." Her father now had regained his footing, assuming his usual lecturer monotone. "You're still young. Unlike us, who just had to settle for simple jobs people think we could barely learn. We're too old, too tired to be taking on new credentials, pursuing better opportunities. But you—"

"I don't need any more guidance about my career."

Her father shook his head, making a huge X in the air with his hands. "I know. We get that. We just want you to try. With our support. At our expense. You could, maybe—" He couldn't stop gesturing with his hands. "Well, we know you've been struggling financially, but it's not too late to cut your losses. With you not marrying anytime soon, there is opportunity to rediscover yourself."

She couldn't believe that even now, as a grown woman running her own hair salon, her parents were still hoping she could be controlled through some glittery offer of a sabbatical slash career do-over. All those years of defiance had taught them nothing. The whole scene would have been annoying but somewhat manageable by its tiring familiarity, but the problem was Sophia was oddly moved by the offer. They had finally noticed all her hard work, her struggles, but then they were also using them to topple her resolve.

"Dad." Sophia wanted the walls around them to crumble, the narrow space was becoming oppressive. "I need you to understand that I'm happy now. Things are all right. I am all right."

"But you're not. We can see you are devastated about Adrian," her mother said.

Sophia blinked her brimming eyes. They had nudged a barely healed wound.

"You know what I think," her mother continued. "He saw who you could be, someone clever and ambitious. Beautiful." There was something infuriating about the way she added the word, beautiful, like a consoling after-thought. Sophia had to draw a sigh.

Her mother wasn't finished. "But then, he saw you're stuck. The salon is weighing you down. And that's not your fault, of course. Running a business is hard, we understand. But your father and I are not going to stand here and watch him discard you just like that. We want to lift you up."

So this was about Adrian. The great catch that got away. Try as her parents might to make it about helping her, it was just a validation of their belief that she wasn't enough for him. She was just a hairstylist with a failing beauty parlour. Her body quivered beneath the weight of this realization. Her father was still speaking. "Nobody's asking you to stop styling. It's a skill that you will always have, maybe do it on the side as you think about your other alternatives. You're going through something really hard, and it's a good time to step back and re-evaluate things."

Her body had turned cool, the red energy of rage leaving her. This lack of anger was unsettling, for what-ever sensation had replaced it had robbed her of strength and voice. At the foot of the stairs was the older, more weathered version of her parents whom she had resented for years. Faces that used to brim with pride and author-ity, now gazed at her sad and helpless. In their discarded and miserable daughter, they saw their wilted potentials and stunted careers. They wanted to raise her up, make her *so much more*. Sophia recalled their stories about rude clients and condescending co-workers, the menial, mind-numbing tasks, and seeing their imploring expressions it seemed as if she was partaking in their shame, experiencing their lowly existence.

Her father sighed. "We only wanted to help."

Sophia wanted her harsh and proud father back, not this one with a whiny voice. "I'm fine. I really am." It came out as a whisper, so faint. Her parents gaped; their daughter not fighting back was new to them too. She felt the rough carpet of the stairs at the back of her shins; she had sat down without realizing it. A hot teardrop was rolling down her cheek. For a moment, it seemed as if she were paralyzed, pinned to the spot. Then, like a toddler learning her first steps, Sophia clambered up the stairs. Her body was rigid, gripped with humiliation, but she managed to reach the top landing and stand up. She retreated to her bedroom, feeling the most defeated she had ever been in her entire life.

15

Hi Sofi,

I received the pera. No word from Auntie Rosy still. I'm getting worried, but I'm afraid to visit her. Just passed by Aling Soledad's today, said she and Auntie Rosy went drinking with their kumpares two nights ago. But you can't be sure if she actually knows what she's saying these days.

Erwin

Sophia actually began to draft a response, but found she was unable to sit still and think of what to say to her friend. Although her bedroom was tiny, she had learned it was possible to pace in it, three strides from one wall to another. How pathetic her parents were, seeing her as a failure like they had become. If there were anyone they should feel sorry for, it was themselves.

On the bed sat her backpack where she had put in rolled up tops, two pairs of her best jeans, some underwear. She didn't have a clear plan; her body was mechanically reaching for clothes she would need for an undetermined number of days. At first she was quick, like fleeing a disaster. All instinct without thought. Then she calmed down, started folding her clothes, arranging them to maximize the space in her backpack. There was no shower in the salon. Shampoos and conditioners, yes, but there was no place to wash herself. Sophia decided to take a shower before leaving home.

She couldn't stand being in that house, hearing her parents' voices, thinking their thoughts. She needed to be elsewhere. Alone.

The salon looked like a different place at night. Counters and chairs cast shadows when Sophia turned on the light. Her reflection moving about on the mirror and on the front window appeared starker, and there were a couple of times when she turned half-expecting an intruder hiding in the corners. That she was there alone and didn't expect anyone to appear till the next day was comforting and scary at the same time. The cold air was almost tangible. After turning up the heat, Sophia pushed the stylist chairs and trolley against the counters, freeing up the floor in the middle.

More than a year ago, she and Adrian had gone camping up at Squamish. It was his idea; Sophia herself was not keen on the thought of being isolated in the wild. Her family had never gone camping before. But she raised her eyebrows, nodded gamely at Adrian who had been talking about it all summer.

Matches and batteries. Chips, hot dogs, cans of beer. Sophia truly did feel excited when they had stopped by at the grocery store. Adrian was taking charge, diligently inspecting every aisle to ensure that they were fully equipped for the next twenty-four hours—they were only camping for one night as Sophia didn't want to be away from the salon for more than two days.

How he had enjoyed himself at the campsite, securing the pegs and smoothing the flaps of their tent. He gathered branches, started a fire, carved the end of twigs to serve as hot dog skewers. Quick and tireless, but he did repeatedly check to make sure she was happy, and Sophia assured him she was, though she suspiciously eyed the woods from time to time for any unwelcome guests. It was when the bonfire crackled brightly, and the dark spaces between the branches let in the sound of night creatures, that Sophia felt relaxed, secure. Adrian's face flushed pleasantly against the flames, talking about the ingenious ways he had convinced his sister during a camping trip years ago that there was a monster preying on her in the dark. How he and his brothers spent most of the night in the tent kicking each other's legs. More stories from his childhood spilled out that night. She had ended up not using her sleeping bag because he brought a two-person one. Their pooled body heat shielded them from the mountain chill. As she slept with the feel of pebbles and earth pressing against layers of polyester, she decided it was not a bad experience. She could do this again. For him.

Sophia exhaled as she rolled out her brand-new sleeping bag on her salon's floor. A corkscrew was working itself within her heart. She should stop thinking of Adrian.

There was no internet connection in the salon. She should have responded to Erwin's email from home. Glancing up at the clock, Sophia noted it wasn't even 9:30. Not too early to turn in for the rough night. There was a bright patch on the floor when she turned off the lights; her front window didn't have a shade. Sophia crawled into the rough polyester cocoon that smelled of some chemical treatment. Her body registered the hardness of the floor. The chair legs were at her eye level, illuminated by street lamps. The tiny holes of the electrical outlets looked like unhappy faces on the wall.

She distracted herself from the strangeness by thinking of Auntie Rosy, who was sleeping in her own salon. For a moment, Sophia was disturbed by this coincidence, revolted by the sameness of their plight. You chose this, she reminded herself. *You had a perfectly comfortable bed at home and you had to come here.* A van or some other huge vehicle drove by and the floor beneath her shook, deflating her will. How arrogant Sophia had been, how insensitive toward her friend's ordeal.

She woke up before her alarm, promptly rising to tidy up. Wary of the open window and her being clad only in an old T-shirt and underwear, she scurried to the washroom with her backpack. She changed into work clothes, washed her face and brushed her teeth. She quickly folded her sleeping bag and sat at the station to curl her hair.

"Morning!" Erica greeted too happily, walking in with takeout coffee in her hand, the aroma reminding Sophia that she hadn't thought about breakfast. "Hey, what's that?" She nodded toward the folded sleeping bag and backpack leaning against a corner.

"I spent the night here."

"Huh?"

"I couldn't stand being at home so I spent the night here."

"Uh, okay." Erica nodded, slowly. "How long are you planning to do this?"

"Not for long."

"Are you looking for an apartment?"

"Wasn't planning to. This just sort of happened last night." Sophia shrugged her shoulders. Erica must be thinking how weird she was, but she didn't care.

"I'd offer you our couch, but my roommate probably won't like it." Erica put down her coffee on the counter. "But if you need a place to shower, you can come over. If you want."

Sophia's stomach grumbled. "That would be great, Erica. Thank you."

⫸

ON SUNDAY, SAMUEL ARRIVED JUST BEFORE THE SALON opened. He looked reluctant when he stepped in. Sophia understood he didn't want anybody to know he was there. He even felt shy around Erica, who was aware of Sophia's plans to skip work that day to attend the convention. Sophia had omitted the part that she was hoping to run into Adrian—she had instead used her brother needing her support as an excuse.

Samuel continued to look around curiously as he sat on Sophia's styling chair. "Talaga? You sleep here?"

"Saves me a lot of time. I have everything I need." Inwardly, Sophia worried about all the money she had been spending on takeout meals. But whenever she thought about going home, her resolve only hardened. Besides, the past couple of nights had been easier. She actually started to enjoy the solitude and the simplicity sleeping in her salon offered. The surfaces and the floors get cleaned every day as part of their chores. Being surrounded by the same things she saw and used at work was somehow calming, making her forget the world outside.

"I almost slipped, you know?" Samuel looked warily at the window. "Ma was telling Pa she's worried about you. I was about to tell them I'll see you today, but stopped myself."

"You didn't say anything?"

He shrugged. "Nothing. I'm studying with friends today, 'di ba?"

Their reflections both melted into sly smiles. Sophia was enjoying the fact that her salon had become a hiding place, like Cine Star. It seemed unbelievable that Samuel was the first person in her family to have stepped foot in her salon. He had relaxed a little bit. Behind them, Erica was chatting with a client, but Sophia would sometimes catch her stealing glances at her and her brother.

"Have they mentioned anything about dropping by here?"

"Pa was thinking about it, but Mama said you might get even more upset."

"Good. Some common sense."

"They seem scared of you." Her brother's tone fell somewhere between envy and accusation, and Sophia felt a sisterly protectiveness in return. She remembered that he was burdened by the hopes and expectations of their parents.

"This is what Daiki looks like." Samuel handed over his phone to Sophia. Daiki was an old man with thick jet-black hair arranged in two flame-shaped towers on his head. His eyebrows were long, winding along his wrinkled forehead, giving him a sinister shrunken expression. He had white skin and dark lips set in a thin smile. Only then did Sophia realize the difficulty of her assignment. She never had to style someone by following a cartoon character.

"I can't figure out if his hair is flat or bulky." Sophia tousled her brother's hair. It was longer than usual. He had obviously grown it for the occasion.

Samuel shrugged. "I don't understand. Obviously, it's not flat. Don't you have hairspray or something?"

"No, what I mean is do you want thin flame-shaped spikes or, I don't know, bulbs?" Sophia gestured shapes with her hands. On the mirror, she could see Erica's client looking at them.

"What do you think looks cooler?"

"I don't know." She was running out of patience for this. "I'll see what works. You don't have enough length for this anyway."

"I can go and buy a wig. A cheap one."

"Are you out of your mind? It would take hours to put that up. Why did you choose this character anyway?"

"He's one of the most powerful characters because he doesn't need the sagacity and vitality spells," Samuel said.

"Aren't you too old to be doing this?"

He shrugged. "You might be surprised."

"Video games are for kids."

"It's a stress reliever for a lot of working professionals. It's also a billion-dollar industry, one of the few that survived the recession. I read somewhere that its annual profit can exceed the growth rate of the entire US economy."

"I see." Sophia marvelled at her brother's manner of speech, which was very similar to their father's.

"Adrian wanted to break into it. As well as many other guys I play with online. Some of them already have kids. You'll see some of them in the convention. Adrian told me a while ago he's thinking of attending one of the career workshops."

A pang of jealousy made Sophia swallow. How could Adrian share these things with Samuel and not with her? She would have been supportive about it. He had always given her the impression that he was content with his job, straightening out budgets, tweaking accounts into a balance. Sophia contemplated how to get more information from her brother.

Samuel was watching her reflection. "Sorry about what happened between you guys," he muttered.

The two soft tufts of her brother's hair would not end up as towering as Daiki's, but Sophia knew she had some purple temporary hair dye and white face powder. She noted her brother's features: the sharp angles of their father's forehead and nose, the thoughtful eyes of their mother. "I can't believe I'm doing this to you."

"Don't worry." Samuel leaned back as if settling in for a massage. "You're doing great so far."

>>>

THE CONVENTION WAS BEING HELD IN A HILTON HOTEL. During the drive, Sophia felt like she and her brother were partners in crime. They laughed as they talked about the possibility of their parents, who were driving back from the dim sum place around that hour, passing them by along Kingsway, recognizing their daughter but not the ageing punk in the passenger seat. They would be so horrified. Sophia thought she did an amazing job, using eyebrow pencils to trace wrinkles on Samuel's forehead and cheeks. His eyes practically disappeared beneath thick layers of makeup, and she slimmed and lengthened his lips using a combination of liquid eyeliner and lipstick. An excessive amount of hairspray was used to achieve the Daiki hairstyle, finished with endless pats of hair shiner. They had agreed he would look more mystical if his hair glistened.

To complete the look, Samuel carried a longsword, with a carved sheath. "It's not real. I got it online," he told Sophia, who was more fascinated with how invested he was with his costume rather than with the actual sword.

"So you're not working today?" Samuel asked.

"Your voice is young. You should sound like a wise old

man," she said, trying to avoid the question.

"Are you going to check out the convention?"

Even though he was a smart guy, Sophia wasn't ready to be explicit about her hope to see and be seen by Adrian that day. "I'm giving myself a break."

"Must be cool to work for yourself."

The remark made Sophia somewhat defensive, but she decided to let it slide. A part of her felt her brother was doing her a favour. She trailed behind his superhero cape across the hotel parking lot and the marble lobby where people standing by their luggage stared at them. They checked the event listing on a digital screen. "There," Samuel pointed: "West Coast GameCon Costume Contest."

Sophia's eyes were trained on a workshop held at a lecture room. It was scheduled to begin at 2:30, the same time as the costume contest. She turned to see Samuel already at the escalator, along with other people in costumes. "Are you coming?" he called out.

They walked side by side through the carpeted hallways, alongside people in heavy dark coats and armour finished with metallic colours. They passed a few participants clad in nothing but body paint or nylon-like bodysuits with sparse prints that mimicked scales, stripes, and other animal attributes that also served to strategically cover parts of their bodies. Many others wore masks or heavy makeup. Others had wings that flapped rigidly and smelled of glue. There were a lot of elaborate hair arrangements, men and women with braids, coils, and curls dyed in forest and ocean hues. Samuel was right. They were around her age, not kids at all.

Even the two people at the registration table looked like they were in their thirties. The woman wore a shiny blazer and talked to the registrants in a friendly tone. The man had a logo T-shirt and was nodding to a participant with a thick scaly tail. The room was buzzing with excited voices. Sophia searched the crowd for other people who were not in costume.

Samuel handed a printed ticket to the woman, who asked him to sign beside his name on a registration list.

"Ticket, please." The guy maintained a cheerful tone as he eyed Sophia quizzically.

"Oh, how much is it?" Sophia glanced at Samuel who had gone past the registration table, joining the massive crowd of supernatural beings. "I'm with him."

"Oh. For non-registrants it's forty dollars."

What a joke! Sophia suddenly felt ridiculous for having tagged along. In a svelte top with geometric cut-outs that revealed her shoulders, tight dress pants, strappy sandals that were torturing her feet, she was obviously out of place. She wasn't going to pay forty dollars to watch a geeky costume contest.

"Oh, you know, that's fine. I just wanted to check it out." She backed away, wishing she would dissolve into the swirly patterns on the wallpaper along the entryway. Through the door streamed more participants, a flood of strange distorted faces blocked her way to the exit. God, what was she doing here?

Back in the hallway, Sophia straightened her back, walked in long, purposeful strides. Recalling the name of the lecture room, she followed the overhead signs.

A thought struck her: what if she ran into Adrian right then? What would she say? How would she act? She had been looking forward to the moment, but hadn't thought through what she would do if it happened. She arranged a calm expression on her face, relaxed her brows, and softened the tightness in her jaws. Reminded herself it wasn't a lie that she was there with Samuel.

The double doors of the lecture room were open. A group of men in casual shirts and jeans walked in. Near the door there was a standing sign: *Exploring the Landscape of Game Design.* By the entrance, there was a registration table manned by a wiry young man who by one look dismissed Sophia as a non-registrant, going back to his seemingly important task of contemplating his list. She could see that the front rows of upholstered chairs were mostly vacant, but she could hear the murmur of a small waiting audience. She didn't spot Adrian as she did a quick scan of the faces. Some of the chairs were partially hidden from her view. Sophia didn't want to look in for too long; the idea was for Adrian to spot her while she was seemingly unaware, not while she was looking for him.

She decided to wait a few steps from the door and relaxed her stance, paced a little bit, making herself look like she was just passing by. More people came. A chubby college-aged man hurriedly speaking to his phone. A couple talking about something purchased by Sony. They all looked at her briefly before walking into the room. A few moments later, someone inside the room said, "Good afternoon, everyone," in a miked voice and the doors were pulled closed.

Just like that and she had no reason to be there. Sophia looked longingly at the end of the hallway, hoping to see latecomers. But she was alone. The speaker behind the doors had an earnest voice, as if the topic of the lecture had something to do with saving lives. Sophia waited for another ten minutes, during which she only spotted two uniformed hotel staff and tourists with searching faces. With heavy feet, she looked for the ladies' washroom.

16

I N THEIR FIRST DECEMBER TOGETHER, ADRIAN HAD INVITED
Sophia to his office holiday party. It was an after-work
reception at a pub close to his office. He picked her up
from the salon.

"So what happens there? Do you guys have lots of
fun?" Sophia asked during the drive.

"Nothing exciting. Just my co-workers mingling."
Adrian squeezed her leg above the knee. "I don't really like
going to office parties. They're mostly lame."

"Why is that?" Sophia didn't really need to ask. Adrian
was not a party person. But she was pleasantly baffled by
how eagerly he had wanted to attend this year when she
had agreed to go with him.

"Because nothing really happens. To me, it's just about
showing up."

Sophia discovered another layer to Adrian's lukewarm
feelings toward office parties. Most of his colleagues had

a partner in tow. Grey-bearded men and sophisticated ladies. The younger ones in the crowd also had dates and were gathered closer to the cash bar. People smiled warmly as Adrian introduced her. He was eager and proud, and Sophia felt the same. His clasp on her hand was tight as they met more people and grabbed bites from appetizer trays being carried around.

After a drink they found a group of people from his department, three young men and a woman.

"Whoa, you're still here?" one of them called out.

Adrian introduced Derek, Baldeep, and Nina, who was with her boyfriend, Andrew. Sophia repeated their names, as she would with clients at her salon.

"Usually he's already gone by the second hour." Derek smiled knowingly at Sophia before asking where she worked. She told him about her hair salon. "That's cool," Derek nodded.

Nina's eyes were wide. "Your hair looks amazing! Lemme see!"

Sophia had fixed her hair into a dishevelled halo braid that looked complicated, but was actually simple for her to put up. She had weaved a thin silver ribbon into the French braid running around her crown and applied glittered gel to the spiky tufts she had pulled out from the braid. She turned her head so Nina could see her handiwork.

Baldeep asked how she and Adrian had met. Sophia told him the story.

"Are you serious?" Baldeep smiled mischievously when she came to the part when Adrian asked her out. "I didn't know that guy had game in him."

Adrian playfully pushed Baldeep away. "Do we know you?"

Sophia had known her boyfriend to be aloof at gatherings, but Adrian seemed lively that night, approaching everyone, gamely joining conversations. She knew it was because she was with him.

When the party thinned around suppertime, Sophia and Adrian went for their coats. "I don't know about you," she said, "but I'm ready for real food."

Adrian chuckled. "I know. Cheese cubes and shrimp cocktail won't do it for me, either. Where do we go?"

Sophia's excitement for the evening had made her ravenous for something hearty and familiar. She asked Adrian to drive to a Filipino eatery on Fraser Street. The small dining space was heavy with the fat aroma of sauces and meats. The steam from the dishes displayed side-by-side fogged up the glass display case. There were three kinds of fried fish. Stews brimming with fat-laced cuts of meat. Eggplants, squash, and other colourful vegetables floating in rich broth. In their first months of dating, Sophia had held back from suggesting that kind of place to Adrian, worried that he'd find the atmosphere unappealing, the food too strange. But he seemed enthusiastic, asking the server behind the counter about the dishes, not even bothering to consult Sophia. Most of the customers were coming from work, grabbing takeout for supper. Adrian told Sophia, "I think I'll get the beef and soy sauce one. You know what it's called?"

"I'll order for you," she said. "Save us a table."

He kissed her on the cheek before leaving the line.

Sophia could feel the woman standing next in line watching them. She beamed at Sophia. "Swerte mo naman." You're lucky.

Sophia grinned to offset the iciness of her tone. "Siya ang swerte." He's the lucky one.

❦

AT THE HOTEL'S BAR, SOPHIA TEXTED SAMUEL TO APOLOGIZE for suddenly disappearing at the costume contest. He texted back telling her not to worry, he'd catch a ride with a friend.

She had wolfed down an expensive roast beef sandwich with surprising gusto. Sophia didn't believe in sandwiches. They hardly satisfied her hunger, but the one she just finished did the trick today. Her body was still in the phase of reclaiming its appetite, making her feel open-minded. Unmoored. Sophia shook her head. It was pitiful, the thought that having a sandwich was her idea of being open-minded.

Sitting there, furtively watching the diners, she felt guilty for skipping another workday, leaving Erica to fend for herself. But it was already late in the afternoon; the salon was about to close. She asked the bartender for a glass of red wine. The hope of seeing Adrian had practically vanished. Samuel had mentioned it was a three-day convention, this being the third. Maybe Adrian had come in on another day.

She had a vague feeling that she was being watched. Sophia looked around and met the look of the guy at the other end of the bar.

"Oh, hey it's you." His eyebrows lifted with recognition.

Sophia was certain she didn't know him and stared mutely.

"I thought you'd left. Sorry I couldn't waive the registration fee."

It was the guy from the costume contest table. Sophia's face heated with embarrassment.

"It's no big deal. I didn't really come to watch," she said evenly. She wondered how long he'd been watching her.

"Have you seen your boyfriend?"

Sophia gaped, stupefied. A fresh wave of humiliation washed over her. How could he possibly know about Adrian? She sipped her wine, slowly, delicately, buying time to create a different explanation for her presence in the convention.

"Or is he too busy being Daiki?" he pursued.

Of course! How stupid of her. "Oh, God, no," she said, relieved. "That was my brother."

"Oh!"

Sophia laughed so hard that the alcohol pooled in her throat, rose in her sinuses. She turned away to cough.

He approached her. "Are you okay?"

By the time it passed, the tiny bar napkin was drenched with wine and her saliva. The guy asked the bartender for a glass of water.

"Here you go," he said.

"Thank you." Head low, Sophia drank from the glass.

He went to retrieve his bottle of beer and smiled as he approached her.

"I'm Bryan."

"Sophia." She immediately regretted giving her name. She wished she had given a fake one.

"Do you want another drink, Sophia?" He was eyeing her empty glass.

"I'm driving."

"Ah."

"Thanks for your help." Sophia held up her glass of water.

"I'm sorry. I'm sure I would have seen the resemblance without the Daiki get-up," Bryan said. "Are you waiting for him? The costume contest's almost finished."

"No, just hanging out. I was hungry." She looked behind her. More people had come to the restaurant. Two greying women, both wearing scarves. An old couple. A bunch of guys talking loudly, not one of them Adrian. She wished he would walk in now, see her speaking with Bryan.

"When I saw you walk in for the contest, I thought you were coming as Adora."

"Who is Adora?" She narrowed her eyes, allowing a hint of annoyance to creep into her voice.

"The hot chick from *Wielding Wizards*. She roams the earthly expanse, casting enchantment spells."

There was pretend-seriousness in his voice. Sophia now couldn't help smiling, yet it hadn't escaped her that he was using a video game to flirt with her. She tried to silence that part of her that firmly believed that video games were not for grown-ups. "So, this Adora character walks around in blouse and pants."

"She has this long, shiny, black hair that she wraps around her enemies." He sat down on the bar stool next to hers. "She carries a deadly potion for the cruel man who stole half of her heart."

Laughter was welling up within her, the dangerous kind that might be accompanied by tears. But the wine was still working its warm, glowing magic. "This has got to be the cheesiest story I've ever heard."

Bryan laughed, looking down. Sophia was intrigued by his sudden self-conscious behaviour. "You're right, actually," he confessed. "Storylines for games don't have to be brilliant. They work as long as the games make sense. Mind you, *Wielding* is not my favourite, but it's very popular right now."

"Hmm," Sophia was unsure what to say. Should she ask him about his favourite game? She couldn't even work up the feigned enthusiasm needed to pose that question. She scrambled for a witty remark.

"Do you always come with your brother to events like this?"

"No." Sophia wondered if she should tell him about Adrian. A terrible idea! "I helped him with his hair and makeup, that's all."

"You're the coolest sister ever."

The compliment was not appealing at all.

"My ex-boyfriend was going to be at the contest too. I wanted to make sure my brother won," Sophia said, amazed at how she easily formulated the lie.

"An ex? Not the smartest guy then."

Sophia now felt at ease enough to study him. Thick, wavy, brown hair shadowed his eyes. The boldness of his gaze arrested her. It must be the dim lighting, or the alcohol, but he looked more manly than she remembered. She shifted on her seat, turned her body toward him. "So aside from having long hair, what does Adora look like?"

He paused, considering something. "She's a really powerful woman."

"Does she have a weapon?" She remembered a term she had learned from Samuel earlier that day. "What does she *wield*?"

"Her spells and her hair, like I said. With her revenge spell though, when she uses it too much, it clouds her judgement. She loses sagacity points."

She was starting to lose interest in this wizard business, but decided to indulge him. The animated glimmer of his eyes was addicting, like it was something Sophia had the special power to bring about. "And what does she need to do to gain sagacity points?"

"She needs to wander into the wilderness of darkness, battle a few monsters." He leaned forward, as if finally convinced that Sophia was really interested. "Pick up a few precious items along the way. I guess you're new to *Wielding*?"

"Fairly. Daiki gave me a crash course this afternoon." Sophia was careful not to mention the word "brother" in this conversation.

"Getting tips from the wisest of them all," Bryan mused. "But who cares about these games, anyway."

"It's a billion-dollar industry." Sophia took a sip, giving herself a break from his stare. "My ex wanted to venture into game design."

Bryan whistled. "A super competitive field. Job forecasts tell two contrasting stories: that it's a rising lucrative industry, and that it's lousy for game junkies who lack creativity and the technical know-how. You've got to know your stuff in there."

They had shifted to shop talk, which Sophia didn't want. But she sensed something promising—they were both steering the conversation toward some place outside of gaming, somewhere more ... grown-up? It was just a matter of finding the right words. The noise of the early suppertime patrons was growing, encroaching on the thrill of the moment. The lounge music was now more sedate, but playing at a higher volume. Sophia craned her neck to see all around, but it had gotten dimmer in the restaurant. There were more people, but their faces were in the shadows.

"You're looking for him." Bryan hadn't bothered phrasing it as a question. He frowned as if she should know better.

Sophia felt a dizzying glow embracing her. It was digging into her skin, seeping into her bones that had been taut, anxious. Bryan's face came closer, his breath warm. When they kissed, he pushed on her with a force that made Sophia lean backwards. His soft lips and the rough stubble reminded her he was a stranger, and at the moment that seemed like a good thing. For a second, she sensed the danger of falling, but then there was a strong arm supporting her back. Still she gripped the bar top when their faces parted.

"Do you want to grab something?" he asked.

"I just ate," Sophia said. Something told her that he knew she was full, that he'd been watching her since the sandwich. "And I'm starting to really hate this place."

"I live nearby." A casual tip of a shoulder. "It'll be quiet there."

Turned out Bryan's apartment was less than four blocks away. Sophia offered to drive, just so she could remove the car from the hotel's parking space. During the short drive, she cherished the male presence in her otherwise lonely car. She also liked that she was driving. It gave her a feeling of control over the situation.

Bryan seemed to know exactly what to do, what she needed. When he ushered her past the door, her eyes landed on dark forms barely illuminated by the settling dusk streaming through the window. There was not much to see, but the bed was pretty evident. A bachelor suite. She took a step back and bumped into him, the slight collision making Sophia question whether she would go ahead with this.

"Do you want something to drink?"

Sophia sensed him turning around, perhaps to turn on the light. She hated the feeling of his flesh drifting away from hers. It felt like something was being severed, left in the air, unfinished. Sophia went after him, grabbed his shoulders from behind, and turned him to her. He responded quickly, wrapping her in a brusque embrace, his hand making its way to places that hit her with the reality of what she half-wanted and half-feared. Somehow, they found the bed in the darkness.

17

LIGHT, STARK AS REGRET, TOOK HOLD OF THE ROOM and pried into Sophia's eyes. She had no idea what time it was. Dazed, she lifted her heavy head and saw Bryan ambling toward the kitchen. He had put on his pants. With his back turned to her, he seemed older, like someone who had children. *Small children*, Sophia consoled herself. A ring of thick flesh bunched around his belt line.

Just what had she done? This wasn't like her at all. Every cell in her body was sluggish, but Sophia forced herself to roll out of the strange bed and pick up her clothes. The carpet looked old with its orange and brown 1970s pattern. She suddenly ached for her own bedroom.

"Do you want some water?" Bryan was standing by the sink.

"No, no thanks. I have to go."

"Cool. I think I'm gonna head out for a bite."

His tone had a weariness that annoyed her. As she

fumbled with her sandals, Sophia had the vague sense that he was impatient for her to leave and might be wondering whether it was rude not to ask her number. She felt like she should say something before goodbye, but what were the right words for a situation like this?

"What time is it?" She cared more about breaking the silence than the hour.

"About 8:30."

Sophia met his eyes. "Thanks for having me over."

"Thanks for coming over." He looked relieved. "You're really cool."

"Bye then."

In the car, she checked her phone. Eight missed calls. Two from her mother. Six from Erica, who also sent a text message. Sophia froze as she read the message. Her mother had dropped by at the salon around closing time, looking for her. Her chest pounded as she drove to Erica's home. It was not like her mother would make a scene— she with her friendly smile and nervous way of talking to people she didn't know. Erica would have been nice and polite as well. But what words had been exchanged, what hints had her mother picked up? She scowled at the third red light that delayed her from finding out. Bryan had been a horrible idea. Everything that had looked strong and firm when they had been at the bar turned flabby and hairy as she held him in the dark. The smell of beer was expected, but there was a dank mix of stale deodorant and dried-up sweat. His surprising attempts to slow things down, caressing her contours with his fingerprints, his tiny kisses on her neck and shoulder, all came across as clumsy and nibbly; his body was not designed for tenderness, unable to disguise its greed. Kisses pressed too hard, the grunts he made were beast-like. With how suave he was at the bar, Sophia briefly wondered whether she had gone to bed with a different man. There had been a couple of instances when she had stiffened, rethinking this escapade. Bryan didn't notice—he was a machine who had found its rhythm. Adrian's face drifted against the ceiling, his voice rang in her ears, making her reach for Bryan's fleshy sides with a boldness that he excelled at reciprocating. She pushed Adrian's presence away by thinking of Tino and Mon, but it only made her feel worse. Bryan's moist, lumbering form blocked the sight of empty spaces, her moans drowned memories of familiar voices. Sophia cringed now, remembering that whenever he had done something that put her off, her body had responded by acting eager, wanting more of it.

By the time she pulled over in front of Erica's place, Sophia was ready with an apology. Erica looked worried when she opened the door. "Jesus, are you okay? What happened to your phone?"

"I'm fine. I got your message. Erica, I'm sorry about my mom. I should have known. I should have been there."

"Where have you been?" Erica glanced anxiously at her car as she stepped aside to let her in. There was a pile of soapy plates by the sink. Sophia felt bad for intruding into her home life. To make matters worse, she also realized she could kill for a shower. Bryan's scent seemed to stick on her body.

"The event that we went to took too long. Did she give you a hard time?"

"Your mom? No, not at all."

"What happened?"

"She just wanted to talk to you." Erica sat down on the couch, wiping her wet hands with a jaggedly torn paper towel. "I told her you went on some errand and would not likely to be back. But I was too busy to mind her. But she waited for a while."

A stab of something like pity went through Sophia's heart. "Did she say anything?"

"She asked about how the salon was doing. I said we're doing okay, we have highs and lows. I was careful not to mention Samuel being there today."

"Thank you. And I'm sorry for the trouble."

"No worries."

The sound of running water could be heard from the bathroom down the hall. Sophia remembered with dismay that she hadn't brought a towel. She would have to borrow one from Erica. The favour felt too personal though. God, only she was capable of putting herself in such a situation. What did she want to prove by running away, camping in her own hair salon? The news of her mother coming to look for her didn't reward her with the satisfaction Sophia thought she would feel. It didn't feel like she had successfully proven a point. Instead, the whole situation came across as petty and unnecessarily dramatic.

"Are you planning to go back and figure things out with them?"

"At some point I'll have to do something, but I'm not sure what."

"Hey, I don't really care. I just don't want to be between you and your folks." Erica was using the casual tone used to mask a more unpleasant feeling. She pulled at her tuft. "And I got worried when you didn't pick up the phone. How was Samuel's thing anyway? Did it really go that long?"

"I'll make sure I'm in the salon next time my mother comes around." She hoped Erica would stop asking about the convention.

The door to the bathroom opened, and Erica's roommate stepped out, clad in a towel. "Oh, hello again," she muttered to Sophia. Coldly.

Sophia nodded. "How's it going?" This was her third time to take a shower at Erica's place. She hoped it would be the last.

⁂

THE FOLLOWING EVENING, HER MOTHER CAME TO THE SALON straight from work. She said hi to Erica like they were friends and beamed at the sight of Sophia. "There you are!"

"Is Dad with you?" Sophia worried that something like what happened the last night she was home would repeat in her own salon. But her mother shook her head, eyebrows lifted meaningfully.

"Don't be silly. I came here for a haircut."

This Sophia didn't expect. Her mother started to settle herself on her chair, doing so without being invited, while not being fully comfortable as well. She sat holding her purse close to her body, only remembering that she didn't need to when Sophia gestured to a nearby stool where her clients usually placed their belongings.

Her mother's hair was always of the same length, a couple of inches past the shoulder. With her head propped backwards against the shampoo sink, her scalp shifting beneath Sophia's fingertips, she looked vulnerable and helpless. There was a time when Sophia thought she was the most elegant woman she knew. As a little girl, she would glimpse her mother sitting at her dresser, leaning toward the mirror, tracing dark lines around her eyes, brushing vibrant colours onto her face before she went to work. The shape of her hair, her pointed high heels, and the crisp smell of her leather purse commanded looks of admiration and respect from people she passed in the college hallways and out in the streets. It was hard to reconcile that memory with the lines on her mother's face, the knitted sweater draping shapelessly on her fleshy midsection. Sophia found herself working carefully, paying more attention. Aside from her occasional directions, they did not exchange any words.

By the time they returned to the chair, Erica had cleaned up her station. "Good night, ladies!" She smiled at Sophia and her mother.

"Do you stay at her place?" her mother asked once Erica had left.

Sophia wasn't prepared to tell her mother she slept in the salon. "Yes."

"When are you planning to come home?"

Sophia was eager to come home, to sleep in her own bed once again and eat home cooked food. Her resistance of sorts was flailing, on the verge of crumbling. But a part of her wanted to hold on to this power for little bit, to see what her stubbornness had bought her.

"I don't know. When I feel like it."

A troubled frown emerged on her mother's forehead.

"Did you just want a trim?"

Her mother nodded. Slowly.

Sophia took refuge from the awkwardness in the hair, the firm hold of its roots and its silkiness against her fingers. She concentrated on her work, avoiding her mother's eyes whenever she looked up at the mirror. It was as if her mother sensed the unease because she sat very still.

"Your Dad is heartbroken. I am, too."

"I'm fine. You don't need to worry about me."

"He drove past your salon every morning. But he never stopped by, knowing you wouldn't want to be bothered while working." Her mother was looking sideways, as if she couldn't care less about how her haircut was turning out. "But I couldn't stay distant anymore. I didn't tell him I was planning to visit though."

"Thanks, I guess."

Nobody spoke during blow-dry. Sophia had made it her goal to make her mother look ten years younger, twirling sections with her brush to create flattering forms. When they finished, it pleased her when her mother took a moment to admire her looks. The supple bell-shaped layers near her cheeks swayed gracefully as she turned her head from side to side. At this point, Sophia would usually give pointers on how to maintain the form, but she found herself unable to speak, her eyes brimming for reasons she couldn't identify. She was feeling warm on the inside and she knew her mother felt this too. But as soon as it came, the moment passed. Her mother slowly rose from her seat, turned to Sophia.

"Come home with me."

Sophia turned away. "No."

"Why are you hurting us like this?"

She started cleaning up her station. "I'm not doing this to hurt you. I just needed to be away."

"I'll tell Dad not to bug you about your job again."

"Then we would have nothing else to talk about and his life would be pointless."

Her mother didn't reply. Sophia dipped her scissors and combs into the disinfecting solution. When she looked up at the mirror, her mother had a trembling hand on her mouth and her eyes were rimmed with tears.

"You are always welcome to come home. And I, for myself, am sorry. Really sorry."

She turned and left the salon.

⟫

DESPERATE FOR INTERNET CONNECTION BUT NOT QUITE prepared to come home, Sophia headed downtown with her laptop. The SkyTrain was almost empty; she wondered if she looked as aimless as the handful of passengers onboard. She was exhausted, judging by how comfortable she was finding train seats. She was heartened to see some lighted signs downtown, remembering those rare late nights she had been out as a student, tottering on platform sandals, following Tino and the rest of their friends to night-club queues. Sophia was grateful for her sneakers, allowing her to cover more ground quickly, but she missed the company. Spotting a coffee shop with a few preoccupied-looking patrons, Sophia pushed the glass door and met the scent of caffeine and sugary pastries.

She settled with her tea on a table close to the window, anxiously eyeing the café staffer who was mopping the floor. The place would probably close in less than an hour. But if the world were kind to her tonight, she would be able to catch Erwin before he went to work.

Please, please, Erwin, be online.

He was.

"Good timing." He lit up when he saw Sophia and scanned her surroundings through the screen. "Where are you?"

"I sort of ran away."

"What?"

Now that she was facing her best friend, Sophia couldn't figure out how to begin. She had kept so much from Erwin, with whom she had always shared everything. Bringing him up to speed felt like an overwhelming task.

"Adrian and I are breaking up. I like to think it's not for real. I found out he's been unsure for some time three weeks ago. I couldn't stand my parents, so I've been living in the salon. Three days now."

"Sofi, sandali." Erwin held up a hand. "What happened with Adrian?"

It tortured her to have to recall her last conversation with Adrian, but Sophia dove into the thick tangle of it all, pulling one excruciating strand out after another. Hot tears streamed down her cheeks; she was practically voiceless when she mentioned Gretchen. She was well aware she was making a scene; people were watching her. But it didn't matter. Erwin was listening intently.

"I really wanted to get back at him. Bwiset, he wasn't even there when I drove away with Bryan."

"Are you out of your mind? Something could have happened to you."

"Nothing worse could happen to me now, I swear."

"You could end up dead. Kidnapped. Or your salon could burn down." When Sophia didn't laugh, Erwin regretted his attempt at morbid humour. "Sorry, Sofi. Was he cute?"

"He's not bad. But I still wish Adrian saw us."

"Okay, then I'm less angry now. But seryoso, use your head next time."

Sophia rolled her eyes in pretend annoyance. "You have no idea how rough things have been."

"You could have talked to me."

"I was hoping Adrian would come back."

It was Erwin's turn to act annoyed. "Who needs a guy without a pair?"

Sophia let out a whimper that swelled into a sob. By this time, the onlookers were no longer hiding the fact that they were staring, holding the line between bearing witness and getting involved. The paper napkin was already drenched with her tears; it reminded her of Bryan approaching her at the bar. In midst of her tears, Sophia started laughing.

"Hala! Are you okay?" Erwin asked. "I think you're losing your mind."

"I really wish you were here."

"Diyos ko, Sofi. I would fly there if I could. Why don't you come here?"

⁂

ERICA WAS THE FIRST TO BE TOLD.

"Okay, let me get this straight. You want to leave for Manila the day after tomorrow. And you'll be away for, what, a week?"

"Eleven days," Sophia said. It was all clear to her now that she needed a break. Everything she thought she had known was becoming unknown, things that were in her control slipping out of her grasp. Running away to squat in her salon had seemed like the easiest way to escape.

Of course, she hadn't thought things through. How it would affect Erica, for instance. But Sophia trusted her, and if she were going to be honest with herself, she also wanted to be away from her competent and reliable colleague who had witnessed her slowly falling apart. Since Maggie's wedding, it seemed that Erica was tiptoeing around her, watching out for the next meltdown.

But now Erica was clutching her temples. "You're kidding, right?"

"I trust you, Erica. And I'm sorry for the short notice." Sophia wavered on the inside but she had already made up her mind. "I really need the time to sort things out for myself. I only have a couple soft appointments, I checked. And I just placed an order for some supplies."

"Okay, I think I'm gonna be fine. Just surprised, that's all."

"You're going to be okay. And you can send me emails. Text me if it's something urgent."

"Look, it's been pretty quiet, which may not be a good thing. You need to do some sort of promotional stuff when you get back. But till then, I'll hold down the fort. Take a break. You need it."

Erica, straight to the point as ever. Last night, Sophia had stayed in the coffee shop as the closing shift workers counted their tills and cleaned the kitchen, looking for the cheapest flights and working on her budget. She chanced upon a discounted ticket, only valid for the week. Yes, a trip to the Philippines was not helping her financially, but then she didn't have to worry about saving up for a wedding. Her salon's income had been low the past two months, but Maggie's gig would keep them just above the surface. She would really need to step up on the online promotion and drum up other ways to bring in business once she was back. Maybe she could sign the salon up for those email deals offering their services at a discount.

That Erica also recognized she needed the break—it offered such relief. Sophia wanted to give her a hug—another thing they didn't do as work friends. "I promise that I'll be the same old after the trip."

"Nah, after everything that has happened, you can't be the same old."

Sophia drove home that evening. Her father, who was watching *Jeopardy!* practically sprang from the couch when she walked in, but managed to still look displeased. He looked more tired than she remembered.

"You have finally decided to come home."

Her mother emerged from the kitchen. "Sophia!"

They all looked at each other mutely, as if they were in a poorly prepared school play where they were all waiting for a forgotten line.

"I'm sorry for getting you all worried," she began. "I needed to be away."

Her mother approached her. "We're just glad you're home. Aren't we, Dad?"

Her father wore a withering stare, and his body couldn't decide whether it wanted to sit back down or remain standing. "I don't know why you're making us to be the ones against you."

"I booked a flight to Manila." Two thoughts ran through Sophia's mind right after she said this. One was that it was jarring news. There had been talks about them visiting home as a family, but they never actually made a plan. The other was her father's words; she realized her mother might have been right when she said he was heartbroken.

"When are you leaving?" her mother asked.

"Thursday, 11:45 p.m."

Her mother's eyes widened. "That soon? For how long?"

"Eleven days."

"How about the salon?" her father asked. Sophia almost laughed at the irony—her father showing concern for her business.

"Erica will be there."

"Who is Erica?" he demanded.

Oh God. Sophia shook her head. Even her mother frowned at him. He was that clueless about her work.

"I will phone Mila." Her mother was backing away from the living room. "She'll probably ask you to stay with her."

Sophia contemplated booking a hotel; she wasn't sure if taking a break from her family only to live with her mother's sister was a great idea. But to be away from all of this was reward enough. Over the next two days, her parents were careful around her. They avoided asking her questions about the days she was away, as if Sophia's answers would be covered with barbs. Adrian was never brought up. Sophia knew she should be grateful for this new respect, though it made her uncomfortable. At the dinner table, her mother filled the tentative silence with questions about her hair salon. Could she really work with two clients at a time? What was their busiest season? Day of the week? Time of the day? Did she really buy all those expensive-looking products, all the equipment? How was she managing all of these? Sophia found herself giving patient and detailed answers. Her mother nodded at her father from time to time. "It seems like a lot of dedication, what she's doing." He simply nodded.

After dinner on Thursday, Sophia was surprised by her father, who offered to drive her to the airport.

"I can take a cab, Dad. It's okay."

"Why waste your money? Let me take you."

They called Samuel from his room to help Sophia bring down her suitcase. "Why are you going to Manila?" he asked.

"To be away from us," her father said, hauling Sophia's backpack onto his shoulder.

Being in her father's car made Sophia feel like a little girl. On her lap, she gripped the purse containing her passport and printed ticket. Her face was trained on the window, watching the trees with sparse branches flying past. It was a wet night; small puddles glinted on the pavement, reflecting store signs and street lamps. Sophia was thinking how she would soon be in a place with a completely different climate. A part of her was pleased that Adrian didn't know about the trip. She was gradually departing from her old self, the one that tried to bridge their differences, involving him in every aspect of her life. But there was a tiny stream draining in her heart. In the past she would dream about flying back to Manila with Adrian, showing him the place she grew up in, introducing him to Erwin, Auntie Rosy, and her relatives.

"Watch out for thieves." Her father's voice was low.

Sophia turned to him and nodded. His face was vacant, and his eyes had a faraway look.

"Don't go around waving your phone, wearing jewellery."

"I know, Dad. I used to commute through Manila."

"It gets worse there every time. Are you planning to go places? Up to Baguio?"

"No. Just staying with Auntie. See friends." Sophia was weighing her words, aware that her father was always assessing her, hunting for flaws. She could practically hear him think, grumbling about this extravagant throwing away of money for ten idle days in their old, unremarkable neighbourhood. The idea of her seeing Erwin and Auntie Rosy probably irritated him now.

"How about swimming?"

"Huh?"

"I taught you how to swim, right? In case you decide to go to some resort."

Sophia turned to the dark window, saw her bewildered expression. Did he really think she could drown in a swimming pool? A memory surfaced: a sweltering summer. A new pink bathing suit that pressed against her thighs. She was probably six or seven. Her mother was sitting at the side of the pool, legs submerged in the water. Sophia and her father were drifting farther and farther away from her.

"Don't scare her!" her mother called out.

Sophia's feet could only feel water but she wasn't scared. Her father was a solid wall and he was holding her in his arms. "Lie on the water, baby," he said, loosening his grip. His arms letting go made her cling to his neck, her legs thrashed, feeling her father's bare stomach. "It's fine. Just relax. Lie down, like on a bed." He spoke kindly but urgently, letting Sophia lie on his arms, which were stretched forward like a sleepwalker's. But the water wouldn't hold her; she felt it rising around her ears, closing around her face. She closed her eyes.

"Just relax. Really. Like you're on clouds."

Sophia opened her eyes and saw the clouds, floating against the sky. Nobody had ever actually been on a cloud, and she liked the idea that her father could show her a similar experience. Her body softened, becoming one with the lapping waves. Parts of her were underwater, but her face could feel the sun, and she could see her stomach and knees. She turned to her father, and seeing his arms up in delight and not supporting her from beneath made her toss about in a panic. "*Hoy!*" he called out, alarmed but not angry. Water got into Sophia's nose and she gripped her father's shoulders hard. But moments later, she was ready to let go and lie on the clouds once again.

Against the night sky, Sophia sighted a plane taking off, soaring above the scattered lights beyond the overpass. At the airport's entrance, her father took her luggage out of the trunk. Sophia quickly put on her backpack, and cast a wary look at the oncoming cars pulling into the drop-off point. Hoping her father would take the cue and drive away.

But he stood there, looking at her with shining eyes.

"Give us a call when you get there."

⁂

IT WAS NOT UNTIL SHE HAD SETTLED IN HER ECONOMY SEAT that Sophia felt the excitement of seeing Erwin again. The airplane was wheeling endlessly around the runway. The other passengers were already comfortable in their flannel blankets, staring at their entertainment sets. She had emailed him to let her know the day she was arriving, but hadn't confirmed when they would meet up. A mischievous smile spread over Sophia's face. She would surprise her best friend.

Of course, Auntie Rosy had not been forgotten. Sophia had been pushing her out of her mind, not wanting to dampen her excitement for the trip. Though they had not discussed anything in their last chat, she felt Erwin was counting on her to confront Auntie Rosy about the future of Cine Star. Would it be easier done face to face? Would Sophia waver and give in upon seeing her in person after all these years? How would they go about convincing their fallen heroine that it was time to give up what she cared about most?

III
HOMECOMING

18

AMP HEAT, THE KIND THAT DRAPED ON THE LIMBS and clung to the skin, told Sophia she was home. At the passport control booths, people in the line were standing too close to one another. She had barely slept on the flight, but there was a restless beat in her, an eagerness. She felt very awake. The man behind her complained about the slowness of the immigration officers. "Everything here is so inefficient," he muttered crankily. Sophia drew herself up despite her aching shoulders, summoning patience. The workers behind the counters looked as surly as the newly arrived passengers.

Every spot in the airport was packed with people, the walkways, the ticketing booths, the escalators at the foot of which the crowd swelled and dispersed with a seemingly hazardous slowness. Miraculously, nobody was trampled upon; people reached the baggage claim area in one piece. Even there, in a large sprawling space, Sophia found herself trying to manoeuvre between tired and sweaty bodies. It was like being on a dance floor where everybody had gotten bored with the music but had nowhere else to go. She reached the assigned carousel for her flight, strained her eyes at the clumsy procession of belongings. Boxes wrapped in thick masking tape, dark suitcases with vibrant ribbons, other curious-looking loads emerging from the mouth before tumbling onto the conveyor belt. After a lifetime's worth of possessions paraded before her watchful eyes, Sophia's own suitcase was still missing. Her feet hurt, sweat trickled down her forehead and her armpits. When her suitcase finally appeared, the same one Sophia had brought to Canada nine years ago, she felt embarrassed by its oldness.

Beyond the exit sign was the blinding sunny morning, and air that slapped a layer of particles on her face. Sophia spotted Auntie Mila in the crowded waiting area waving her thin arms, which turned out to be mighty as they gripped her in a tight embrace.

"How was your flight? Ay, you look different! So sophisticated-looking! You need to tell me everything. When your mother told me the news, I was surprised, you know? I wondered what was wrong." Her aunt was still as chatty as she remembered. And she looked so young. Sophia couldn't help admiring her slim figure and her choice of outfit: a floral peasant blouse with ruffled straps, sea-green cotton skirt, thick wedge espadrilles. It was hard to imagine how she fought for a spot in such a feminine outfit through the crowds, but the same strong arm stayed around Sophia's shoulder, eager and welcoming, as if it had been her and not her mother that Auntie Mila had been in contact with all these years. An ambivalent memory flashed in Sophia's head: a rainy Sunday afternoon when she was a girl of seven or eight. She and her mother were visiting Auntie Mila. The two women traded gossip in the living room as they polished their nails, and when Sophia became the topic of the conversation, they spoke of her as if she weren't sitting right there, in the same room—her remarks, manners, achievements, and offences doled out and dissected.

"I'm okay," Sophia affected casualness by shrugging. "I just need a break."

"So you're still thinking of taking him back? Tarantado! He's not worth it, darling." It stung to hear this vehement criticism of her former fiancé, but a part of her was grateful. Auntie Mila was looking around frantically, her ponytail whipping the back of her neck. She smelled of something flowery. "Goodness, where is Paul? Paul! Paul!" Her aunt was calling out over blaring horns and cries of greetings. Sophia, feeling drained by the bustle and the heat, had a hard time convincing herself that it was only around eight in the morning. A man with a kind and narrow face emerged from the crowd.

"There you are," her aunt said playfully. "Let's take my niece home before she passes out. She's so pale, look!"

Sophia wanted to ask Auntie Mila if Paul were her boyfriend, but they were now heading to an unpaved parking lot where vehicles were parked in no particular arrangement, strewn like giant confetti. They continued to bicker as they carried Sophia's suitcase and backpack. Paul led them to a white delivery van marked with a blue and green decal of a waterfall flanked by coconut trees. This illustration of a tropical paradise was enclosed within a circle formed by the words Fresh Springs in thick inflated letters. Paul slid the door open to reveal ten-gallon water bottles—their pure-looking contents made Sophia long for a cool drink. Her suitcase and backpack found a place among these enormous containers.

"Is there not a place for my niece there?" Sophia felt uneasy by the demanding way her aunt said *my niece*.

"I haven't done my delivery yet." Paul scratched his head. "You wanted me to come early so—"

Auntie Mila drew a low flat line with her hands, closing the matter. "Okay, okay. She'll sit with us in the front."

The front compartment of the van stored heat that seemed solid enough to clog one's airways. Auntie Mila, whose moist knees were pressing against Sophia's, started fanning herself with a folded newspaper. Paul fiddled with the aircon. Sophia exhaled and wished the drive would not be long. But the van was painfully slow even in navigating out of the airport parking lot. Exhaustion from the trip started to set in once they merged into the highway traffic. The rays that bounced off the roof of the vehicles hurt Sophia's eyes. Gigantic billboards of grinning celebrities blazed against the white sky. The roadside hosted cramped colonies of umbrellas, banners, gates, and signs with bright colours aged by traffic smog and monsoon splatters. In every corner or so there were flapping advertisements for mobile phone loading stations. Huge bubble gum-coloured signs warned against death by jaywalking.

On the pavements marched commuters, a mix of virginal uniforms, crisply-pressed business wear interspersed with the patched and grimy garb of street beggars. Most people had wet hair—with this hot weather it was stupid to use a hair dryer after showering. The roar of the engines and the frustrated chorus of honking from the jeepneys, trucks, taxis and tricycles sharing the narrow lanes swelled in her ears. Sophia was finding all of these dreamlike—how else to describe a familiar scene that was foreign to her senses?

"How are they?" Auntie Mila was referring to Sophia's parents.

"They're okay. They haven't changed much, except for gaining some weight." Sophia wondered if her aunt knew about the events that drove her to live in her salon. She didn't feel like talking about it right now.

"I saw photos of Samuel on Facebook. He has gotten so thin."

She remembered her brother in his Daiki costume. "He's busy at school."

The van was at a standstill, inching forward only to stop again for five or ten minutes. Sophia started to doze off, her head propped against her aunt's shoulder. The air-con chill was feeble against the searing heat beating on the glass. Traffic noises, along with snippets of songs and jingles from the car radio, seeped into her light sleep.

It was noontime when they reached her aunt's home. When Sophia got out of the van, it struck her how the neighbourhood looked smaller than she remembered. The row of uneven dwellings threatened to invade the road and the horizon it led to; the view had the appearance of a makeshift backdrop for a stage play. Paul, who had gotten out of the van, had to squeeze himself between the vehicle and the concrete wall of her aunt's apartment building. The houses and gates, the parked vehicles, and even the neighbours milling about or squatted on the pavement, seemed to encroach on her personal space. Sweat dripped down her spine and her scalp had grown sticky. Auntie Mila hurried to turn on the electric fan in the living room as Paul carried in her things. The place was still how it was years ago, but Sophia couldn't remember everything looking so old and faded, from the red-tiled floor to the rattan living room set. It was as if she had walked into a photograph with colours that didn't fully set.

"You must be tired." Auntie Mila handed her a chilled bottle of Fresh Springs water. "I cleaned up the other bedroom—I prepared some clothes in there so you don't have to unpack right away."

Sophia sat down on a couch, observing the brownish stains on the lower part of the walls. Her aunt followed her gaze.

"Those are from the flood. Ondoy was terrible. We never had floods that high in this area before. Paul helped me clean up."

Sophia traced the path of the stains around the living room, the legs of tables and chairs, the bottom half of a chest of drawers. It surrounded them like a scar. "That must have been scary."

"It wasn't too terrible here." Auntie Mila was looking about wistfully, as if she didn't believe her words. "The worst part was the dirt and the mud that came with the flood. Diyos ko, you wouldn't want to know what else the water brought in. It was really disgusting. Fortunately, it didn't reach the second floor."

"Oh, no," Sophia uttered, noticing the photo albums stacked on the bottom shelf of the coffee table. The edges of the covers and pages were stained and shrivelled. "The water got these!"

"I know," Auntie Mila sat down, eyeing the albums sadly. "A lot of them are ruined, but I don't have the heart to throw them away."

Sophia carefully opened one of the albums, recognizing familiar faces through the layer of dirt. The plastic pockets were stained with yellow marks that made some of the pages stick to one another. There was a creaky, peeling sound whenever she turned a page. Through the stained surface, she could make out a photo of her aunt with her parents. Sophia took it out of its pocket.

To her surprise, the photo was still intact. Her mother appeared to be around Sophia's age, smiling next to her father who was wearing a tight, collared shirt over high-waisted pants. Even with his huge dark sunglasses, Sophia could make out his proud, confident expression. Her aunt, the third wheel, was still a young girl, beaming in a dress with large prints and high shoulder pads. They were standing near a low wall bordering a flowering shrub—the photograph was too old for Sophia to determine the colour of the blooms.

"That was taken outside the church where they got married," Auntie Mila explained. "They had just talked to the priest about the date."

There was a whirl of contrasting sentiments: admiration for her parents' enduring union tinged with envy for the sense of security they felt in each other. Sadness for their middle-aged disappointments and a sense of triumph for defying them the past few days. Sophia slipped the photo back into its pocket and flicked the dust off her fingerprints.

In the shower, she scraped off the dirt that she imagined coating her whole body, enduring the ice-cold water. Her teeth clattered with each splash from the plastic dipper, but the clammy heat wrapped itself around her body as soon as she dried herself with a towel.

"I have some food, but I thought you'd like to sleep first," her aunt said. She had set up a tiny bed in the room that she used both as storage and office space. Sophia knew that this used to be her mother and aunt's childhood bedroom; she could see faint outlines on the wall where posters of their favourite bands and movie stars used to be displayed. The mattress was thin; she could feel the metal bars of the bed frame as she sat down. The pillows were lumpy, the linen stiff. She didn't mind the discomfort; she mostly welcomed how different everything was. It reminded her that she was far away.

Sophia was starting to fall asleep when she heard a knock on the door.

"Auntie?"

Auntie Mila entered holding a cell phone. "Your mom has called to check if you made it safely. You can go on Skype if you want."

"No need." Sophia reached for her aunt's phone, still lying down. "Hello, Ma. I'm okay."

"How was your trip?" Her mother's voice echoed slightly.

"It was fine. Kind of tiring." Sophia wished the call would end soon.

"Okay." There was hesitation in her voice. "I'm passing the phone on to Samuel. I don't know what he wants to talk about."

Sophia's heavy eyelids flew open. "What's up?"

"Wait!" She could hear Samuel racing up the stairs for privacy. "Ate, just so you know, Adrian was looking for you."

Sophia sat up. "Huh?"

"He just asked where you were. I think he went to your salon too."

"Okay." Sophia paused. She was grateful for the information, but she didn't want Samuel to sense how much it excited her. "What did he say?"

"He just asked where you were. I said you went on a holiday."

Sophia was pleased with this; she wanted Adrian to visualize her having fun without him. She wanted to mine for more information, but her body was surrendering. "Salamat," she said, casually.

"No problem." Samuel promptly hung up the call, forgetting to ask their parents if they still wanted to talk to her. Good boy.

THE CLUTTERED BEDROOM WAS STEEPED IN THE ORANGE and purple hues of the sunset when Sophia opened her eyes. As she felt for her slippers, she wondered if it would be possible for her to fall asleep again in a few hours, actual Manila bedtime.

The living room looked different at nighttime. She now noticed the hanging plants, the batik table runner, the cozy arrangements of books on the side table and the magazines—*Cosmopolitan, Glamour,* some other title featuring a glittering collage of the Manila elites—fanned on the table. The thought of her mother constantly worrying about her aunt's singlehood now made Sophia laugh.

She was ravenous. On the table, her aunt had prepared a takeout feast: fried rice, charcoal-roasted chicken, and deep-fried pork rolls. "I rarely cook around here," she explained as she hurriedly tossed a vegetable salad. "Sus, don't wait for me. Kain!" Auntie Mila, said noticing Sophia was hesitating.

"Thanks for picking me up today." Sophia started to fill her plate. "Didn't you have to go to work?"

"It's okay. Good thing you arrived on a Saturday. Though I would have called in sick if you arrived on a school day." Auntie Mila raised her eyebrows sneakily as she sat across the table. "There's Red Horse in the fridge. Do you drink beer, Sofi?"

"Ha?" Sophia was not sure how to respond to her aunt acting like they were girlfriends. "No, not really."

Her aunt groaned. "Don't be such a killjoy. I mean, look at you. You are so thin. Chic yes, but in desperate need of nourishment!"

"Okay, fine."

Auntie Mila clapped like she had won a prize and went to grab two cans. "I know you're jet-lagged so I got the perfect antidote. You're going to have to tell me stories then sleep soundly tonight. Your mom told me about you running away. Really, I don't blame you."

This chummy attitude was suspicious. Sophia wondered how much of tonight's conversation would be eventually shared with her mother. The walls between women's secrets were permeable. "So what did Mama tell you?"

"That you got fed up with them." Her aunt said this cheerfully as if she believed they deserved this treatment from their daughter. Sophia pulled the tab off her drink; the chilled bitter smell was inviting, as her palate was now coated with delightfully oily flavours. She thought of Adrian, who from time to time would drink beer when they were out, how Sophia would playfully pat the modest paunch once they were in the privacy of his car.

"I have to admit when I learned that you'd been spending all your afternoons at Cine Star years ago, I was shocked. How could I not know? I lived closer to Cine Star. Your house was at the next barangay over." Aunt Mila seemed more sour about how she was kept out of the secret, than about Sophia's violation.

"Auntie Rosy told some folks here she was my nanny." Sophia recalled the gazes she had received from the neighbours whenever Auntie Rosy walked her home years ago. Strangers' eyes that were intimidating at first, but grew familiar and even friendly after a few nights. Those shadowy figures in the evening could keep secrets as easily as they could spread rumours.

This revelation earned a nod of smug admiration from her aunt. "What were you doing there anyway?"

"Not much. Listening to stories, watching them work." She couldn't be bothered to put into words how memorable, how *fun*, those afternoons were. "Watching TV."

"Sometimes, she tells people she was your first hairstyling mentor."

Sophia groaned. "It's not like she actually taught me. Just little things."

"She takes pride in it." Auntie Mila had a teasing look on her face, enjoying Sophia's discomfort. She daintily bit on a spring roll.

"Is Paul your boyfriend?" Sophia trained her eyes on her aunt's throughout a long refreshing gulp.

The question dented Auntie Mila's composure, but she recovered by smiling coyly. "He seems to think so."

"How long have you known him?"

"A few months. Are you interrogating me?"

"Just examining his intentions." Sophia smiled sweetly before realizing her error. She had exposed a weakness, opened herself for an attack. Auntie Mila seemed to sense this but settled for a merciful blow.

"This Adrian of yours, what's his problem?"

"There's not much to tell, Auntie. He proposed and he backed out."

"Ay! What an idiot."

Sophia lifted her eyebrows in agreement, though she inwardly wondered what her aunt would say if, by some miracle, she and Adrian managed to patch things up. As if to hint at a truce, Auntie Mila announced she would get more beer.

"Your mom was so impressed with your salon," Auntie Mila said when she returned to the table, sliding another can toward Sophia. "She can't stop talking about all the cool styling stuff you own, that you run two stations and that someone's working for you."

Sophia chuckled. "She probably imagined the place in chaos. And me running around, pulling my hair."

Auntie Mila gave her a mild scolding look, making Sophia feel like she was her little niece once again. "I like the cut that you gave her. Too bad I just had my hair cut. It was already up to here." Her aunt patted her arm, right above her elbow. "But have I known that you were coming home I would have waited." She smoothed her own hair, a bouncy shoulder-length cut. "I used to go to Cine Star too, but Aling Helen died. My current stylist keeps me looking hip. Really important if you're teaching high school."

"So you never returned to Cine Star after Aling Helen died?"

Auntie Mila pressed her lips tightly. "Maybe it's just me being picky, but I just never trusted Rosy. Sorry."

"I know. No need to say sorry."

"I just didn't think she's that good, you know? Don't tell her when you see her, ha."

"Don't worry about it." Sophia finished her second can of Red Horse, wincing at the bitter aftertaste. The alcohol swirled in her head, loosened her muscles, but thinking of Auntie Rosy roused a part of her that was cautious and responsible. "Auntie, can I have the Wi-Fi password?"

"You're not thinking of getting in touch with *him*, are you?" Auntie Mila gave her a disapproving look.

"I just want to check if there's news from the salon."

They chatted until close to midnight, and Sophia ended up having to remind Auntie Mila to give her the password after they cleaned up the dinner table. Sophia took out her laptop, fighting the rising anticipation as she entered the code and logged onto her email. As expected, there was a message from Erica.

> Hi Sophia,
>
> Thank God it's slow today. Angie
>
> dropped by but said she'll be back.
>
> Queens called to say your order will be
>
> delayed. It's ok, I guess.
>
> Adrian came by to talk to you. That guy
>
> has the worst timing ever. Told him you
>
> were in Manila for holidays. He didn't
>
> seem to believe me.
>
> -E

There was no email from Adrian. The curiosity surging within Sophia made her consider giving him a call. But her anger was still there, cresting upon the elation in finding an ally in her aunt. Whatever it was that Adrian wanted to talk about, it could wait until Sophia felt like listening.

≋

BY THE FOLLOWING AFTERNOON, SOPHIA WAS READY TO explore the neighbourhood. Though she had been away for many years, she still remembered the directions to Erwin's place by foot. But the hellish heat of the afternoon made her hail a tricyle. It was a bumpy ride. The two wheels of the motorcycle and the one for the sidecar scurried through muddy craters on the neglected parts of the road. Sophia bounced off her seat. Her body slammed against the metal frame of the sidecar, and her head kept hitting the thinly padded roof. It was hard to believe that she had taken a ride like this many times as a child.

She could still picture Erwin's home. She had dropped by a few times years ago. The dining area and kitchen served as the living room, and there were two bedrooms hidden from view by curtains. The bathroom was blocked by thin plywood behind the kitchen sink; Sophia remembered feeling self-conscious when she had to pee while Erwin's mother was washing the dishes.

After paying the tricycle driver, she walked eagerly toward the house, which looked more worn down than she remembered. Sophia knocked. Loudly. Only then did it cross her mind that Erwin might not be home. Or he might be catching sleep from his graveyard shift.

But the door opened, and Erwin's face through the gap made Sophia squeal with joy. "Uy! Kumusta na?"

"Diyos ko, Sophia!" Erwin opened the door wider and gave her a hug. "You nearly gave me a heart attack. Pasok."

Sophia entered the house, grateful for the shade. "Are you busy? Are you working tonight?"

"No." Erwin's voice lowered to a whisper, and he tilted his head toward the bedrooms. His face and body were more solid, but his gestures were light, graceful. "It's siesta time around here. Maybe we should go out, go to the mall or somewhere."

"Later. Please, it's so hot outside." Sophia was sweating even though she had come by a tricycle. She sat on a chair by the dining table as Erwin trained the electric fan toward her. It made small ticking noises as if it were broken.

"I'm sorry I can't offer you something to drink. I know I'm not supposed to offer you water from the tap, di ba? I have heard of people coming from abroad after a long time who had stomach problems after drinking water here." Erwin was frantically moving about the tiny kitchen, searching the cupboards and the fridge. "I don't have anything for us to snack on."

He was being too fretful, unlike the Erwin Sophia remembered and came home for. He was always the one who was more confident, the one who took charge in uncertain situations. She wished he would just relax rather than fuss over her. Feeling bad for the hassle she had caused, Sophia stood up and hugged him. "It's so good to see you. We can eat later. Just tell me how have you been?"

"Well, you know about me." Erwin shrugged as she released him. "Busy with work. I rarely go out with friends. I'm trying to save some money so I can move away." He was looking at her from head to toe, as if he couldn't believe Sophia was standing right before him. "Why didn't you tell me you were coming over? We could have planned something fun."

"I'm excited to see you."

He seemed embarrassed by this. "Naman. So sentimental."

"You look kind of ... buff." Sophia patted his arm and used her flirtatious voice. "Have you been working out?"

"No time for that." Erwin smiled. "I'm a natural. And if you think your charms will work on me, you're hugely mistaken."

"That's a shame."

"You arrived yesterday?"

"Yes. Everything looks ... smaller."

Erwin laughed again, voice still whispery. "You're going to be like the other balikbayans who complain a lot. I should get you some snacks. Let's go to Aling Soledad's store. Tara!" He started toward the door. "You know, I heard she has totally lost her mind. People would sometimes buy things from her and not pay her at all. Or those who didn't know her condition would pay and then not get any change back. Then there are days when her head is clear and she's doing everything right. Let's see how she is today."

"Please, let's wait for it to get a little cooler." Sophia sat back down on the chair. She was dreading the heat. "I want to pass by Cine Star, but I don't want to run into Auntie Rosy for now. You know, I really think that accident with her client was her fault. Don't you think?"

"Shush! Your voice."

"Has she been in touch?"

A thud was heard from one of the bedrooms, which still had curtains instead of doors. Erwin's eyes widened. Sophia felt bad that she had woken someone up, but she was prepared to apologize. Surely, whoever was home would understand. Hopefully, it wasn't Erwin's father. The curtain darkened with the shadow from within, and through the flimsy partition Auntie Rosy emerged, looking every bit as upset as a person roused from sleep.

19

I T WAS AS IF A COLD GUST SWEPT INTO THE LIVING ROOM, the kind to accompany a ghost. Sophia herself felt disembodied, floating, merely witnessing the moment unfold.

She was a young girl again, in her awkward teens, a time of feigning curves and confidence. Out on the streets, she had noticed the lingering stares from men, and women sizing her up. She had learned to wear her school uniform a certain way: the two topmost buttons of the white blouse undone, the waistband of her long plaid skirt—that hideous, matronly skirt—hiked higher up her waist so that the hemline floated above her knees. She and Auntie Rosy were walking side by side after another afternoon at Cine Star. A wolf whistle pierced the dusk, followed by some brash hooting and laughter. Sophia knew to frown and toss her head, but she glowed on the inside. Auntie Rosy was locating the source of that offending greeting, her gaze eventually landing on a huddle of young men across the street. She strutted toward them, hands on hips. Sophia followed behind. She was used to these encounters; to Auntie Rosy everybody who reigned over the sidewalks past six was family. They had ugly leering smiles but Auntie Rosy gave them high-fives. They talked about some upcoming basketball match, then someone they knew throwing a birthday party that coming Sunday—there will be videoke and drinking, and more names and events Sophia didn't know.

"Won't you introduce us?" one of them said to Auntie Rosy as he winked at Sophia.

Auntie Rosy turned to her quickly, as if surprised that Sophia was right behind her. "Not her. She's not right for you." She said this in a severe tone because they had crossed a line. Sophia sensed that Auntie Rosy, while being protective, also envied her for being the one who had caught these rascals' eyes. The past months she had refused to eat full meals, surviving on Diet Coke and SkyFlakes crackers each day because she wanted to get rid of the bulge around her stomach, the soft, wobbling flesh around her thighs. Auntie Rosy's momentary glance had a mixture of fondness and resentment, conveying that Sophia was welcome but she didn't belong.

This was the same look Auntie Rosy bestowed with her still puffy eyes as she emerged from the bedroom. Her yellow housedress was rumpled from sleep; it was so loose it hung to one side, exposing a scrawny shoulder. A strong tangy odour emanated from her. She peered briefly at a framed mirror hanging on the wall and smoothed her hair.

"You shouldn't be talking so loudly when someone's taking a nap," she said gruffly.

"Sophia flew in yesterday," Erwin said.

Auntie Rosy pulled over a chair, sat right across the table from Sophia.

Sophia's mouth felt dry. "Kumusta na po, Auntie?"

"I'm getting by. You're all grown up, no longer that girl who's so unsure about herself." Auntie Rosy wore an acrimonious look. When both Sophia and Erwin didn't say anything, she raised her eyebrows meaningfully. "Go on. I think I heard my name."

Erwin was standing by the sink, fidgeting with the hem of his shirt. Sophia decided to meet Auntie Rosy's eyes. "I was just telling the truth."

"So you believe all of it was my fault. You were not even there when it happened."

As Sophia quietly contemplated the details she had heard, Auntie Rosy turned to Erwin. "Who do you think is the better stylist? Sophia or me?"

Oh God, Sophia thought. Poor Erwin looked nervously at her, then rested his eyes on the table.

Auntie Rosy shook her head. "Don't worry, I am used to all of this. Not being believed in. Being seen as a burden." She paused, noticing that the electric fan was trained on Sophia. With a surprising vigour for someone newly risen, Auntie Rosy strode toward the appliance and pulled the knob behind its head. The electric fan swivelled, its weak breeze reaching her side of the table where she sat down lazily, blinking like she could return to her nap, but she settled her stare on Sophia. "Aling Helen was the same way. Let me tell you, that woman was so full of herself. She expected everybody to be an unhappy spinster like she was." ·

"Auntie, naman. She meant well. She wanted you out of trouble," Erwin said.

"When she took me away from my hometown, I was full of hope," Auntie Rosy cut in. "I envisioned big things happening to me in Manila, meeting interesting people, seeing places. Everybody knew that she used to work on movie sets. I was lucky to be going with her. But no, she was full of rules and conditions. She criticized everything I did outside the salon. She never approved of any of my friends. It's not like she was a joy to work with. Don't you remember?"

Silence set in, during which Sophia imagined Aling Helen as a cruel slave driver, and finding that her head didn't agree with the image. She was remembering a completely different person, someone sensible and loving. Serious, maybe, but certainly not mean.

"When I got pregnant, I got nothing but blame from her."

"She wanted you to be a good mother." Erwin sounded firmer this time.

"What did she know?" Auntie Rosy huffed. "It's not like she knew anything about caring for people. All she wanted was to control me."

"She wanted to make sure your baby would be provided for," he responded. Sophia was grateful he was doing the talking for them.

"I sometimes wonder what would have happened if I had my baby." The corners of Auntie Rosy's eyes glistened.

"Even if she didn't say it, I'm sure Aling Helen thought the miscarriage was also my fault. Or she probably believed I deserved it. If only my child had lived, there would be someone who would look after me, someone who would love me no matter what. Unlike both of you."

Sophia was provoked by this. "Auntie, Erwin and I have been helping you."

Auntie Rosy held up a wilted hand. "You clearly want me out of your way. Both of you so young and selfish—I was like that myself. You probably think I'm just someone you can send back to my old life. That I'm too old to want things. But this is not just about my job. This neighbourhood *needs* Cine Star. I care for every single woman who walks through its door. I've lived here for twenty years."

Or, they could go to a different salon. Sophia thought back to her tricycle ride during which she had passed several hair salons, from makeshift shacks advertising the most basic of services on a piece of cardboard to air-conditioned chain boutiques named after celebrity stylists who had built illustrious careers in the beauty industry. The neighbourhood was changing. People were moving away, and those who remained were attracted to the newer, flashier enterprises taking over. One could opt to buy a bag of morning pan de sal from franchised bakeries that advertised their use of wood-fired brick ovens, shifting support from the neighbourhood's greying home-based baker. The corner street-side eateries had to up their game against the shiny cafeterias with glass door entrances, upholstered seats, and combo box specials. Sophia didn't know how to point all of this out to Auntie Rosy who was deluded by a conviction of her permanence amidst all these merciless changes. But she was right about her and Erwin being absorbed in their own lives. They failed to recognize that in fighting for Cine Star, Auntie Rosy was also holding onto the community she had lived in for many years and her reputation within it; the place she had left her impoverished origins for, her toehold in the city that promised greater things. Sophia felt stupid for not agreeing to go out with Erwin earlier.

Auntie Rosy noticed her shifting. "You're getting married and will have a family soon. Good for you."

A look passed between Sophia and Erwin.

"You'll have everything. A job that you love. A man caring for you."

"We've split up," Sophia blurted.

Auntie Rosy's eyes grew round, and for a second, Sophia spotted a look of dismay passing over her face. Erwin pulled a chair beside Sophia and sat down, feeling safe to fully join the conversation. Nobody spoke and the sporadic ticking from the electric fan filled the humid air.

"Why? What happened?" Auntie Rosy's voice was laced with concern.

Sophia shrugged. "He changed his mind." She was tired of explaining what she herself couldn't comprehend.

Auntie Rosy nodded. "Men. They are the same everywhere."

The turn in conversation emboldened Sophia. "Auntie, we care about you."

"Tse! You think I'm just a useless old hag."

"You don't have to be alone. You have family in Bicol," Erwin said.

"Maybe it's time to retire," Sophia added.

"If only people knew the truth," Auntie Rosy sighed. Then looking at Sophia, she said, "Tell me, Erwin, who do you think is the better stylist?"

"Sophia," Erwin replied meekly.

"You're on her side," Auntie Rosy said smugly. "But what about the neighbourhood? What if they knew the truth?"

Erwin and Sophia stared blankly at Auntie Rosy.

"I saw an updo competition on TV once. The styles were just out of this world!" Auntie Rosy said dreamily. "I bet I can create something as dazzling and beautiful. You see, you are making assumptions. Like the people out there. If Sophia and I compete, they will see who is the best stylist."

"Auntie, naman, let's talk about the salon." Sophia was mildly irritated.

"We *are* talking about the salon," Auntie Rosy replied. "Imagine this, an updo competition at Cine Star. The neighbourhood will watch and vote for the winner."

Sophia was convinced Auntie Rosy was partly crazy. "Are you serious?"

"I will invite the neighbours. Soledad will be my model. You will need a model as well. People will decide the winner by the sound of applause."

"Auntie, I don't think people will show up for this." She chuckled to convey how ridiculous the idea was. "You'll just be wasting everybody's time."

"People here have time for real entertainment, darling," Auntie Rosy said evenly. "Besides, you're just afraid that I will defeat you. I will let you choose the theme, if you want."

"Theme?" Sophia's mouth dropped open. This conversation could not get any more ridiculous. How much did Auntie Rosy know about professional updo competitions? How flashy were the styles she was envisioning to create? "Auntie, those competitions take the entire day. Including prep and makeup."

"We can do a simpler version. Say for one hour."

Erwin whistled. "That's not realistic at all."

"Sige na, Sofi," Auntie Rosy sounded like those times she was offering Sophia a treat when she was a little girl. "Choose a theme."

"Auntie, I'm not doing this."

"You're afraid to go against me."

"Are you out of your mind?"

The insult didn't affect Auntie Rosy. "Everybody will see that with everything you achieved in Canada, you are still no better than your mentor."

"Diyos ko naman." Sophia pushed herself away from the table, the chair scraping against the floor. The heat was making her impatient. She strode toward the electric fan and shook her damp blouse by the collar to let in some of the breeze.

"I don't see why you can't help me with this." Auntie Rosy actually looked confused.

Sophia's gut was against the idea. Even without looking at Erwin, she knew he felt the same. *Don't do it! Don't do it!* But with her jet lag and the stifling air in that tiny house, she was losing the battle of wills.

"Okay Auntie, let's do a garden theme. Very simple, okay? For one hour, but we will prep beforehand." Sophia stepped away from the electric fan, allowing cool air to reach Auntie Rosy.

The glint in Auntie Rosy's eyes took on a combative shade. "Agreed!"

"Wow, are we really doing this?" Erwin flattened himself against the chair, as if a truck were barrelling past right before him.

"It's meant to be." Auntie Rosy looked wide awake now. "Cine Star needs a fresh start. Sofi is back here from Canada. People will see how skilled she has become, how much she has learned all these years. But they will also know that she can't surpass my experience."

"You seem so certain of winning," Sophia remarked.

"If you don't believe me now, that's fine. But after the competition, you'll realize you are doing this neighbourhood a disservice by asking me to sell Cine Star and retire to the province." Auntie Rosy gave a self-satisfied shrug. "Both of you will have to let me. I will use the money you sent to help pretty things up, restock supplies." She paused, making sure to glance severely both at Sophia and Erwin. "You wouldn't hear me asking for help anymore. I'll manage on my own when Cine Star opens once again."

SOPHIA, NOW ALONE WITH HER THOUGHTS, CONTEMPLATED what she had just agreed to. The ticking of that stupid electric fan—which she had trained to herself again—was getting annoying, but she needed what little relief it could offer. The vinyl tablecloth was still moist with the sweat of her forearms, making her think of germs. Her eyes pored over the dark grout visible between the chipped tiles around the kitchen sink. On the bare cement wall, the calendar featured the sexy starlet for the month of October who stared at her with glassy sensuality, the incongruous form of her huge breasts and well-defined rib cage pressing against a red, glittery swimsuit, her lustrous hair tangled with her outstretched arms. The piles of aluminum cookware and enamel plates, next to a row of cloudy bottles of cooking oil, and condiments crammed on the shelves and counters made her feel more like an intruder rather than a visitor. Overhead, a fluorescent lamp hung from exposed beams by wiry cables. Sophia decided against turning on the light in that darkening living room.

The water pipes made a gurgling sound as they facilitated Erwin's showering in the adjacent bathroom. He would be finished soon, so Sophia hurriedly collected her thoughts. Surely, he was disappointed that she had accepted Auntie Rosy's challenge.

It was a relief that Auntie Rosy chose not to join them that evening. Her presence had been too oppressive, and Sophia wanted some time alone with Erwin. When it became clear to Auntie Rosy that they were heading out for the night, she had smoothed her loose dress and announced that she was going back to Cine Star. She sensed she wasn't invited, though Sophia wouldn't have had the heart to say no if Auntie Rosy had asked to join them. "I'm going back to my salon. Make sure everything is ready for the competition."

Erwin emerged from the bathroom wearing a dark

blue striped polo shirt and tight dark jeans. As they waited for a jeepney at the main road, Sophia asked, "Do you think we should have insisted that she come along? She would have loved a good meal."

He shrugged. "One moment she's feeling so helpless she'll ask for whatever she wants without shame. The next moment she's too proud to receive something being freely offered."

"I feel bad for not inviting her to come with us."

"She's really game about this," Erwin mused, ignoring her thread of thought. "Preparing a week ahead."

Sophia punched his arm lightly. "Loka! Why didn't you tell me she was staying at your place?"

Erwin averted his eyes by turning to the oncoming traffic. "It started last week. She comes over for a siesta because the heat is unbearable at Cine Star in the afternoons. My family is out the whole day, so she tries to catch some sleep on a real bed. Sleeping on the floor at nights is hurting her back."

"What happened to her bed?"

"Her landlord locked up the apartment with most of her things in it. She owed two months' worth of rent. And electricity and water bills."

"The money I sent the first time didn't help?"

"Who knows how long she's been behind on her bills?"

Sophia recalled the days when she lived in her salon, how inconvenient it was to have no kitchen and to drive to Erica's place to shower. But her experience was nowhere near Auntie Rosy's situation.

"The truth is I was kind of afraid to tell you." Erwin

raised an arm to hail a jeepney. "Here, let's catch this one."

Why would Erwin hold back from her? They climbed onboard the jeepney and wriggled into the remaining seating spaces between the tired-looking passengers. He reached for his wallet, but Sophia was already holding out a ten-peso coin toward the driver's compartment. "I got this." He promptly added more change to the driver's waiting hand. "That's not enough for two. Have you been gone that long?"

"You were afraid to tell me things about Auntie Rosy?"

"You have always been strong-minded about when to help and when to cut her off. Which is fine. I understand where you're coming from. I mean, she stopped speaking to you years ago and she came crawling back just because she needs money. It's irritating for sure. Maybe if I wasn't stuck here, I would react the same way. I guess a part of me envies you. I don't really have that option. I hold back from telling you about the hassle she's causing me because I don't want to be another person you'd pity. And eventually avoid."

Sophia took this in, suddenly aware of the curious gazes from the other passengers. "I was feeling terrible about leaving you alone to deal with her."

Erwin rolled his eyes, an expression that stung Sophia. "And now, you're helping her with her publicity stunt. Let's say her clients come back. Things will be good for a while, but it won't take long until she will fall apart again. We both know that. I appreciate you feeling bad for me, okay? But now, you're just maintaining the situation. Do you know that when she showed up at our place, she was hungry and smelly? It was like she had been living in the streets. I couldn't turn her away." His face seemed to age with the troubling memory. "That's when I told her the hours when I would be alone at home, so she could come over to clean herself and sleep. It's been going on without a hitch for a few days. Until today. You visited without calling ahead. I thought I could convince you to step out. I didn't want to talk about her when she was right across the wall."

"I'm sorry."

"I'll feel better if she goes back to her family."

"I know." Sophia didn't know what more to say. The jeepney lurched into an open lane, its blaring motor drilling into her ears. Sophia winced but Erwin was too deep in his thoughts to be bothered by the noise. She leaned forward as her friend spoke again.

"I just want her to give up, you know? Cine Star had been going downhill even before the accident."

"The money she mentioned, was that the same amount she turned down?"

"Yes. I'm actually surprised she hasn't spent all of it yet."

A few passengers alighted, allowing Sophia and Erwin to sit more comfortably. She glanced out the window, letting the air whip her hair against her cheeks.

At the mall, she was taken aback by the security guards checking each person at the entrance and searching the bags with a wooden baton. The lady guard patted Sophia's sides and back pockets.

Erwin took Sophia's hand as she gaped at the massive atrium. "Why do you look so lost?"

They were swept in by the loud multitudes of shoppers

who strode in all directions. For a while, they were mostly dodging rather than strolling, at times getting separated to make way for a rowdy group of college students, young couples holding hands. At least there was air conditioning; she no longer felt like she was melting. They made their way through endless passages of brightly-lit boutiques. Flowery scents hovered near the entrance of women's clothing stores, headless mannequins jutted out their hips for a glamorous pose. They passed a gigantic patchwork of gleaming widescreen televisions showing the same field of sunflowers. Rows of platform heels beneath the spotlight. Erwin pointed out the expanded sections of the mall—the outdoor promenade overlooking the highway, a new wing toward the end. Everything around them seemed bigger, so shamelessly opulent.

They were lured into a restaurant that smelled of grilled seafood. It was busy, but the dim glow from the light bulbs in woven lampshades mellowed the diners into quietness. Sophia looked around. A well-dressed couple was out on a date. At another table, a mother was busily serving food to four small children as her husband poured water for everyone. She was suddenly homesick for Vancouver, which she was surprised to feel in the place she had been missing for years.

"That talk with Auntie Rosy made me hungry," Erwin said.

She realized that she was feeling the same. They quietly pored over the glossy dishes on the menu, with Sophia adjusting to the three-figure prices.

"So, are you still missing Adrian?"

"Oh! I wanted to tell you. He was looking for me the day after I left Vancouver."

"Wanting to get back?" Erwin's tone was smug.

"I don't know." Sophia smiled as she entertained this possibility. "He talked to Samuel, and Erica saw him at the salon."

"Sounds like he's regretful. Don't take him back."

"Why not?" Sophia asked before she could stop herself.

"Can't you see? He left you hanging all this time. You should be with someone who knows what he wants."

"But what if he knows now that he wants to be with me?"

"Go ahead, take him back. Just make sure that you'll feel safe being with him. That you won't always be wondering what he's thinking. Or whether he's really happy."

The frank, all-knowing way Erwin spoke now was familiar but not what Sophia wanted. "You don't even know him. He can be so sweet, so supportive. You would have liked him." She paused. She was talking about a person from a long time ago. Adrian no longer fit her memory of who he was.

Across the table, Erwin seemed to read her thoughts. "I just want you to make the best of the situation."

"I'm trying."

The server was a young girl with a toothy smile. She talked about the specials in a pinched, singsong tone, her gaze landing more on Erwin whom she perceived to be Sophia's date. Erwin, who seemed accustomed to this kind of error, asked about the portion sizes. His way of asking questions intimidated the waitress, who fidgeted as she responded, adding more po's in her sentences. She left with their order of garlic rice, grilled pork, stuffed grilled squid, and sinigang with milkfish and prawns.

"Well, enough about me." Sophia beamed at Erwin. "Anybody special?"

He scoffed. "Like I have time for that. A few cuties at work, that's just about it. Loving in silence so to speak."

She felt callous for steering the conversation in this direction, so Sophia attempted a different topic. "How about your plans. For the future. Do you want to go abroad or something?"

"No. Imagine my family and all our relatives looking up to me to raise them from poverty." Erwin flattened his lips in a pretend-frazzled expression. "I don't want that kind of responsibility. I just want to be on my own. When I get a better-paying job, I will move out."

"I want to move out too," Sophia said.

"Why don't you? Isn't it easier to do over there? Grown-up kids moving out."

"My father wanted me to stay. Till I got married."

"Not that you're known for following his rules."

"For once, I want to get it right. I let my parents down." Sophia traced a finger on the chilled surface of the iced water pitcher. She drew a heart, which she promptly shaded off. "They couldn't hide their disappointment about me losing Adrian. After the split, all they could think about was to have me go back to school. Upgrade myself so a good catch wouldn't be driven away."

"Naman, I'm sure they mean well." Erwin's face softened. "They're on your side."

"You don't know them." She looked up to see him

drumming his fingers on the colourful paper placemat, looking sombre.

"Sofi, at least your father truly cares about you. He has it in him to steer you toward what he thinks is better for you. My father could never look at me without hatred."

Erwin sat back, as if the confession had drained him. Sophia itched to tell him about how her parents had begged that she explore other career paths, and their being convinced that she was not suitable for a kind and attractive man who had a stable career. It was infuriating to think of it all, but Erwin would never understand. Homesickness, work stress, and heartache he could sympathize with, but when it came to who had the worst parents, Sophia had to surrender the title.

Adrian had been the one who understood this.

When their dishes arrived in clay pots and rattan serving plates lined with banana leaves, they eagerly dug their forks into the supple flesh, filled their plates with rice, which they soaked with the sinigang's tamarind broth.

"What will happen on Saturday?" Sophia was more wondering to herself, than asking the question.

"You will do a great job." He paused, chewing while deep in thought. "Auntie Rosy will do her best. Will try to outdo herself, actually. She will go for something flashy and elaborate. You better come up with something to top that."

Sophia licked the taste of prawns off her fingers. "Who's going to be my model?"

"I can ask some friends."

"But you were against this competition."

"There's nothing I can do now," Erwin replied. "Maybe

you're right. It's the kind thing to do, give her another chance to bounce back."

Sophia was eating fast, her appetite propelled not just by that afternoon's incident, but by the brewing dread over the competition's outcome. "I am nervous," she admitted, "but not in the way you think. It's just that there are so many ways things could turn out. First of all, she could pull herself together, do a fantastic job, and win the contest. She has the skills and experience after all. But that doesn't mean Cine Star will survive for long."

"Right."

"Or she could end up doing something really stupid in front of everyone. I don't know how she'd take it." Sophia shook away a mental picture of Auntie Rosy throwing a fit in front of everyone after losing the vote. For some reason, this reminded her of the time she threw her scissors at Adrian that last time they saw each other. She cringed at the memory.

"If that happens, she'll be so humiliated she'll leave town." Erwin grinned.

"Or sue us," Sophia said. They both laughed.

Between them, the food went fast. The restaurant didn't have many diners by the time they finished, so they stayed, chatting over barbecue that have been reduced to bare bamboo skewers, squid to its greasy tentacles, sinigang to a murky broth of fish bones and prawn carcass. Sophia ordered desserts.

"I understand what you're saying," Erwin said after a moment. "As much as I'd like you to win—and I'm pretty sure you will—I would hate to see her get hurt."

Sophia nodded. They were children again, their lives

steered by the complexities of the grown-ups around them. Erwin's face brightened, remembering something. "You know, when I brought Auntie Rosy to our place during the typhoon, my father could only manage angry glares at her. He couldn't say anything even though she didn't have any sharp objects with her."

They were still laughing when a platter with thin slices of biko and maja blanca arrived. As Erwin remarked on the tiny servings and checked the prices on the menu, Sophia pondered Auntie Rosy's plight. Though hungry and battered by a typhoon, she never lost her formidable spirit. There was fight left in her.

And here she was, running away from her troubles in Vancouver, leaving her thriving salon in someone else's hands.

They stayed in the mall until closing time. When lights blinked within the shops and the dolled-up but sleepy-looking sales attendants started locking up the stores, Erwin declared he had an idea. They took a cab, alighted at a nightclub in Cubao. He insisted on treating Sophia as she had paid for supper. Hand in clammy hand, they lost themselves in the twisting and shaking crowd. Some ear-splitting techno music was playing. It wasn't her first time in a nightclub, but Sophia wanted to cover her ears. Had she gotten so old? Through the wandering rays of strobe lights she spotted young faces; she felt like she didn't belong. But Erwin was grinning, twirling, pounding the dark, sweaty air with his fists. He threw her a puzzled look, conveying she looked even more silly by standing there, doing nothing. She started dancing to the ugly music. She remembered her younger self in Vancouver, and for a moment, it seemed that her two selves were sharing space, dancing with each other. Only, the body Sophia inhabited now was tired, longing for a seat in the sidelines. Then quickly, she realized that her younger self had felt the same—she wasn't really having fun even back then. While she was younger, letting out hoots and shaking her much more energetic body, she had merely been drowning her exhaustion, her loneliness. She wondered if Erwin came here to do the same.

He bought her drinks, some cocktail with a weird blue colour, which she drank thirstily. Then they were dancing again; the floor had gotten more crowded so their bodies grew close to one another. But Erwin's hold on her waist was barely there, mere fingertips on the side of her shirt, just enough to let her know he was there when the frenetic rays wandered away and left them in the shadows.

During the cab ride home, Erwin explained that it was a favourite spot among friends. Sophia nodded, stopped herself from asking if he truly found that kind of place fun. There was no sense in shattering other people's fleeting pleasures. She felt a tap on her arm; Erwin was pointing to a convenience store they had just passed by. "People who took shelter in there during Ondoy all died. They were trapped when the water rose. After the storm, there were handprints on the ceiling and along the top edges of the glass walls."

"Oh my God!" Her skin lifted with goosebumps.

"Nobody knew it was going to be that bad. I was lucky to be heading home at the right time."

Sophia could still see the store, its orange lights fusing

with the brightness from the street lamps. Her ears were starting to get used to the traffic noises, her body settling into the environment and the energy around it. Erwin's story reminded her of the city's ruthlessness. Year after year, it plucked from its alleys the weakest, the most helpless. Luck was what decided life and death. Moments ago, she had been marvelling at Auntie Rosy's strength, and now Sophia saw her in a different light: fragile, careless, and alone.

Auntie Mila was already in bed when she got home. Sophia was not feeling sleepy so she checked her laptop. When she saw the email on the top of her inbox, her heart stopped. She blinked. Once. Twice. It was from Adrian.

> Hi Sophia,
>
> Finally gathered my thoughts and mustered the courage to talk to you, but found out that you have gone to the Philippines. I'm really sorry for hurting you. And for wasting your time.
>
> I owe you an explanation. The last time we talked I couldn't express myself very well. But my head has been clearer since. There are things I understand better now.
>
> First of all, I've always cared about you. But I want a different life from the one

we were planning together. I want a career change. I'm going to study game design. Maybe it's not fair that I didn't tell you about this, but it didn't feel right to involve you either. I have looked into schools and I might have to move. I don't feel like committing to anyone as I embark on this plan. Things are up in the air at the moment.

It was you who inspired me to have the courage to make these changes. Thank you for showing me how life should be lived. Right from the day I met you, I have always admired your will and sense of ambition. We became each other's joy and future, but I couldn't be that person for you anymore. The life that you found me in is not fulfilling for me.

I'm really sorry about everything. I hope you'll find someone who can love you better someday.

Adrian

20

SOPHIA WAS REMEMBERING THOSE TIMES WHEN ADRIAN would ask her questions about her workday. Wide-eyed and expectant, he appeared eager to hear everything in detail. Her stories were full of pauses when she had to recall bits that escaped her, because she didn't want him to miss anything. Now, she turned this look over in her mind. In her salon, she observed faces as she worked, and Adrian's had now become one of those that could be read many different ways. Suddenly, those loving questions he had asked about her life seemed canned, a dogged formation of habit.

The lights were off, but the bedroom was not dark—the glow of the street lamps directly across the window bounced against the jalousies, illuminating the walls, her aunt's desk, the computer, the old dresser. Intense heat clung to her newly washed skin despite Sophia having kicked off the blanket, and there was the occasional tricycle that blistered the silence. She resigned herself to a sleepless night.

She wished he were right there, lying next to her. There were too many questions. She craved the truth more than the company. When did he lose sight of himself within their relationship? Which sweet moments made him question things? Which milestones gave him a pause? In his typical tender way, Adrian had even thanked her for showing him how life should be lived. Mulling this over, something in Sophia broke, the last of her inner shields cracked and shattered. Her tears drenched a spot on her pillow. Why did the one person who truly saw her, who knew how to make her feel her best, have to leave her life?

She woke up angry. There was nothing like being lied to and being controlled in such a sweet, almost blameless, way. He was probably feeling good about finally having done the right thing. And coming clean, before they married, was the right thing to do. Still Sophia wanted to slap Adrian's bright, dishonest face.

Over breakfast, she mentally listed parts of her life untouched by Adrian. It made her happy that he and Erwin had never talked. Auntie Mila, along with their other distant relatives, had not met him. She was now grateful that he had not been present in their family outings. The city she grew up in, also, was Adrian-free.

She left the house. The neighbourhood no longer felt strange. But she was hesitant still; when she had been out with Erwin the day before, he had guided her when they crossed the busy roads that had no pedestrian lanes or traffic lights. On her own, she had no sense of timing for the oncoming motorists. It took time for her to cross safely. She could feel the looks coming from people idling along the pavement. Sophia wondered if they sat on those storefront benches all day. Didn't they have jobs? There was no attempt to hide their curiosity and lower their voices as they wondered amongst themselves.

"That's Rosy's little pet?"

"She's all grown up."

"Uy, Sophia! When's the competition?"

Sophia turned, not sure if she heard right. "Ano po?"

The woman was in the middle of collecting clothes that had dried on the pikes of her gate. "Aling Rosy told me about the hairstyling contest."

"It's this Saturday."

"Mang Simon and his kumpares down the road are betting their money on Rosy," the woman prattled. "She refused to drink with them until Saturday. To keep her head clear."

Sophia's joints turned to jelly. "Good for her," she murmured.

A man sitting on a nearby bench overheard them. "You're trained in Canada, right? Think you can beat her? I haven't placed my bet yet."

"I guess we'll find out."

Sophia walked faster, as if trying to outpace the spreading of the news. As Auntie Rosy had promised, there was an audience for this competition. People were even planning to gamble. It was just like her to drum up the hype to attract a bigger crowd. Her pace turned rapid. Discarded by Adrian and now being used by Auntie Rosy.

She truly wanted to help, but Sophia wanted to kick her-self. She couldn't stop walking—why was it so crowded everywhere? Alleys and dark entryways. Decrepit build-ings and storefronts hosting loitering customers fanning themselves in the heat. Something cold dripped on her scalp and she looked up to see another droplet hanging from the edge of a rusty gutter, on the verge of detaching itself from the roof. She ruefully felt the top of her head, hoping the dripping liquid was just some leak, not some discarded waste. She had only walked a few blocks, but her hair, which she had hastily put up in a ponytail, had gone limp, clinging to her nape. Her feet took her to narrower and more crowded sidewalks. Smells of greasy food, diesel, cleaning fluids, coils of dog waste. Reaching the end of a block, she had an idea.

She turned around, heeding a familiar impulse from her girlhood. Having a destination calmed her. On the way to Cine Star, she passed the same people who had earlier inquired about the Saturday's event. Some nodded in her direction, but others had turned to their day's preoccupa-tions. After making it past her aunt's home, she was met by more neighbours who couldn't wait for Saturday. "Aling Rosy told us you have your own salon. In Canada!" "She thinks she's better than you—she has more years under her belt." "Who do you think will win?" She shrugged and smiled her way through these inquiries, her stom-ach churning. There was no way out of it. She kept her eyes on the ground, willing away looks from these famil-iar strangers. Walking in such a manner made her almost miss Aling Soledad's store. Its window no longer teemed with bags of snacks and jars of candies. Sophia couldn't see anybody through the screen. The sight of frail vacant benches beside the store made her a little sad.

Another few blocks and she came upon a tiny roadside eatery. Huge aluminum pots were lined along the storefront, next to a glass food display case containing platters of fried fish and meats. A man was hungrily finishing his bowl of rice porridge on a makeshift counter precariously attached to the storefront with chains. Sophia called out to the woman behind the pots. Over a good meal, she had found common ground with Auntie Mila, cleared the air between her and Erwin. Things needed the most fixing between her and Auntie Rosy.

She bought three cups of steamed rice, beef and onions cooked in calamansi and soy sauce, and pork stew with potatoes and carrots in tomato sauce. These were not enough—Sophia still felt guilty about the meal she and Erwin enjoyed without Auntie Rosy the night before. Fried tilapia. Stir-fried vermicelli noodles. The dishes were ladled and forked into clear plastic bags. By the time the woman handed over the bigger bag containing all the dishes ordered, a lineup had formed behind Sophia.

She hesitated across the street from Cine Star. The sign she remembered was gone, replaced by a dusty, pink banner, with "Cine Star Beauty Salon" printed in stick-like letters with curly ends, like a teenage girl's handwriting. Aling Helen wouldn't have approved. Sophia crossed the street, knocked on the door. Auntie Rosy instantly opened for her. She held up the bag of food. "Hi Auntie!"

Auntie Rosy gazed at the bag, swallowed, and looked back at Sophia. "Are you bribing me?"

"Naman, Auntie!" Sophia laughed, inwardly feeling caught. Her rival was still in a proud mood. "I don't want to compete with someone who's not sufficiently nourished."

The hinges of the door whined as Sophia was let in. After the storm and everything else Auntie Rosy had gone through, Sophia had expected to find Cine Star looking neglected. But she found herself gazing at polished mirrors reflecting a pristine and orderly space. Everything around her looked new: the metallic trolley, the chrome armrests of the chairs, the bevelled blades of the Japanese styling scissors. A soapy fragrance hung in the air. The floor was also spotless. There were all the indications of a recent thorough cleanup. Auntie Rosy had begun to wage the battle.

The grating sound of metal legs being dragged against the floor broke into her thoughts. By the window, Auntie Rosy was hastily setting a folding table with plastic plates and cutlery. She transferred the dishes Sophia brought from their plastic bags into small bowls. The rice was served on a bigger plate. Sophia recognized the red floral design around the plate's rim, now faded to pink, the very same plate on which Auntie Rosy had placed their snacks of fried bananas and pastries years ago. The battleground in her head collapsed as she settled in this cherished sanctuary. If a client had walked in right at that moment, proving Auntie Rosy correct that her business could be revived, Sophia would have been pleased.

"Let's eat, Sofi." Her nemesis had a softer voice.

"No, go ahead, Auntie."

"I'll wait for you then." Auntie Rosy stood up, stepped away from the table.

Sophia realized Auntie Rosy wasn't going to eat alone—that would just make it seem like Sophia had brought all the food out of pity, not as a feast to be shared between friends. With the swiftness with which she had set the table, it was clear that Auntie Rosy had not enjoyed a hearty meal for some time.

"Actually, I'm kind of hungry now. That mechado smells good." Sophia hoped she sounded convincing enough.

Auntie Rosy's face brightened. "Here, sit down."

In the wordless moments that followed, amidst satisfied slurps and scrapes of cutlery against the plates, Sophia racked her head for a safe topic. She was still edgy after their sour reunion from last evening. Auntie Rosy was eating fast, her proud facade crumbling with each warm spoonful.

"It looks great around here," Sophia remarked.

Auntie Rosy glanced around them. "It should be like this. Clients have to feel special."

"Have there been any clients?"

Auntie Rosy waved a spoon. "I have told people about the competition. Are you getting ready?"

Sophia squared her shoulders. It was the moment she had been waiting for. "Syempre, I'm ready. But Auntie, I want to add a condition."

Auntie Rosy looked concerned but quickly hardened her stare.

Sophia continued. "The last time we talked, you were very sure about winning. You said once that happens, people will come back here. Erwin and I will just have to agree that you'll continue to run Cine Star."

"I can already see that happening."

"Fine." Sophia smiled. "But we never set a condition on what would happen if *you* lost."

"Aba!" Auntie Rosy's steely expression turned jovial, as if hearing a joke. "Name it, darling. I am not afraid."

"Okay. If the audience vote me as the winner, you will sell Cine Star and move back to your province."

Auntie Rosy pounded a fist on the table, shaking their half-finished plates. "Game. I like it very much, Sofi. Threats make me stronger."

"It's not a threat. It's a condition."

"And I agree to it."

Then they were quiet again, intent on their food. Sophia couldn't tell if the air between them had become hostile again. Making her voice friendly, she asked, "Are you ready, Auntie?"

"Aba! Soledad's already knows she's going to be my model. Who's going to be yours?"

God, she didn't even have a model yet.

Now that she had settled in, Sophia saw the signs of deterioration: rust stains around the electric outlets, the bare merchandise shelves, the water stains on the walls. By the nook near the backroom, she noticed a rolled-up bamboo mat resting against the wall. Beside it were two pillows, sheets, and a single pile of folded clothes.

Then her eyes landed on the far end of the station. A

glass holder crammed with the basics: combs, scissors, brushes, and clips. The blades were so old and tarnished they didn't catch light. There was gradual recognition followed by a current of memories. Sophia approached the glass holder and picked up Aling Helen's pintail comb.

"I could never throw them away," Auntie Rosy said. "The combs are still in good shape. You could use them this Saturday."

"Thanks. I didn't bring mine." Grateful, Sophia turned to Auntie Rosy, who was cleaning up the table. She was putting the dirty plates and bowls in a plastic bag.

"What are you doing?"

"There's no running water here. I'm going over to Erwin's to wash the dishes."

IT HAD TAKEN SOPHIA TWO DAYS TO WORK UP THE COURAGE, and her aunt didn't disappoint with the vehement resistance.

"No!" Her Auntie Mila sat up from her sluggish pose on the sofa—she had just arrived from school. "Are you out of your mind? I'm not going to be your model!"

She was still in her teacher's uniform: a slim-waisted navy blue blouse with white rounded collar and trims around the short sleeves paired with a pencil-cut skirt in the same colour scheme. Auntie Mila carried the outfit well and Sophia could tell she was one of those rare popular teachers that were both loved and respected by teenaged students. She herself enjoyed her aunt's youthful, edgy energy. "It will be fun, Auntie. I will give you an amazing updo!"

"Is that why you're cooking our supper tonight?"

The truth was Sophia was getting tired of her aunt's store-bought meals. That she never cooked anything except for rice had not been an exaggerated warning. "No, I just really felt like making something. Please, I need someone who's easy to work with."

Auntie Mila ruefully massaged the toes of her stock-inged foot. "Sophia, darling, you are asking me to be styled in the salon run by a drunk woman who hurt a client. My students will make fun of me."

"I will be the one styling you."

"Why don't you just style me here at home before heading over to Cine Star?"

"It's not the same. The audience has to see us in action."

"I've been hearing about this competition for the past few days. I told myself, 'Okay, I'll stay out of it. Let Sofi deal with whatever it is she has gotten into.' I don't even know why you're doing this." There was a sharper note to her tone now. The uniform had an effect: Sophia felt like she was a student being chastised for missing homework.

"Auntie Rosy wants to prove to the people that she's still a great stylist. Just look at it as something fun." Her idea was to present it like a game to her aunt, skipping the part about the fate of Cine Star being decided. "A friendly neighbourhood contest. A story you can regale your students with for the coming years."

Auntie Mila had switched to massaging her other foot, pressing its toes and heel. Sophia waited for a moment before saying more. "I know how silly the idea is. But it will mean so much to me if I have you to go through this with. You told me I could tell you things. You would keep secrets for me. Because you're cool and more fun, right? This is something we could go through together. It will be fun. No one in Vancouver has to know."

Her aunt sighed as she picked up her pair of high-heeled pumps, a task through which she tried to hide her half-amused, half-annoyed expression from her niece. Sophia pretended not to notice that she had won and managed a deferential nod when Auntie Mila said, "Promise me I will look really, really good."

IN A RUNDOWN DUNKIN' DONUTS EARLY IN THE MORNING, Sophia read Adrian's email to Erwin from her phone. She had thought that she would cry on her friend's shoulder, but she was still too outraged to do so.

It was also an awkward space—the entire café was about the size of a cubicle. The people standing in line were brushing against the shoulders of those drinking coffee in the tiny booths that could only seat two diners, one at each side of the table. It was too cold: the air-conditioner machine stationed near the entrance had leaked a puddle on the floor, and some thoughtful worker had padded the area with a flattened cardboard box. The damp chill smelled of caffeine and icing sugar. Amidst this wakeful hubbub, Erwin was bleary-eyed, but perked up as Sophia read.

"A coward to the very end," he muttered as he sipped his hot chocolate.

"I was away, so he wrote me."

"He could have waited for you to come back. Say all of those things to your face."

Sophia scoffed. "Give him the chance to reject me once again. In person."

"Sofi," Erwin reached for her hand, "you're going to be okay. I promise."

They left with a box of doughnuts for Auntie Rosy.

"You're a dangerous competitor," Erwin remarked. "Upping the stakes and giving gifts at the same time."

"She is still my friend. I care about her." Sophia paused. "But I can't let another person I care about disrupt my life anymore."

"I have a good feeling about tomorrow."

"It's been a while since I felt good about anything."

Erwin's hand was resting on Sophia's shoulder as they walked. She liked its weight; it reminded her that she was still whole.

"There'll come a time when you'll just laugh whenever you think of him," he said.

"I could laugh now. To think he could break up with me through my brother. And now across the ocean."

Erwin gripped her shoulder. "It's a blessing, trust me."

As they approached Cine Star, they noticed a large white cardboard sign posted on the window, the words written with a thick black marker:

CINE STAR
presents
UPDO COMPETITION —
GARDEN STYLE
ROSY Of PHILIPINES VS.
SOFIA Of CANADA
11:00, SABADO
OKTOBER 22, 2009

Sophia almost dropped the box of doughnuts to the ground. "If my aunt sees this, she'll change her mind about being my model."

Erwin was laughing, cradling his stomach like he was in pain. "The marker's probably inside. I'll fix it."

21

THEY ARRIVED AT CINE STAR A FEW MINUTES BEFORE eleven. Auntie Mila and Paul led the way, holding hands. Sophia followed a few paces behind, feeling uneasy about the fact that her aunt had once again convinced Paul to delay his morning delivery so he could support her during the competition. She wasn't even sure what kind of support Paul would be there for. They walked slowly, a reluctant parade. Sophia could detect nervousness in her aunt's tone as she spoke to Paul.

A boisterous crowd had formed in front of Cine Star. Their neighbours were huddled together in earnest exchanges, groups nodding among themselves as details were offered and corroborated. With their milling and pacing, the crowd gave off the impression that they had been waiting in their spots for some time. Some had taken advantage of the opportunity: a taho vendor was kneeling before a growing queue, hurriedly filling plastic cups with soy pudding, tapioca pearls, and syrup, while another man was selling bottled water, going around with a Styrofoam icebox slung by a strap across his scrawny body. "Fake brand," Paul whispered half-resentful, half-cautious. Sophia was more troubled by the young man collecting money from another group of men. "*Aling Rosy o kay Sofi?*" He marked a scrap of paper with each response he got. Those closer to the salon were straining to see through the window, elbowing one another for a better view. The cardboard sign, to Sophia's relief, had been torn off the glass. Sophia, Auntie Mila, and Paul squeezed through the outer group of spectators who were craning their necks forward. Upon seeing Sophia, the throng quickly parted around the open door.

"She's here! Make way!"

"I heard she's marrying a Canadian."

"Didn't she promise to bring Aling Rosy to Canada?"

"Good luck, Ma'am Mila," someone called out from the crowd, followed by cheers of young voices. Auntie Mila smiled at her students who had heard of the competition and moved closer to Paul.

A wave of oppressive heat met Sophia as she stepped into the salon. There were people inside, crowding around the stations in a tight semicircle. Their reflections on the mirror made it look like there were spectators all around the room. The lights were on, but the salon was dark with the shadows of those peering through the window. Small children playfully pressed their faces against the glass.

Auntie Rosy, who was standing by the station closer to the window, nodded at Sophia with a ceremonial look on her face. She was wearing a dark red dress with thick lace ruffles running along her chest. Sophia wondered if it offended her that she and Auntie Mila had chosen the comfort of light T-shirts and shorts. Aling Soledad was already sitting on her chair, her slinky jersey top showing off jutting shoulders and elbow joints. The fair and once supple skin had shrivelled and sagged, smattered with tiny red blisters. Her eyes were dazed and glassy. But her hair— Sophia was gaping now—gloriously flowed to the small of her back, lush and shiny. She and Auntie Mila approached the other styling chair. Paul, feeling out of place, withdrew into the crowd. Camera clicks could be heard in the din. Sophia looked around for who could be chronicling this event, and saw at least three people with their phones held up. *Oh God.* She noticed Aling Soledad had also turned to the direction of the self-appointed photographers, teasing her hair to give it more volume. Then she met Sophia's eyes and her face turned sour, as if they were rivals for the spotlight. Jovial greetings heralded the arrival of new people who managed to get into the tight salon and claim a spot within the crowd. Aling Soledad would turn to the direction of this commotion, looking pleased.

"Uy! You didn't tell me I'll be up against Aling Soledad." Auntie Mila looked anxious.

"Why? Are you threatened by her?" Sophia giggled to lighten her mood.

"I'm a teacher, Sofi. You are placing me alongside ..." Auntie Mila trailed off, conscious of the audience trying to catch their conversation. She leaned closer to Sophia. "You know she's a call girl, right?"

"Of course. So what? Don't take this too seriously now, Auntie." Sophia nudged her, playfully. "I thought you were cool. Where's your sense of fun?"

Incredible effort had been put into setting up the stations identically: each equipped with a curling iron, an assortment of combs, brushes, sectioning clips, hair elastics, and bobby pins—all of these were spread out on a folded towel. Between them were two piles of towels that looked faded but freshly washed. A styling cape was draped over each of these piles. Each station also had a bottle of hair shiner, mousse, and holding spray. Sophia wished there were more products.

The only difference was the accessories. Auntie Rosy had chosen butterflies, tiny metal clips and bigger ones made of capiz. The colourful wings glittered against the mirror. *So 90s,* Sophia thought. On her counter, she laid out hair clips adorned with satin daisies of different colours, and a bunch of fresh baby's breath. She and her aunt had braved the hot, jam-packed halls of Divisoria Market the day before, pushing their way through displays of clothes, footwear, and beauty accessories. Auntie Mila had picked up hair clips encrusted with dainty crystals, ignoring Sophia's repeated reminders that they needed something bolder and more visible than the usual accessories. "These are pretty, why can't we use them?" her aunt had demanded. Between them, the aggressive seller of the desired ornament waved more items toward Sophia, who flashed an apologetic look before turning away to join the moving throng of shoppers. They were both exhausted and crabby by the time Sophia settled on silk flower clips being sold alongside bolts of textiles. The fresh flowers had been an afterthought at the market's exit.

"Sofi!"

Sophia turned to see Erwin pushing his way through the audience. He approached Sophia and whispered, "Good luck. Don't let her get to you."

She nodded at him, suppressing her nervousness.

A deep male voice dominated the din. "We're for Rosy! She's going to win!" Then there was a mixture of hooting and cheers. Auntie Rosy waved gamely. Despite the sweltering air in the salon, cold beads of sweat formed on Sophia's forehead.

"Hello! Hello!" Auntie Rosy had one arm up, addressing the crowd, which quickly quieted down. It was exactly eleven o'clock.

"Salamat, maraming salamat, for coming to this momentous event. I know you have all been looking forward to this. Today, you will watch two talented stylists not only display their skills, but outdo each other." Auntie Rosy face gleamed with assured triumph. "Many of you know that Sofi and I go way back. She was the little girl who came here to the salon and learned from me and Aling Helen, God bless her soul. This is the place where her passion for hairstyling was shaped and nurtured. May you have an enjoyable time watching us show our skills."

The speech sounded prepared, more formal than Auntie Rosy's usual language. Even the audience who were mostly rapt could sense this because some wore the quivering expression of suppressed laughter. Many of them stared at Sophia as if holding her responsible for her weird behaviour. She looked down at her slippers, fighting the urge to push her way out of the salon and run away.

"After finishing a hairstyling program here in Manila, our dear Sofi moved to Canada, where she received a more sophisticated training. She runs her own beauty parlour in Vancouver. I am incredibly proud of her. But now, she's here to challenge me!"

Murmurs of admiration rose from the spectators, accompanied with a ripple of applause. Auntie Mila nudged Sophia teasingly. Sophia nudged her back.

"And now, over to Erwin, who will explain the rules."

Erwin's eyes widened. They didn't really talk about his role in this event. Everyone was looking at him. He recovered and stepped out of the crowd.

"Hello, everyone. Thank you for being here. It's been agreed that the stylists will be given an hour to create a garden-themed updo for their models. As you can see, they are equally provided with the necessary tools and products. We ask that you don't approach the chairs so that the stylists can concentrate on creating their best work."

Erwin paused for a moment, thinking of what else he needed to say. "When the hour is up, all of you will vote for the winner by the sound of applause."

The ecstatic roar that followed was mixed with ear-splitting whistles. The people standing outside rapped on the window. Sophia felt certain that the salon was shaking beneath her feet. Auntie Mila flinched at the noise.

Erwin glanced at the clock between the two mirrors, which showed that it had just turned 11:13. "We will begin promptly at 11:15."

The clamour subsided into lowered voices. Auntie Mila sighed, settling into the styling chair. Sophia exhaled her mounting stress. She caught Aling Soledad giving her a haughty look from the mirror. She looked away.

Auntie Rosy stood motionless, hands clasped in front of her as if she were praying.

Erwin was watching the clock. "In ten, nine, eight ..."

The crowd echoed him at seven. Sophia shook her tensed shoulders loose, and suddenly felt embarrassed at making this boxer-like gesture.

"*Three, two, one!*"

Auntie Rosy leapt for the styling cape folded on the counter. Sophia grabbed hers and put it on her aunt, who was snickering at Auntie Rosy's rapid movements.

Taking Aling Helen's comb, Sophia smoothed her aunt's hair, parting it in the middle. There had been a humid breeze during their walk, so she had to work through a few tangles. Her hands were shaking a little. *Relax, Sophia.*

She made a shallow half-moon part, letting the front-most section of Auntie Mila's hair cover her face. Then she rolled this section up, securing it with a sectioning clip by the forehead. Sophia's plan was to create an assemblage of coils and buns interspersed with flowers, making Auntie Mila's head resemble a garden. She would divide the rest of her hair into half-inch sections to be curled and twirled either into a loose spiral or a tight bun. Sophia had to make sure that each curl would be oriented differently for a lush, spread-out finish, a realistic outcome given her aunt's mid-length hair. Auntie Rosy had an advantage in having a model with longer hair. But it all came down to skill.

Sophia sprayed some hair shiner on her palm, rubbed her hands, and ran her fingers through her aunt's hair. With the pintail comb, she lifted the topmost section of the loose hair and brushed it toward the left side of the head where she secured it with an elastic behind the ear. A neat horizontal part now ran between the newly tied ponytail and the remaining loose hair. From the corner of her eye, Sophia noticed the brisk strokes of Auntie Rosy's hand as she back-combed a section above Aling Soledad's ear, teasing out volume. Some spectators were praising her technique.

Taking a deep breath, Sophia worked her way through the rest of Auntie Mila's loose hair, pulling each horizontal section toward alternating sides of her head. After tying an elastic around the last ponytail resting on her nape, she glanced up at the clock. To her surprise, ten minutes had passed. A ribbon of chill slid through Sophia's body. The curling iron was ready. She took a lock of Auntie Mila's lowest ponytail and wound it around the base to hide the elastic. The rest of the ponytail she twirled around the hot barrel. Her aunt had thick hair so she had to keep the hair around the curler for a few extra seconds. Sophia misted the coiled hair with holding spray before releasing a bouncy curl. Then she started working on the next ponytail.

A quick succession of camera clicks made Sophia glance at Auntie Rosy's station. She saw half of Aling Soledad's hair was swept up on one side. Erwin had been right in his prediction that Auntie Rosy would go for something ostentatious.

Another curl unfurled in Sophia's hands. It felt like she was moving in slow motion. The steamy air was pungent with body odours and the cloying scent of hairspray. The people around them didn't seem to mind. They had fallen into steady chatter.

"Yes, I heard! I missed last Friday's episode—I had to work. Kainis!"

"Your boy was sick, 'no? He'll fatten up soon."

"I think she's doing something too simple," someone said. Sophia knew she was the subject of this remark.

She finished curling all of the ponytails. There were six all in all. Her eyes darted to the clock: it was almost 11:40. She took the lowest curl near the right ear, combing it gently before twisting it into a bun, which she held down with a bobby pin. Her fingers had broken into a rapid, adroit rhythm. For the next curl near the left ear, Sophia made a quick decision to wrap it around itself to create another mound to balance with the other side. She used a daisy hairpin to secure the tip.

"She works so fast," someone said.

Through the mirror, Sophia spotted Erwin gazing intently at Auntie Mila's hair, calculating her odds of getting the winning vote.

She loosely folded the next ponytail into itself, forming a soft, delicate loop, and pinned its base on the back of her aunt's head. Its ends curled up, making Sophia pause to debate whether to use a bobby pin or another flower pin to hold the tips down. Worried about the overcrowding of accessories, she opted to leave it loose for now. She twisted the next curl into an identical loop. As with the last one, she oriented it toward the back of the head, and its ends also curled up, as if reaching for the ends of the other loop.

Sophia smiled. They looked like suspended vines. She would leave them as is.

When she had used up all of Auntie Mila's ponytailed curls, Sophia realized that it was going to be hard for her to insert the flowered clips without displacing some of the loops and buns. This was what she deserved for not taking the time to map out the accessories. She pulled out a few bobby pins, releasing the last three curls. Auntie Mila flashed her an apprehensive look in the mirror. "Anong problema?"

"Wala ... okay lang," Sophia said. She took one of the just-released curls, fashioned it into a loop higher up on Auntie Mila's head, where there was space for a daisy pin. She gave this formation a quick spritz of holding spray.

"Wow! That is so pretty," someone uttered from behind her.

"Thirty-minute mark, stylists," Erwin announced.

"Come on, Sofi!" Paul called out. A few voices followed him. "*Sofi! Sofi! Sofi!*"

This brought out a response from Auntie Rosy's camp, which seemed to have more male voices in it. "*Rosy! Rosy! Rosy!*"

Sophia added more daisies. She decided to fashion the last two curls into fan-shaped coils that would sit on top of Auntie Mila's head. She twirled each ponytail, gently pushing down the loop to spread out the strands before sliding a bobby pin beneath. They wobbled. Sophia unpinned the curls and reached for the hairspray. After a generous spritz, she attempted to form the fan-shaped formations again. They felt a little brittle but held nicely even as she fashioned their tips to form tendrils coiling around the base. Sophia almost whooped with relief.

The children who had been watching through the window were gone. But the grown-ups remained; judging from the noise streaming through the open door, Sophia sensed that there were more people gathered outside than when they had arrived. She added more pins and gently adjusted the satin petals. As she stepped back to check Auntie Mila's updo from a distance, Sophia caught Aling Soledad's confident look in the mirror, her hair a tall, dishevelled mass.

"She's turning her into Marie Antoinette," Auntie Mila remarked, looking amazed.

Auntie Rosy was moving slower now, face flushed and forehead glistening with sweat. She had lost the adrenal energy she had when the competition began. But the desperation was still there—Auntie Rosy seemed to have shut the world out, and all that mattered was Aling Soledad's hair. Sophia had a fleeting desire for her opponent to win. If only she were just among the audience, which had swarmed closer. Someone with sour breath was giving a detailed commentary: "She has twirled some strands and arranged them to resemble vines, bushes maybe ..." Her friend commented, "Enough with the talk, we can see clearly." The commentator turned quiet as Sophia struggled to keep an even face.

"It's beautiful." Her aunt bobbed her head carefully as Sophia lightly sprayed the crown.

"We're not finished yet," Sophia said, plucking little stems from the bunch of baby's breath. She slipped the tiny blooms at the base of the mounds, spaces not obstructed by the flower clips.

"Fifteen minutes!" Erwin's voice seemed to have a panicked edge to it.

Sophia studied Auntie Mila's style. The coils and buns looked elegant with the satin daisies nestled between them. The baby's breath stood out nicely against the black, shiny hair. The horizontal lines of exposed scalp at the back of her head resembled the pathways of a labyrinth. An understated yet beautiful arrangement. But Sophia wondered whether she had done enough to defeat Auntie Rosy. The style was elegant but from the spectators' point of view, it might appear too simple compared to Aling Soledad's updo.

And there was still the front section to work with. Sophia removed the sectioning clip, debating whether to curl or leave it straight. Possibilities raced through her mind. She stood motionless, holding Auntie Mila's hair on her palm.

"We're running out of time," Auntie Mila warned her.

Sophia imagined using the section to create a thin braid that would run around Auntie Mila's temples. No, it wasn't the right look. It was too girly, and might collapse the existing arrangement. She needed to keep the look unique and classy.

She brushed the section backward, twirled its ends before pushing them toward the forehead, forming a pompadour perched above Auntie Mila's hairline. Sophia held this down with a couple of bobby pins, which she concealed using another daisy clip. She stuck a few branches of baby's breath into the pompadour.

Sophia stepped back to study this addition. The white flowers looked awkward and overdone. What was she thinking? As Sophia removed the blooms of baby's breath, a few strands pulled out of the pompadour. "Tsk, tsk!" She unclipped the section.

"Five minutes!" Erwin was looking at Sophia. From the corner of her eye, she saw Auntie Rosy straighten her shoulders and quicken her movements.

She could feel a tingling in her upper arms as she restored the pompadour. It wavered and some strands threatened to unravel. Why was she being so clumsy? Heart racing, Sophia twirled again and managed to make it firmer and bouncier. Relieved, she reached for the hairspray, but the can slipped from her hands. It made a loud, clattering sound on the floor.

"*Oww*," the crowd chorused.

"We're doing great," Auntie Mila reminded gently.

Glancing up at the clock, Sophia saw that it was about 12:14. Time had practically sprinted by, but she was almost finished. Her aunt looked stunning. From the crowd, Paul tilted his head to one side, trying to get a better view.

At the next station, Aling Soledad's hair was majestic. The rolled-up sections on her crown formed a lofty bouffant. It was adorned with shiny butterflies of varying colours and sizes at the sides and back. The lengths at the back of her head had been arranged into loose chignons at her nape. Auntie Rosy was rolling up one last section at the back, bobby pins dangling from her mouth.

Sophia inspected Auntie Mila's hair one last time, making

sure the blooms of baby's breath were staying in place.

Erwin roused the crowd. "Okay, ten, nine ..." The crowd ceased chatting and joined in the countdown.

Sophia watched as Auntie Rosy gave Aling Soledad's hair a generous spray and hurriedly placed the bottle on the counter. She clipped on more butterflies.

"Four, three, two ..."

At *one*, the crowd burst into a volley of clapping and shouts. Sharp whistles pierced the air, which had turned stuffy with the hairspray fumes and collective breathing in the tiny space. The tapping on the window deepened into a drum-like rumble.

"Time's up, stylists!" Erwin yelled.

Auntie Mila looked up at Sophia and said something inaudible. Sophia tilted her head down and only caught the tail end of her sentence "... or do I stay seated?" Sophia nodded, not really sure what to say.

"Okay, okay," Erwin held his hands up. "It's time to vote for the winner." Auntie Rosy's fans were first to claim the air. *"Rosy! Rosy! Rosy!"* To Sophia's relief, she heard people rooting for her as well. *"Sofi! Sofi! Sofi!"* The cheers melded into a thundering babel.

Auntie Rosy was waving her arms to be heard. "The models must stand up!"

The models stood up slowly, as if balancing delicate objects on their heads. Aling Soledad's hair, high forehead, and triumphant expression made her look queenly. Auntie Mila tipped her head and gave a small wave. More cell phones were held up. Sophia blinked against the onslaught of camera flashes.

"I feel like a star," Auntie Mila giggled. Her face was red with the heat and all the attention.

"Our models will turn around to show the stylists' handiwork," Erwin announced.

To Sophia's surprise, Auntie Mila gamely planted her hands on her hips and did a couple of turns. Right after, she winked flirtatiously at Paul. Wolf whistles pierced through the hooting and applause. Sophia laughed at her aunt's sudden enthusiasm.

But Aling Soledad was not to be outdone. She fixed a pout on her face and spun a few times, swift and rhythmic like a dancer.

Whoooa! The crowd rewarded Aling Soledad with her own salvo of cheers.

Both models were now facing the crowd with Erwin standing between them. Sophia, who was right behind Auntie Mila, glanced at Auntie Rosy. Her rival was standing far back, leaning against the counter, with what seemed like a petrified look on her face. With a shot of pity, Sophia realized that the moment that would decide Auntie Rosy's fate had arrived.

Then Sophia glanced at Aling Soledad's hair.

From the crowd's point of view, the finished updo appeared flawless and extravagant. But from behind, the towering formation was giving way, splintering against the weight of capiz and metal butterflies. One of the heavier clips had tumbled halfway down, letting loose some strands. Another shiny butterfly was partially dangling sideways, awkwardly perched behind Aling Soledad's ear. Sophia realized that Aling Soledad's quick turns had spoiled her updo. Whatever the reason, whether there was too little holding spray, or the hair was weighed down by excessive accessories, Auntie Rosy's creation was going to fall apart right that minute!

Auntie Rosy looked at Sophia with fearful eyes, her chin trembling. Sophia grasped the dread gripping her dear old friend, who had been struggling for so long and had given up so much. All the cheers and praises would turn into merciless jeers once the spectators discovered that Aling Soledad's updo was crumbling. The men who had counted on her winning would despise her. The women would nod their heads as if they knew all along she was a failure. Everyone would mock her when Auntie Rosy had been convinced that every single person watching them that moment would eventually judge her worthy of keeping Cine Star.

But now came humiliation.

Sophia frantically tapped Erwin's shoulder, who was trying to make himself heard through the competing chants. He turned to her with an exhilarated look—he was also caught in the thrill of the moment. But his expression changed when he saw Sophia's. She tilted her head toward Aling Soledad. Erwin glanced at her direction, but because he was standing right beside Aling Soledad, he couldn't see what was wrong.

Sophia spoke into Erwin's ear: "Auntie Rosy's updo is collapsing. We have to finish. Now!"

Stunned, Erwin whipped his head to get a better look at Aling Soledad's hair. Then he faced the crowd and shouted in a deep, booming voice Sophia had never heard him use before. "Hoy! Hoy! We have to vote! Quickly now!" He clapped his hands loudly. This got some people's attention, but it took an unbearably long moment for everyone to quiet down. Sophia watched helplessly as Aling Soledad, who had sensed something was wrong, gingerly touched the back of her head. Two more butterfly clips had fallen down her back, precariously hanging by loosened strands. Her eyes widened but her smile remained and even grew wider. People were debating among themselves who had the winning hairstyle.

"Let's hear it for Sophia!" Erwin shouted.

The applause for the vote was intermingled with their names. "*Sofi-Mila! Sofi-Mila!*"

Auntie Mila had noticed the frantic exchange between Sophia and Erwin, but didn't understand what was happening. She smiled tentatively and gave Sophia a puzzled look.

"Okay, okay!" Erwin's voice was still powered by panic. "Let's hear it for Aling—"

The pandemonium that followed rocked the salon, swallowing up Erwin's voice. Sophia knew her updo was beautiful and cleanly done, the intricate arrangement of hair and flowers better appreciated at close scrutiny. But for the audience, the winner was obvious. Auntie Rosy's work had more height and volume. It resembled a black tidal wave suspended in the air, wild and graceful at the same time.

At least for now.

Auntie Rosy shrunk against her station as if her victory had terrified her. The voices had taken on one name:

"Rosy! Rosy! Rosy!"

Smiling, Sophia walked over to Auntie Rosy, took her hand, and raised it like a prizefighter's. Whooping and whistles weaved in with the crashing applause.

This was the salvation Auntie Rosy had been waiting for. Right after shaking hands with Sophia, she flung her arms around Aling Soledad for a tight hug. When this passionate reaction to a victory pushed Aling Soledad's beehive hair to one side, and some clipped sections fell down her shoulders, the crowd didn't suspect anything at all. They were too ecstatic for the victory of Cine Star Beauty Salon's owner.

22

A RUSH OF SPECTATORS LEFT THE SALON WITH ALING Soledad, who walked with a proud, queenly air despite her half-destroyed updo. And there were those who stayed, approaching Auntie Rosy to congratulate her, while others complimented Auntie Mila's updo. People who had been standing outside were pushing their way into Cine Star, latecomers hoping for scraps of the spectacle they had missed. Someone was calling out for those who lost the bet to pay up. It took a superhuman amount of effort for Sophia to not glance in the direction of the voice. She hoped she wouldn't come across a disgruntled spectator before she flew back to Vancouver. She focused on granting requests to pose for photos next to her aunt, and sometimes with Auntie Rosy. She was too overwhelmed by the events to worry about where her images might end up later. Auntie Mila enjoyed the attention at first, nodding gratefully at her admirers—mostly her students—and cordially responding to fatuous questions. "Do you agree with the decision?" "Do you wish that Aling Rosy styled you instead?" She finally grabbed Sophia's wrist at one point, hissing, "Can I go home now?" Sophia nodded, saying she needed to stay behind.

When the last few spectators finally trickled out of Cine Star, Auntie Rosy collapsed on her styling chair, looking at Sophia and Erwin with a trapped look in her eyes.

"I don't know what happened. I felt so weak."

"You put up a good match," Erwin said.

"My heart was beating so fast. *Ta-dug, ta-dug, ta-dug.*" Auntie Rosy pounded a fist against the ruffles on her chest. "Everything was happening too fast. And it felt like we were in an oven."

"There were a lot of people here." Sophia was cooling herself by shaking the collar of her T-shirt. The rubbish strewn around made the salon resemble a classroom at the end of the day. She joined Erwin in cleaning up, squeezed juice boxes and half-empty water bottles; candy wrappers, plastic bags, empty and flattened corn chips foil packets that still smelled of their salty contents. A useful distraction from watching Auntie Rosy grapple with the contest's outcome.

"You're probably glad I messed up," Auntie Rosy sighed, her shoulders hunched.

"No," Sophia said. "We didn't want those people to make fun of you."

Auntie Rosy looked pained by this. Erwin was still searching the corners of the salon for more trash. Not being able to find any, he sat down on a chair and looked at Sophia blankly, unsure how to proceed.

"I worked hard. You probably don't believe me but I did."

"Everybody saw—" Erwin began but Auntie Rosy cut him off.

"I looked up to Aling Helen." She flinched. "But she never believed in me up to the very end."

"She didn't." Sophia had meant for this to come out as a question, but her tone instead betrayed the truth that she wasn't surprised.

"I was taking care of her, visiting at the hospital. She knew she was going to die. She told me her strength was gone." Auntie Rosy was gazing downwards, as if her recollection was unravelling on the floor. "She said I needed to do her a favour. She asked me to sell the salon."

"Sell it?" It was Erwin's turn to pretend.

"Sell Cine Star. She was being kind about it, telling me I could keep the proceeds. Up to the very end, that old woman didn't trust me. But I told her to lay her worries to rest. I will take on the business. I will even open up branches."

"Why didn't you sell it?" Erwin asked. Sophia shot him a stern look, making him stammer. "I mean, you could have used the money. Started somewhere new ..."

Auntie Rosy glanced at him feebly and Sophia was compelled to come to her rescue—the role was growing on her. "She wanted to stay with Cine Star."

Then there was silence, each of them retreating to their own thoughts. Sophia visualized Aling Helen in her last days. Bone-thin with rattling breath, she was still sharp. And worried about her salon, her eager and rash assistant.

Was it her death wish to uphold her impeccable reputation as a stylist, or protect Auntie Rosy from her imminent downfall? At her bedside sat Auntie Rosy, sombre and caring but not without a dream. Sophia could not judge her for envisioning a shining future in Cine Star at Aling Helen's deathbed—her own salon, after all, came about through an older woman's failing health. Demise made dreams possible. Sometimes, the reverse was also true.

Auntie Rosy spoke: "Years ago, when she came to our hometown, she was telling everyone about the movie stars she had worked with. She was my mother's distant cousin. We were all intrigued by her stories, amazed at her experience. She was this incredibly successful stylist living a big life in Manila. Watching filmings, being around celebrities. She told me she had made enough money to open her own business. There were other young girls who wanted to work for her, but she only wanted one. I fought for it, you know?" Auntie Rosy voice was a mixture of shame and pride. "I pleaded with my mother to persuade her to pick me. I offered to style her—I could tell she wasn't impressed. Looking back, she probably thought I'm someone easy. Someone she could control. I thought I'd be surrounded with glamour and entertainment. The other girls were jealous when I left with her. Only when we got here, I realized that she had turned her back on showbiz."

Sophia couldn't decide whether to defend Aling Helen or press Auntie Rosy for details. Auntie Rosy had told many stories about herself, but not this version where she had put herself forward for Aling Helen's approval only to find herself mislead. What did she truly know? Perhaps everything she remembered about Aling Helen was a just a patchwork of flawed impressions. Who better to trust than the person who had worked for her?

Auntie Rosy now cradled her face into her gnarly hands. There was no sound at first, but her wrist and shoulders convulsed. "I'm so tired—"

Her voice trailed and crumbled into a soft, plaintive cry that tore at Sophia's heart. She and Erwin had seen Auntie Rosy in all swings of emotions, but they had never seen her weep quietly. She blew up, she guffawed, she snorted and wailed loudly. People and things she loved and hated were kindling to her fires. But Auntie Rosy never fizzled.

"Let me unfold the mat so you can rest for a bit." Erwin stood up. "Or maybe we should get you some food."

The rims of Auntie Rosy's eyes were red when she looked up. "I want to be left alone for a while."

THE FOLLOWING DAY, ALING SOLEDAD WAS STILL PARADING around the neighbourhood, talking about Auntie Rosy's victory. People cheered whenever they saw her, and she bestowed playful bows as acknowledgment. Auntie Mila was telling Sophia about this.

"I still can't believe they won," Auntie Mila grumbled. "I was prettier."

Sophia was amused that her aunt was taking the competition seriously now that it was behind them. "It wasn't a beauty contest, Auntie."

"We should have gone for a bolder style. Maybe we should have gotten peacock feathers. Bigger flowers. Rosy won by being grand. Too bad my hair wasn't very long. Maybe we should have gotten extensions. Or would that be cheating?"

"It's very hard to work with extensions."

Auntie Mila clucked her tongue. "The problem with you, Sofi, is that you're afraid of risks."

Sophia debated whether to tell Auntie Mila what actually happened. She now adored her in a way she never had as a child. But her aunt was too competitive—she wouldn't understand. The secret needed to stay within Cine Star. Erwin and Sophia protected the precious little left of Auntie Rosy's pride.

That afternoon, she went with Erwin to the cemetery to visit Aling Helen's resting place. It had rained a little in the morning but it was sunny now. Mud clung to their shoes as they made their way through the crooked labyrinth of tombstones. Sophia had brought a huge bouquet of flowers. She lovingly placed it on a marker so plain and small that the surrounding wet soil and grass had found their way through the engraved letters of Aling Helen's name. In that sea of grey and white, she was just one tombstone among many. An injustice. Not that she expected a mausoleum, but surely the woman deserved something more ... beautiful. "Was this all she could afford?" Sophia asked.

"She had always wanted things simple," Erwin replied.

"You think she really used Auntie Rosy? Took advantage of her?"

"Who knows? It was so long ago."

"But what do you think?" Sophia pressed. Why was Erwin being so apathetic? "You knew her better than I did. You spent more time with them."

"I was just a kid like you. A kid pretending to know a lot. But I'll always remember her as a good person." There was an unmistakable lightness in his voice. He sounded relieved. Liberated.

Sophia nodded, looking ahead to hide the tears forming at the corner of her eyes. She understood where he was coming from, and she also believed that Auntie Rosy was better off leaving the city. But all these great changes they had orchestrated, from Auntie Rosy's departure to Cine Star closing its doors, along with questions about Aling Helen's true nature and intentions—they sat heavy in her chest.

"In the meantime, Auntie Rosy can't be there. We can't sell the place while she's occupying it. Maybe at the end of the month, when her lease is up? I can post an ad online about the salon. I know some websites." Erwin was all business. He had it all planned out. "That will give her time to decide what she wants to take with her."

"I can help you with the inventory. I guess the new owner can handle the mayor's permit, licence, and stuff." Sophia struggled to control her trembling voice. "It's just hard to believe that it's finally closing."

"It has finally set all of us free," Erwin said. "Think about it, Sophia. Aling Helen opened it so no one could boss her around anymore. We escaped to it when we were children. Because of it, you went to do what you really wanted to do. I love Auntie Rosy—she gave me something my own family couldn't. But it has really been difficult helping her. Now that she'll leave town, I can think about going someplace far."

⫸

THEY HAD BOTH WORRIED THAT AUNTIE ROSY WOULD BE emotional as they cleaned up Cine Star. Her silence was hard to read. At times, she acted sulky, someone being asked to do something against her will. Then she would giggle out of the blue, remembering something funny that had happened with one of her clients. Sophia and Erwin asked questions and laughed along, wanting to maintain the spark of cheerfulness.

"We could figure out the resale prices for these." Sophia started a list of tools and equipment. "Those chairs and that colouring tray still look pretty new. Do you have the receipts, Auntie?"

"Why would I keep receipts from months ago?" Auntie Rosy asked.

"Well, do you remember how much they cost?"

"Diyos ko, Sofi. How would I remember such things?"

By noon, it had become evident that Auntie Rosy hadn't fully accepted losing Cine Star. All of Sophia's questions about the paperwork and inventory were met with blunt retorts.

"Why would they look for the permit? The new owners should apply for their own."

"Notify the property office? They should just see for themselves I'm no longer occupying the premises."

"So what if things don't tally up? I'm leaving anyway."

At one point, Sophia ran an open palm down her face. "Auntie, I just want you to make the most out of your salon. It will be easier if we know how much everything in here costs."

"Money's not the most important thing in the world, right?"

Sophia fought the urge to scream.

At the back of the salon, Sophia took the moment to remember the times when she and Erwin made it a game to hide there from the grown-ups who could tell on her parents. There were boxes of more hair products. Hot oil tubes, canisters of gels, bottles of conditioning sprays, hair colour, and perm solutions. A set of heated rollers that appeared unused. Stacks of hair salon magazines dating up to five years back. Exhausted, Sophia sat on one of the boxes, shaking her head at the wasteful spending. She wanted to carry every single item out to the front, pile them up to the ceiling to make a point. *See, Auntie, all these things you bought that turned out to be useless.* But she remembered that her friend was already defeated. In Auntie Rosy's eyes, she and Erwin must look like looters, going through her possessions, stripping her of her livelihood.

Sophia ended up showing her the magazines. "How come you never used these? And all the other stuff at the back?"

Auntie Rosy's eyes widened with recognition. "Ay! I bought those with your money, Sofi. I thought I'll bring them to you someday." She paused, her face turning more sombre. "When we stopped talking, I decided to save them for when I open another branch."

"Oh." Sophia looked down at the stack, feeling mean.

"In other words, they're yours," Auntie Rosy said. "You can take them if you want."

⁂

FOR HER LAST NIGHT IN MANILA, SHE WANTED TO TAKE ERWIN and Auntie Rosy out for dinner. But Auntie Rosy had two conditions: one was Aling Soledad would be invited. The second and even more surprising was that they would gather at home. By home, she meant Cine Star. "You don't have to take us somewhere too expensive." Auntie Rosy had wrinkled her nose at the prospect. "It's the company that matters, di ba?"

On the floor mat, they arranged their humble feast of skewered pork intestine, deep-fried breaded quail eggs, rice, shrimp crackers, and buttered sweet bread. Erwin brought beers. This was not how Sophia visualized their last meal together. But how could she protest when the two older women were having a great time? Even just listening to their laughter made Sophia's stomach hurt. She felt almost jealous of their bond. Thankfully, Aling Soledad was sober—that she could walk and speak coherently, albeit slowly, was the best that could be hoped for, according to Erwin. Upon arriving, she had stood gaping at their modest gathering. "Just us? How about our fans?"

Auntie Rosy had responded: "Just us. Sophia won't be here long."

The strange part of the evening was the way Auntie Rosy rubbed in Sophia's defeat. "She was so proud, challenging me like that. Me?" She drawled between gulps of San Miguel. It was as if the competition had taken place many years back, not a day ago—the beer loosening her tongue. Sophia fought the urge to remind Auntie Rosy that her work was as sloppy as the way she ran Cine Star. She had brought about her own downfall.

Aling Soledad was being gracious. "Sus, your Sofi was impressive."

The dying glimmer of the setting sun bounced off the newly wiped mirrors, and with the lights off, the salon felt empty. Lifeless. They were surrounded by bulging bags and boxes, some containing Auntie Rosy's possessions, the others containing salon supplies. Sophia had included the items Auntie Rosy offered to the resale list and had labelled each box with a black marker. Tonight they looked like a family who had just moved into that place, celebrating a beginning. How similar it was, Sophia thought, to a feast marking an end.

Auntie Rosy opened another bottle of beer. "Life is quieter there, simpler," she said. "My sisters and brothers all have children. I will be busy helping raise them."

"They have never met you," Erwin said. His voice, Sophia noted, was infused with forced excitement. He was still convincing Auntie Rosy that a happy life awaited her back home.

"They have never met me," Auntie Rosy agreed.

Predictably, the conversation drifted to remembering old times. But as the night deepened and the food ran out, they became quiet. Auntie Rosy leaned against the wall, gazing about as if to memorize her surroundings. Erwin had stopped asking about her family. He looked bored. Sophia was starting to feel the same. There had been a time when they wished they didn't have to leave Cine Star. Tonight, they could stay till dawn, but they both wished to be somewhere else. Tomorrow they would have nothing in common except from the memories swirling in their drunken heads. But what would have happened if Erwin had not invited her to Cine Star? Sophia was certain her life would be drastically different without these friends of hers.

She stood up to urge circulation through her numb legs.

Auntie Rosy blinked. "You're saying goodbye?"

Sophia was flying back to Vancouver the next evening. "I don't have to. I could stay out late."

"Not like she still has a curfew," Erwin said.

Auntie Rosy made a limp gesture with her hand, which looked beckoning and dismissive at the same time. "It's been a long day. You have a long trip tomorrow. Thank you for the food. For not forgetting us. Your visit." Her words were beginning to slur.

"Are you okay, Auntie?" Erwin stood up as well.

"I'm tired. I get tired quickly these days. Come, Sofi, hug me. Let's say goodbye in a simple way." When Sophia didn't move, Auntie Rosy drew forward, ending up on all fours. For a moment, it looked like she would crawl toward Sophia. "I'll fall asleep soon and we wouldn't be able to do a proper goodbye. Come hug me and go home."

Sophia hugged her friend tightly. Walking home, alone, tears ran down her face.

23

I T RAINED HARD THE DAY SOPHIA WAS LEAVING MANILA. NO storm signal had been raised, but sheets of rain whipped at the pavement, the droplets drummed against the windows and the roof. She wished she were staying for another day. The showers in Vancouver never made the same wonderful sounds.

But Auntie Mila was panicking. Rain, even less torrential than this one, meant flood and flood meant snail-paced traffic. She was late for her seven o'clock class, but she wanted to make sure Sophia got a ride to the airport. Paul was promptly phoned.

"Auntie, my flight isn't until 4 p.m."

"It's better to be early. Traffic's already terrible without rain." Auntie Mila looked anxiously at the dark clouds. "And if the flood rises, you'll fly out tomorrow."

The ever-reliable Paul agreed to give her a lift. Sophia turned her head when her aunt rewarded his willingness with a noisy smooch on the cheek. Then she turned to her niece. "You should come home often. We'll have more fun." They hugged tight as if to compensate for the knowledge that such promises couldn't be made.

The minor downside was that *Fresh Spring*'s delivery list was long that day, so there was hardly any space for Sophia's luggage. There was even a ten-gallon bottle on the front passenger seat, which Paul pushed to the middle to make space for her.

It did end up being a slow drive. Sophia's suitcase was on the floor, pressing against her shins. The bulky backpack sat on her lap. The congested procession waded through murky streams that slapped currents and trash against the wheels of the traffic. Paul turned on the radio, flipped through stations for a storm announcement. Not finding any, he flicked the radio off. "Your typical monsoon," he muttered wearily.

"How long have you been courting my aunt?" Sophia asked.

Paul's nose flared at this question. "We're a couple now."

"I mean how long have you been together?" She knew he would talk to her aunt about her questions later but she didn't care. That would be a good thing, actually. Sophia wanted her to poke around the edges. Find the real face behind that loving, tender mask men found convenient to wear at times. But a frown had emerged on Paul's face. The traffic wasn't helping his mood.

She was relieved when they finally reached the airport. The constant stops did get her a little worried about missing the flight, as she didn't want to spend more money to book another one. Thanks to her trip, her salon would be in the red at the end of the month.

Non-travellers were not allowed past the drop-off area, so Paul helped Sophia haul her luggage out of the van. She didn't need a teary embrace from him, but she thought being deserted right there at the pavement was too abrupt a treatment for someone about to board a thirteen-hour flight. Whatever happened to thoughtful send-offs?

Paul seemed to sense this crudeness too. Keeping a wary eye on the *Fresh Springs* van, which he had parked in a taxicab slot, he patted Sophia on the shoulder. "Can you manage those?" He nodded toward the railed conveyor belt that was attached to an x-ray lodged against the airport's entrance, a partition between civility and security.

"I'll be fine."

"Take care." He sounded nicer when he said this. Dutiful to Auntie Mila, Sophia thought wistfully.

The digital flight list in the terminal showed her flight departing in six hours. It was too early even for checking in her suitcase. Under another sky, the life she had forged and temporarily escaped from awaited. Sophia couldn't wait to go back to her salon, to usher clients to her station, help them uncover their best selves. To run a washcloth over its mirrors and counters after turning the door sign to *Closed*, sweep off the remnants of tired and outgrown appearances, pore over her earnings and losses at nights.

Erwin would write her a few weeks later that on the day Auntie Rosy left for Bicol, the neighbours gathered in front of Cine Star, sending her off. There were women who had been her clients, men she had drinking sessions with.

The taxi driver taking her to the airport had to honk several times to clear the way. There had been a party at Cine Star the night before. *A real* one. Aling Soledad gave away food from her store, and there was lots of drinking and who knows what else. Erwin had been invited, but he had to work that night.

Sophia looked around. The terminal was the vast expanse between her two different worlds. Everyone in that space must be dreading the separation from their loved ones or cherishing the reunion with them. She tottered between relief and emptiness. Cine Star was now just a place in her memory, the comfort and courage it gave her could only be summoned by her own mind. There would be no new stories. Auntie Rosy and Erwin, she would hear from them even less, now that the place that had held them together had closed down. It would have been nice to have Adrian to come back to, but their lives had already splintered into widely different paths. She didn't need him, but it still hurt. She would cry when they turned off the lights in the aircraft, she would press her tear-stained face against the scratchy airline blanket. She would distract herself with Tagalog movies.

She was alone, but there was comfort in that too. She had everything she needed within her. She would move out. Her parents would try to dissuade her with the usual talk of finances and the future. Steer her toward a safer course, a path more familiar. She knew their tune well. It had stirred many storms within her, darkened too many days. This time Sophia would let their words land on her with the lightness of spring rain. Gather them in a lovely, tangled bunch, binding her to her parents wherever the soft and the cruel breezes took her.

In the first hours of waiting, she watched the hall fill and empty of travellers. Every once in a while, she stretched her legs and walked with her suitcase in tow. She circled the terminal as if she were weightless. Poised for a flight. Auntie Mila had been wrong in thinking her niece was afraid of risks.

After yet another round of weaving through restless souls who also pulled and carried various loads, she found a row of vacant chairs facing the terminal's tall windows. Sophia sat down. Through the glass, Manila appeared besieged by clouds, folds of overcast curtains closing off the city to her. She gazed to memorize the darkening view until it offered back her own bold stare.

THE END

DISCUSSION QUESTIONS

1. Sophia feels like the odd one out in her family because of her career choice. Do you think this would still have been the case if she had not befriended the people at Cine Star Salon and had discovered her love of hairstyling later in Vancouver?

2. Rumours play a huge part in the plot. How did they influence your impression of the characters living within the neighbourhood of Cine Star Salon?

3. The book shows the dynamics within Sophia's family when they were living in Manila and after settling in Vancouver. How did immigration change the family? What remained the same?

4. How did you feel about Auntie Rosy's entreaties? Would you have addressed them differently from Sophia? If so, how would you have addressed them? Would you have been more sympathetic, or less?

5. Did Adrian's confession come as a surprise? Why or why not?

6. Sophia's friendship with Erwin is the most enduring throughout the book. How did their relationship evolve from when they were children to adulthood? Do you see it continuing after the events in the book? Can you foresee further changes if it does continue?

7. As a child, Sophia looked up to both Auntie Rosy and Aling Helen who often clashed with one another. How did each woman influence Sophia's choices as a salon owner in Canada?

8. Throughout the novel, Sophia grapples with a sense of not being enough. Thinking about similar instances in your life, how much of it do you attribute to expectations from others against those from yourself? Were you of a similar age as Sophia when you were dealing with the sense of being not enough?

9. Does the novel have an antagonist? If so, who is it? Is there more than one?

10. Before reading the book, how did you imagine a hair salon owner spending a workday? Has your impression changed after reading the book?

ACKNOWLEDGEMENTS

I FIRST TOOK WRITING SERIOUSLY AT THE UNIVERSITY OF Santo Tomas Faculty of Arts and Letters in Manila, and I thank my friends, classmates, and faculty members for everything I have learned and the wonderful memories.

I'm incredibly grateful to Hiromi Goto, who was my first writing mentor in Canada and inspired me to write the stories many know well but are less read about.

Thank you to my fiction workshop group at Simon Fraser University's The Writer's Studio: Timothy Taylor for selecting me for his cohort, Carleigh Baker, Janet Fretter, Romney Grant, Kevin Kokoska, Marda Miller, Eric Torin, and especially to Karen Faryna, Rena Graham, and Joanne Betzler who read completed versions of the manuscript. I extend my gratitude to the rest of the TWS community to which I'm fortunate to belong.

Many thanks to everyone at NeWest Press, most notably Anne Nothof for her kindly and superb guidance, Matt Bowes, Claire Kelly, and Christine Kohler for their enthusiasm and careful attention. For the beautiful cover design, I have Kate Hargreaves to thank.

I gained so much knowledge of and appreciation for the work of hairstylists and hair salon owners through conversations with Lita Roxas, owner of Manila Hair Salon in Vancouver and with Shandie Wattley, who reviewed an earlier version of the novel. Their insights were invaluable.

Much love and gratitude to Mama, Ate Pinky, and Jon for being a source of inspiration and laughter as we forge a better life in Canada. Special thanks to Vitaly for the joy and unending encouragement.

LEAH RANADA was born in the Philippines. She moved to Canada in 2006, shortly after graduating from University of Santo Tomas in Manila. She attended The Writer's Studio at Simon Fraser University in 2013. Her short stories have appeared in *On Spec, Room, Santa Ana River Review, Scarlet Leaf Review,* and elsewhere. Leah has brought her administrative and editorial skills to legal, settlement services, and academic workplaces. She lives in New Westminster and blogs at leahranada.com. *The Cine Star Salon* is her debut novel.